The Island Bride

The Island Bride

by Susan Page Davis

Published by Tea Tin Press

The Island Bride
© 2018 by Susan Page Davis

ISBN 978-1-947079-08-3

All rights reserved. No part of this publication may be reproduced in any form, except for brief quotations in printed reviews, without written permission of the publisher.

Cover design by Lynnette Bonner

Printed in USA.

About This Book

Prince Edward Island, the smallest of the Canadian provinces, has a rich and varied heritage. The Míkmaq people called it *Epekwitk* (Anglicized spellings vary), which means "resting on the waves" or "cradle on the waves," a tribute to the island's crescent shape. The French named it Ile Saint-Jean, or Saint John's Island, when they began to colonize it in 1713. The English took it over in 1758 and gave it the decidedly English name Prince Edward Island, in honor of Prince Edward Augustus, Duke of Kent and father of Queen Victoria. In 1864, four years after this story takes place, Prince Edward Island hosted the Charlottetown Conference, during which the colonies moved toward uniting to become Canada. Ironically, islanders didn't see the move as advantageous to them, and Prince Edward Island did not become a province of Canada until 1873.

The island is now home to about 140,000 people, and nearly three-fourths of the people can claim British ancestry. Prince Edward Island is known for its beautiful coastal scenery, including beaches and red cliffs, and rich farmland. A more recent attraction is the newly constructed eight-mile Confederation Bridge, which, in winter, becomes the world's longest bridge over ice-covered waters. A trip across it from New Brunswick takes about ten minutes.

The island is also home to Lucy Maud Montgomery's most beloved fictional character, Anne Shirley. Anne's home of Green Gables (based on the author's uncle's real-life farm) and other sites related to the author and her books draw thousands of tourists to the island each year. PEI is a popular destination for vacationing Americans who want to experience the gentle island life.

Susan Page Davis

Chapter One

June 27, 1860
Charlottetown, Prince Edward Island

The back door to the kitchen burst open. Molly Orland nearly dropped the wooden spoon she held.

"Mum!" Her brother Nathan loomed in the doorway, panting.

"What is it?" Their mother turned from her worktable and stepped toward him, fear leaping into her eyes.

"Papa's hurt."

"No! What happened?"

"He fell off the wagon. Thinks his leg is broken."

Mum snatched a clean towel off the rack and glanced at Molly. "Get a jug of water—quick."

Her chest aching, Molly filled the small pottery jug her father sometimes took when he went to work in the fields.

"Where is he?" her mother asked Nathan.

"Grandpa and Joe are bringing him in the wagon."

Molly's younger sister, Kate, scurried down the stairs into the room. "What's going on? Nathan, what is it?"

Molly's hand shook as she reached out to touch Kate's shoulder. "Papa is hurt."

Kate's face crumpled.

Their mother grabbed the jug in one hand and held up her skirt and the towel with the other and whisked out the door. Nathan followed her, and the room went still.

"How bad is it?" Kate's lips trembled as she looked up into Molly's face. Her eyes filled with tears.

Molly felt tears flooding her own eyes. She hauled in a painful breath. "We don't know yet. Let's get his bed ready."

She strode into their parents' bedchamber with twelve-year-old Kate on her heels. The bed was made neatly, as always during the day.

Molly seized the edge of the coverlet. "Get on the other side, Kate. Help me lay this back, so can get Papa into bed easily."

"Will he need the doctor? I could go for Dr. Trann."

"I think he might. Let's go meet them and see if we should run to the Tranns'."

As soon as they'd turned down the covers, Molly hurried to the front door and looked across the barnyard and down the field. Kate pushed in between her and the doorjamb. The hay wagon, pulled by Papa's team of big chestnut geldings, rolled slowly toward them. A lithe figure ran from the wagon toward the road of packed red earth.

"Look! There goes Joe." Molly pointed. The youngest of the four Orland siblings at ten, Joe streaked across the hayfield then hopped over rows of potato plants until he reached the road and tore for town. "Mum must have told him to fetch the doctor."

"What else can we do to help?" Kate's weepiness had passed, and Molly decided that keeping busy was the key for both of them.

"Come, let's fill the teakettle. Doctors always want hot water."

"What for?"

"To clean things, I expect." Molly went to the hearth and filled the kettle from the bucket of water on the floor. "Can you run out and draw another pail of water? They'll be nearly here by the time you do it."

Kate seized the pail and ran for the back door. Molly checked the stove's firebox, put in another stick of wood, and went back to the doorway. The wagon drew up outside. Was her father conscious, and if so, how badly did he suffer? Molly swallowed around an aching lump in her throat. If Papa was badly hurt, how would they keep the dairy going, and who would finish getting in the hay crop? Nathan and Grandpa couldn't do it all by themselves.

Grandpa Anson carefully climbed from the seat at the front of the wagon, onto the mound of hay. Mum and Nathan remained kneeling beside the prone form that lay on top of the load. Molly ran down the steps and caught her breath at her first glimpse of her father.

His ashen face was set in a grimace that could not hold back his groans. His left trouser leg was soaked in blood above the knee.

"Molly, bring the blanket off Joseph's bed," her mother snapped.

Molly hurried into the house and dashed up the stairs to her brothers' room beneath the eaves. Nathan and Joe shared the small chamber and the tiered bunks that hugged the wall. Molly grabbed the edge of the woolen blanket tucked over Joe's straw tick on the top bunk and yanked it off. His pillow and nightshirt tumbled to the floor, but she didn't stop to pick them up.

Nathan, her mother, and her grandfather hovered over Papa as Molly ran through the doorway and to the wagon's side. Her mother plucked the blanket from her hands and laid it out beside the injured man.

"Now, Nathan, help me lift him onto the blanket."

"I'll help too." Anson squeezed closer and grimaced as he looked down into his son's face. "David, can you hear me?"

"I hear you, Da."

"We'll move you easy, son."

Nathan looked anxiously at his mother and then his grandfather. "Maybe we should wait until Dr. Trann gets here."

"If the doctor's not home, it could be hours," Mum said. "Let's slide him over onto the blanket, and then we can lower him down slowly. Molly can help."

"Should we put splints on it?" Nathan stood solidly atop the hay mound as though still unwilling to move his father.

"The doctor will tell us," Grandpa said. "Let's get him in the house."

Kate had come to stand beside Molly, and she stepped forward, her brow wrinkled like the furrowed cornfields. "I can help, too."

Together, Mum, Nathan, and Grandpa managed to ease Papa onto the wool blanket. Getting him down from the wagon was harder. Molly's heart wrenched as he let out a cry of agony. They lowered him quicker than they'd planned to the ground, with Molly and Kate trying to ease the landing. Papa lay panting, staring up at the sky, as Mum slid down off the hay load.

"David, did we hurt you more?" Mum wrung her hands as she bent over him. "I should have listened to Nathan and let the doctor tell us how to do it."

"Nay. I'm all right." Papa's clenched teeth belied his words.

"Nathan, there's a wide plank in the byre leaning against the wall," Grandpa said. "I was going to use it to wall off a calving stall. Fetch it, lad. We'll carry your father on it and jostle him less."

Molly wrapped her apron around her hands and squeezed them tight. "What shall I do, Mum?"

Her mother's eyes were dark with determination—no time for weeping yet. "Get down the willow bark and yarrow, in case the doctor can't come. And tear up that old linen towel I said could go for a rag. We'll need strips."

Molly hurried with her little sister to the assigned tasks, terrified to turn her back on her suffering father, yet relieved not to gaze any longer on his face.

*****

Lord Washburn's country estate, outside London

Peter Stark entered the Earl of Washburn's "closet"—the private study where the earl conducted his official business—with caution. His heart always thumped when his master summoned him. Washburn treated him well, but the difference in their stations and the knowledge that his lordship could make life very difficult for him if he desired always kept Peter on edge in his presence.

"Good afternoon, my lord. You wished to see me?" Peter bowed as he spoke.

"Yes, yes, come in." Washburn laid aside the paper he'd been reading. "Have a seat, Stark."

Even more unsettled, Peter walked to the chair the earl indicated. He always stood in the presence of aristocracy—except for that one time several years ago when his master had invited him into his closet and spoken to Peter as one man to another, not as a master to a servant. That had never been repeated, and Peter liked to think they understood one another—but here was the earl inviting him to sit down again. Was he going to talk about Peter's past once more? What would be the point?

Peter sat still and tried not to fidget.

"I've just learned that I'll soon be taking a journey," Washburn said.

Peter arched his eyebrows. "A journey, my lord?" He'd seen the butler usher in the Duke of Newcastle that morning. Newcastle—the queen's colonial secretary—had been closeted with the earl for a half hour and then left, seemingly in a good humor. Was he the one who had informed Washburn of his impending trip?

"Yes. It seems I'm invited to travel to North America with Newcastle and the Prince of Wales."

Peter's heart sank. The earl would be away for several months, which meant Peter wouldn't work during that time unless he went back to his former means of earning a living—hiring out as a day laborer and doing whatever heavy work was available. Or perhaps he'd carry on under the supervision of the earl's steward.

"I wish you a good journey, my lord."

Washburn smiled. "I was hoping you'd consent to accompany me."

Peter blinked. This unexpected news made it more difficult to keep his composure. To travel with his lordship—and to

America! What would his mother say about this? "I…don't know what to say, my lord."

"It's like this." Washburn leaned forward and laced his fingers together on the desktop. "Newcastle has charge of the arrangements for the prince's transportation and so forth. The entertainment—that is, the reception in each city…the levees, balls, and such—will be left to the local officials. But Newcastle asked me to go along as a friend of the prince's family and a representative of the government. Of course, General Bruce will go in the capacity of the prince's personal governor, but I have a good rapport with His Royal Highness, if I may say so, and I'll be able to advise him if it's needed."

Peter nodded slowly. The Prince of Wales, at eighteen years of age, would need older, steadier heads along. He couldn't charge across British North America alone, for certain. The provincial politicians would eat him alive, currying the favor of the future regent—not to mention the mischief the young prince had shown he could find when unsupervised. General Robert Bruce would keep a lid on the young man's behavior, and Washburn would be available as a discreet confidant—a role he filled well, as Peter could attest. But he wasn't sure what part someone like himself would play in this drama. Surely he wouldn't be considered a companion for the prince. A commoner of questionable parentage would not be approved for such a position.

"And you wish me to go?" he managed.

"Yes. Two of the prince's friends are going—soldiers back from the Crimea. They'll be company for the prince, as equerries. But Newcastle thought it would be well to have a young man along whom we could send on errands if we meet with any problems. Someone who can deal with shopkeepers and railroad superintendents if need be, things like that. I told him you are a dependable and personable young fellow. He agreed to let me invite you." Washburn sat back, beaming at Peter.

"That was very kind of you. Thank you." Peter found it difficult to speak, but the idea had grown more real—and more attractive—as his master talked.

"I admit, it was selfish on my part, knowing I'd travel more comfortably with you along," Washburn said. "I'm not taking Varrell, so you'll have to assist with my wardrobe and the like."

"That would be an honor, my lord."

"I'll warn you, though, most of the members of the suite will be middle-aged fogies like me…or journalists from various newspapers. Dr. Acland, the prince's physician, will be along, as well as a couple of other gentlemen, but it will be quite a small party. We don't want to overwhelm the provincial folks with a plethora of guests to put up."

As his lordship explained it all, Peter tried to take it in. He, a common laborer, now servant to an earl, had been chosen out of all the men in England to accompany the Prince of Wales. It boggled the mind. But the description of his duties eased his tension a bit. He could run errands and go behind-the-scenes to settle small difficulties. As Washburn's understeward, he was used to wading through the minutiae of details to make his master's life run more smoothly. Surely he could do that for the prince as well. And if Washburn needed him to brush and press his clothes, Peter was used to doing that for himself. Varrell, the valet, could give him some pointers before he left.

"Of course, I'll stand for your expenses," Washburn said. "So, what do you say? Can I count on you?"

Peter's heart thudded in his chest. The earl was leaving the decision to him, not ordering him to go. That typified the relationship they'd had for the last six years. He was an employee, but he'd served Washburn with a willing heart since he was sixteen years old. This voyage could change his life. What would it mean for him? For his mother? For the future?

He managed to smile serenely. "Of course, my lord. I'd be happy to serve you on the journey."

Chapter Two

Molly tiptoed about the kitchen, helping her mother cook supper while Grandpa and the two boys milked the cows.

"Do you think Papa will wake up for supper?" Kate asked from the doorway.

Mum glanced up from kneading the biscuit dough. "The doctor gave him a good dose of laudanum. He'll likely sleep a few more hours. But the rest of us need to eat."

Kate clenched and unclenched one fist as she hovered. Molly made herself smile in what she hoped was a reassuring manner. "He'll get rested, and maybe you can talk to him in the morning."

"How will we keep up with all the chores?" Kate asked.

"I'm sure I don't know." Their mother reached for her biscuit cutter.

"The boys and Grandpa Anson can handle the milking, now that school is out," Molly said.

"It will test us, for certain." Mum swiftly pressed the cutter into the dough a half dozen times and laid it aside.

"Kate and I will do everything in the house," Molly said. "And I can milk too, if need be."

Her mother made a dismissive sound.

"I know I'm not good at it, but if I practice, I'll get better." Molly reached for a stack of ironstone plates.

"That's probably true, but I think you'd help us more if you tried for one of those jobs at Government House."

Molly stopped with her hand in midair. "Do you?"

"Your father mentioned it to me last night. He didn't want to push you into service if you weren't of a mind to do it, but the truth is, we were scraping the bottom of the cash barrel before this happened. He already wondered if he'd have enough to pay men to help with the hay crop."

Molly walked around the table, setting each plate down deliberately. Taking a job as a domestic servant was far from what she'd imagined she'd be doing at the age of twenty. A schoolteacher, perhaps, though Mum and Papa had coaxed her to stay with them on the farm. She'd even dreamed of marrying and keeping her own house by now. But the young man she'd fancied had turned elsewhere, and she hadn't met anyone else she could love enough to leave her family for.

But scrubbing and cleaning at the governor's mansion? She turned toward the small mirror that hung beside the coatrack. "They would never choose me." She eyed her reflection doubtfully in the old walnut-framed glass her grandmother had brought across the ocean from England. Her grandpa and her friend Allison said she was pretty, but she didn't feel pretty.

"Why not? You're not afraid of hard work," her mother said. "That's what they want at Government House—young ladies who'll be diligent and not lose their heads over the prince."

"The prince." Kate squinnied up her eyes until they became slits with blue slashes glinting at Molly. "Imagine being in the same house with him."

Molly shook her head and turned to get the saltcellar from the cupboard. "I wouldn't be so foolish as to become enamored of an aristocrat. Everybody in this family knows better than that."

Nathan entered the kitchen from the dairy attached to the house, carrying a can of cream. "Fresh from the separator." He lumbered to the churn, and Molly leaped to open the lid for him.

Her mother continued as if the conversation had not been interrupted. "I expect you're right, dear. You'd be fine."

Her brother tipped up the can of cream and emptied it into the wooden churn. "Our Molly is nearly always right, but what is it this time?"

Mum gave him a wan smile. "We were discussing whether she should put in her name for service at Government House."

Nathan eyed his sister with keen appraisal. "Would you go and scrub floors, or what?"

"Probably." Molly shrugged as though it wasn't important, though her pulse had ratcheted upward when her mother suggested it, and she felt like running to her room to escape the discussion. She smoothed her apron. "The governor's wife is going to hire extra domestic staff to get ready for the Prince of Wales's visit. Housemaids and kitchen staff, mostly."

"We could use the money, I guess." Nathan set the cream can on the floor and replaced the churn lid firmly. "With Papa laid up, it might be tough around here this summer. You know the doctor said six weeks at least, maybe eight, before he can work again."

Mum said gently, "Molly shouldn't have to apply if she doesn't want to. We've plenty for her to do here."

"Aye." Nathan gazed at his mother with mournful blue eyes. "We might be all right. Joe and I will work hard."

Molly's chest ached. Go to work at the governor's house, among strangers? She would have people critically watching everything she did. And would others look down on her if she became a servant? But if this was the one thing she could do that would most help the family in this time of need, of course she would do it. She pasted on a smile for her mother's sake. "It would only be for a few weeks. The prince is coming in early August." She went to the large cabinet where they kept the everyday dishes and flatware. Automatically, she counted out seven forks.

"Still, I never expected to see my daughter go into service." Her mother shot another questioning glance at her.

"It's all right, Mum," Molly said. "Allison Johnson is putting her name in. I'll go with her tomorrow." Molly crossed to the kitchen table and laid down the forks. She picked up that week's edition of the *Islander*. "The notice says they want a dozen women."

Her mother's brow furrowed. "If I were younger..."

"You'll be needed here at home," Nathan said.

"Yes," Kate said from the corner near the stove. Molly realized she'd been listening and waiting to see the outcome. "You can't go to work in the city, Mum."

"Let Molly apply." Nathan sounded very like Papa, though he was two years younger than Molly's twenty. "If they don't take her, we'll get by on what we have, though it's precious little. If they do, it will be a help. And as Molly says, it's only until August. She'll be free to help with harvest."

"Will Papa and Grandpa get to meet the Prince of Wales?" Molly asked. Grandpa had talked of the possibility for weeks now.

Her mother frowned. "I doubt your father will be able. He'll be disappointed. But Grandpa will want to go, of course. I don't think you could stop him from going into town when the royal party arrives."

The door that led to the front yard swung open, and Grandpa Anson hobbled in, leaning on his cane.

"Well, then, Da, what's the news?" Mum asked. "I saw you leaning on the fence and conversing with Denny Sayre."

"Denny says Lord Washburn is coming with the Prince of Wales in August."

Molly caught her breath. "Washburn?" It was a name they all knew well.

"Aye. He heard it from Tinen Brophy, and he's a member of the legislature, now there."

Mum eyed her father-in-law narrowly. "Now, Da, you mustn't start anything."

"What do you mean, start anything? 'Twasn't me who started it. All I want is a word with his lordship, that's all. Just a word."

"But…" Mum closed her mouth and turned back to her biscuit dough.

Molly realized she'd counted out enough plates and forks to include her father at the table and took one of each back to the cupboard. "Grandpa, I'm going with Allison Johnson tomorrow to ask for employment at Government House. What do you think of that?"

The old man stroked his white beard. "Well, now, that's interesting."

"It will be a good opportunity for her." Mum looked anxiously at him for a moment.

"Perhaps."

"Perhaps she'll meet his lordship," Nathan said. He ducked out the back door and closed it.

Molly stared after him. What would she do if she came in contact with the earl? The idea was more daunting than that of meeting the Prince of Wales.

"There, we shall have some nice biscuits tonight." Mum placed each one in the pan and set it in the oven. "Katie, after you've set out the cups and knives, go call the boys and your father for tea."

"But Papa's abed, with his leg all smashed."

Her mother's face threatened to crumple. "You're right—I misspoke. Call the boys and let your papa sleep."

"Yes, ma'am."

Molly and Kate hurried to finish setting the table. Their mother poured hot water into the teapot and bustled about the stove. When the last dish was laid, Kate scurried out the back door that led through the dairy into the barn.

Grandpa reached out and laid a gentle hand on Molly's sleeve. "You'd not be eyeing one of those grand fellows who'll be with the prince?"

"Of course not, Grandpa."

He nodded and straightened the chipped cup she'd set beside his plate. "The prince is but eighteen years old—two years younger than you, my girl."

"That's so. he's Nathan's age. But there's talk of a ball in his honor." Molly rounded the table, laying out soft old linen napkins at each place as she went.

"A ball." Her grandfather snorted, and her mother looked their way.

"And why not?" Mum asked sharply. "He's the queen's son, after all, and the heir apparent."

"Oh, yes. Our future ruler." Grandpa looked longingly at the teapot. "I suppose he'll want to dance with the local girls."

"Not with me," Molly said.

"And why not?" Mum asked sharply. "You'd stand up to any of them for looks, even Mrs. Dundas."

Molly smiled at that. "Now, Mum, let's not be comparing me to the governor's wife."

"Well, she's a handsome lady, 'tis true." Again Grandpa eyed the teapot.

"I expect it's brewed enough for you to have half a cup." Molly picked up the teapot and poured some into his cup.

Mum shook her head. "You spoil that man, Molly."

Grandpa laughed. "Too late for that. My Ellen coddled me for nigh forty years, and you've not done such a shabby job yourself, Liza. She's carrying on the tradition."

Mum waved a dismissive hand at him. "There now, don't ask me to give you extra flan because you talk so sweet."

"Well, then I'll ask our Molly. Think you to be a Cinderella, girl?"

Molly chuckled. "Me? I'm like her, I suppose. I've no dress to wear to a fancy ball. But then, I've no fairy godmother, either."

"You never spoke a truer word."

"Besides, if I'm in service at Government House, I certainly shall not be invited."

"Perhaps not." Grandpa sipped his tea and looked over at Mum. "How's David doing now?"

"Still asleep."

"I'll check on him now, before we sit down," Molly said. She stepped to the door of her parents' room and opened it gently, peering into the dim room. Her father lay on the bed as the doctor had left him, breathing deeply as he slept.

The back door opened once more as Molly regained the kitchen, and Kate skipped in. "The boys are washing up."

A moment later, Nathan and Joe came in, their sleeves rolled up and their hair damp, with comb marks lining it.

"If it stays warm like this, we'll get all the hay in," Nathan said as he slid onto the bench on the wall side of the table.

"We may need to hire another man to help us get it all cut," Grandpa said with a frown. "I doubt you and I can manage it alone."

Ten-year-old Joe took the seat beside Nathan. Kate took the other end of the bench. With her mother at one end of the table, Molly took her customary chair beside Grandpa Anson.

"Shall we pray?" Her grandfather bowed his head, and all of them followed his example. "Lord, we thank thee for this food and for our family and farm. We beg thy swift healing for David, and we ask thy providential hand on the young prince as he comes to us. May he prosper if You see fit to preserve him and let him one day rule over us."

The others said, "Amen." Molly shot Grandpa a sideways glance, expecting him to begin talking about the royal visitors again, but he began filling his plate and for once kept his thoughts to himself.

*****

June 28

Molly and her friend Allison stood in line outside the back door of Government House. A chilly drizzle soaked their bonnets and skirts. Some of the women in line had umbrellas, but most did not.

Allison's face pinched up as though she'd bitten into one of Mum's icicle pickles. "We look like a couple of drowned rats. They'll never pick us."

"We're no worse off than most of the others." Molly touched her friend's shoulder with her sodden glove. "Just be glad you wore your warm coat."

"Who'd have thought it, in June?"

"Indeed." The line moved forward, and Molly took a step. They'd arrived early, and she had counted thirty women ahead of her and Allison that morning. Nine were left—that she could see. Others were sheltered inside the kitchen of the huge house, as they'd progressed in the line to that point. Behind Molly and her friend, at least sixty more stood in the rain. The queue straggled down the drive toward the city streets near the harbor, so far that Molly couldn't see the end of it. "We'll be inside soon."

A young woman in a worsted skirt, cotton apron, and gray knit shawl emerged from the door ahead of them, squeezing past those waiting. " 'Scuse me. Pardon."

"Fanny!" Allison seized the young woman's arm. "Were you interviewed?"

"Good day, Allison—or rather, soggy, nasty, wet day." The interviewee laughed. "You're nearly there, so take heart."

Molly knew Fanny Dalton slightly. The young woman had attended the same rural school as she and Allison but had been two grades behind them. Molly kept her peace and let Allison carry the conversation.

"What did they ask you?"

"Hmm. Well, if I had experience in service, and if I could do heavy cleaning, and who my folks were."

"Were you hired?"

Fanny frowned. "The housekeeper said those as are hired will be told on Monday."

Molly let out a pent-up breath. So, they would have to wait four more days before they knew the outcome.

Other women in line were looking at Fanny and leaning in to catch her words. Fanny bent toward Allison and said softly, "Once you're through the door, you'll be in the kitchen. If you're there for a few minutes, you'll warm up and dry out a little. If you're in luck, your hair will dry and not frizz all over like mine did."

Allison smiled. "I brought a comb."

"That was great foresight on your part. You ought to get a moment to use it. Best of luck."

"Thanks." Fanny walked away, and Allison said to Molly, "At least we can run the comb through our hair before they call us. Maybe you can shield me so other people can't see me do it."

Molly, whose locks were pulled back and knotted at the nape of her neck, only smiled. Her hat had at least kept the worst of the water from her hair and she doubted she could improve her looks in a ten-second encounter with Allison's comb, but she was willing to aid her friend.

At last the line moved forward enough for them to reach the back entrance of the mansion. As she stepped into the dim interior, Molly realized they didn't enter the kitchen directly. The line wended through a cold room holding several large tubs and baskets. This must be the laundry. Soon they shuffled to the next doorway. Several women were visible inside the vast kitchen, all diligently tending to their tasks—chopping vegetables, filling the firebox on a huge cast-iron cookstove, and putting away stacks of clean dishes. Although the door had to remain open behind them, the warmth of the kitchen prompted the girls to remove their coats and shake their skirts a little, hoping they would dry quickly.

Four stools had been placed so that the four women at the head of the line could sit down for a few minutes and ease their feet, and to Molly's surprise a girl of about sixteen, dressed in black and wearing a white overall apron, brought her and Allison each a cup of strong tea.

"Thank you very much," Molly said.

The girl ducked her head. "You're welcome, miss." Her soft brogue told Molly that she belonged to one of the many Irish families on the island. "Mrs. Dundas came in an hour ago and saw that the ladies had a long wait. The tea was her idea, to perk you up before you face Mrs. Bolton."

"Mrs. Bolton?" Allison asked in a guarded whisper.

"She's the housekeeper, miss."

"Ah." Allison shot Molly a glance.

Realizing they had an opportunity to gain information, Molly asked, "Do you like working here?"

"Oh, surely." The girl smiled. "It's hard work, but they treat us well, and the pay is good."

Molly smiled back. "What's your name?"

"Jane Lyons. I'm one of Cook's helpers."

"I believe my younger brother was in school with you," Molly said. "Nathan Orland."

"Sure, I remember. He was a year above me. But I'm done with school now that I'm employed." Jane nodded and turned to take empty teacups from those ahead of Molly in the line. On her way back past them, she paused just long enough to say, "I hope you're hired, ladies."

"I wonder how she got her job," Allison said.

"Who knows? Maybe she's related to someone in service here, or perhaps she answered an earlier advertisement."

During their conversation they drank their tea and moved forward until they were privileged to occupy two of the stools. Every few minutes a footman wearing green-and-gold livery came to the doorway near where the first woman in line sat and told her to go in. Finally Allison was called, and Molly sat on the first stool still waiting her turn and holding both their coats.

"Almost there, dear," said the older woman behind her.

Molly turned and smiled at her. "Yes, ma'am. Aren't you Mrs. Chiden?"

"The same. I've known your mother these twenty years."

"So, you hope to get work during the royal visit?" Molly asked.

"We all do, don't we?" Mrs. Chiden grimaced. "I suppose every family can use a little ready money."

"Yes, that's so."

The door opened, and the footman said, "Next."

Molly followed him along a hallway and up a flight of stairs, wondering what she should do with the coats. Another footman, in his green-and-gold livery, stood outside a closed door in the passageway.

"You'll wait here," said the young man who had brought her up.

Before Molly could thank him, the door opened and Allison slipped out. Her face was bright red, and she looked close to tears. She seized Molly's wrist before taking their coats. "Good luck, friend."

"Thank you."

The first footman said, "I'll take you down, miss."

The footman beside the door nodded to Molly and opened the door again. "There, now, go on in, miss."

Molly thought he winked at her, but she wasn't certain, so she decided to ignore him. She stepped forward, into a cozy sitting room crowded with furniture. A thin, gray-haired woman sat regally in a rocker near the empty fireplace. Beside her was a small table holding a teacup and saucer, a pencil, and a sheaf of papers. Not a speck of ash marred the spotless hearth. The furnishings outshone those at the Orland farm in their finery, but Molly wasn't sure the room full of stiff chairs, stands, and china ornaments was as comfortable as the shabby rooms back home.

The woman's black dress crinkled slightly as she pushed the rocker back and forth with her toes. "Come in, then, and sit down. We haven't all day."

Molly scuttled into the chair facing her.

"I'm Mrs. Bolton."

"How do you do?"

"I do fine, thank you. What is your name?"

"Molly Orland."

"Hmm..." Mrs. Bolton consulted the paper before her then raised her chin, giving the effect of eyeing Molly down one side of her ample nose. "You're a farm girl?"

"Yes, ma'am. My father is David Orland, on the North River Road."

"I see. What sort of work do you do on the farm?"

"I keep house with my mother, mostly. I cook and sew and scrub and churn—whatever needs doing."

"And have you a beau?"

Molly's pulse quickened, and she blinked at the abrupt question. "No, ma'am."

The housekeeper nodded. "Wouldn't want your young man coming around while you were working, or making a fuss about it."

Molly was beginning to understand why Allison's face had flushed so while she sat in this chair.

"So you're not afraid of drudgery?"

"Oh no, ma'am. I can scrub and iron and wash dishes—whatever you need."

"Well...I'll keep you on the list." Mrs. Bolton made a notation on a piece of paper. "If you are hired, you'll be informed on Monday. You'll come in that afternoon to be measured for your uniform. You'll provide your own dress and apron for regular work, and you'll receive one dress, black stockings, a white apron, and a cap to wear while the royal visitors are in residence. You must supply your own shoes—black. You can keep the clothing after your period of employment ends."

"Thank you, ma'am. That's very generous."

"Perhaps. You'll be expected to arrive properly clothed and clean every morning."

"Assuredly."

Mrs. Bolton nodded. "Go on, then. If you don't hear on Monday, you're not hired."

"Thank you very much." Molly stood and gave a little curtsy then strode toward the door.

When she stepped out into the hallway, the footman said, "All done, miss?"

"Yes, thanks."

He smiled at her. "Not so bad, was it?"

"I suppose not."

"I'm Eustace. Milton is the other footman. He'll be right along to take you down."

Molly eyed him cautiously. He wasn't homely, but she suspected he fancied himself quite a figure in his uniform. Did he chitchat with all the applicants? She thought not. She looked down the hallway, toward the stairs. Milton and Mrs. Chiden rounded the corner of the passage.

"I work here regular," Eustace said.

"I see."

"Perhaps we'll meet again."

"Yes, perhaps."

Molly was glad when the others came close.

"Go right in, ma'am," Eustace told Mrs. Chiden.

Molly smiled at her. "I wish you success." She scooted after Milton toward the staircase, without looking back at Eustace.

At the kitchen door, Milton swung open the panel and let her pass before saying, "Next."

Molly slid by the waiting women and squeezed through the laundry room door.

Allison waited for her under a tree on the back lawn. She held out Molly's coat when she saw her. "What kept you?" She fell into step with Molly.

"I didn't think anything did. But that footman upstairs—Eustace. Did he want to talk to you?"

Allison curled her lip. "He asked me if my knees were shaking before I went in. Can you imagine?"

"Cheeky, I'd call it."

Allison nodded. "He's supposed to keep the line moving. Mrs. Bolton won't stand for much shilly-shallying."

"I agree, and if he thinks he can flirt with all the new maids, he'll get a surprise when he comes around us, won't he?" Molly slipped on her coat and buttoned it, though it smelled of damp wool and hung heavy on her shoulders. The rain had stopped, but the wind still blew keenly off the sea.

Allison laughed as they trudged down the muddy street. "You're so sure they'll take us on. But what did you think of your interview? Will she hire us?"

"I don't know. She did say that we'd know Monday, and if I was called I should come in for a dress and other clothing. Did she tell you that?"

"Aye. But perhaps she told everyone."

"We'll have to be patient. I thought you looked a bit upset when you came out of Mrs. Bolton's room. What did she say to you?"

Allison shrugged. "Just things like did I have any followers—you know, beaux."

Molly nodded. "She asked me that too."

"And she said I looked a mite scrawny. I suppose she was testing me."

Molly threaded her arm through Allison's. "Well, I don't think you look scrawny, though you are willowy-slender."

The friends walked away from the harbor and the crowded streets of Charlottetown. Their fathers' farms lay about two miles from the official home of the colony's lieutenant governor, George Dundas. The islanders usually referred to Dundas simply as "the governor," though he served under Sir Edmund Head, the governor general of British North America, and as Queen Victoria's official vice-regent of the island.

After the first half mile, the paved streets gave way to roads—normally hard-packed earth, but an oozy red mud today. They kept to the side as much as possible, walking in the grass at the edge of the road.

"This mud will be the death of us," Allison muttered.

"It is a trial. But the sky is lighter ahead, and I believe it's getting warmer too." Molly unbuttoned her coat as she walked and looked out over the fields that already sprouted this year's crop of potatoes in long, regimental rows. "I love this time of year, and Grandpa says it will dry up soon."

"Do you think we'll get to see the prince if we're hired?" Allison's brown eyes had gone dreamy.

"I don't know. We'll probably be kept below stairs and out of sight. I expect the more experienced servants will serve the prince and his retinue."

"You're probably right." Allison's foot slipped, and she stumbled into the spongy roadbed. "Ach! This mud."

Molly smiled and grabbed her friend's hand. "Come on. Let's get home. I'm sure our mothers have plenty of chores for us to do."

"But if we did see the prince..."

"Yes?"

"They say there will be a fine ball at the Colonial Building."

Molly grimaced. "Servants won't go to that, unless it's to pass trays of food and take the ladies' wraps. It will be for the legislators and their wives, and the leading merchants—people like that."

"That's so unfair."

"What would be fair?" Molly shook her head. "I don't think many girls on this island will lay eyes on Prince Albert Edward. That's only for the rich."

Chapter Three

Monday, July 2

Molly woke early on Monday and couldn't go back to sleep. When she heard her grandfather call softly to the boys, she rose and dressed. She filled the coffeepot and set it on the stove. Grandpa and Nathan liked coffee after they finished the morning milking.

As she worked, she tried to imagine herself in her own kitchen. She'd expected to be married by now—had even picked out her husband two years back. Emmet Price. He was reading law then, and her father considered him a fine prospect. Emmet had called on Molly every Friday evening for two months. He'd even spoken to her in general terms about the future. Though Molly wasn't sure she loved him, she had begun to dream.

All that had changed on the evening Emmet questioned her about her family. He'd heard a rumor in town—something about her grandfather being deported from England. It was true, Molly admitted.

But why, he wanted to know. Emmet had pressed her on the issue until she told him everything. It wasn't a secret, exactly, but they rarely spoke of the matter outside the family circle. But Emmet was to be part of the family, wasn't he? Molly felt he had a right to know.

"The man's a felon," Emmet had declared when she'd finished the tale. "A criminal in exile."

Molly had leaped up, flushed with anger. "How dare you! My grandfather is an honorable man!"

That was the last time Emmet had come around. If they saw each other across the church or met on the street, they nodded coldly and then studiously avoided looking at each other. Just thinking about the night they'd had their falling-out still made Molly's blood simmer.

She tore about the kitchen trying not to think about Emmet or the fact that no other suitors had come a-courting since then. Had Emmet warned all the other young men that she was the granddaughter of a felon? Surely not. Any decent young man would see Grandpa Anson's integrity and ignore the rumors.

Molly blew a stray wisp of hair off her forehead and began to chop onions with a vengeance, as though her family's well-being depended on her making the pieces small enough. She had breakfast started—potatoes sliced and frying with the onions, and cornmeal mush bubbling on the stove—before her mother came into the kitchen.

"How's Papa?" Molly asked.

"Fretful. That leg pains him so. I dosed him just now so he'll rest a bit longer. Dr. Trann is due to come and look at him again today."

"That's good. I'll be anxious to hear if his bones have begun to knit together."

"I'm not sure the doctor can know that yet, but he should be able to see if anything's going wrong. Your father hates the medicine. He wants to stay alert and know what's happening around the farm." Mum sighed and tied on her apron. "Can you help weed the garden today? Da and the boys have all they can manage with the milking and the hay."

"Yes, and Katie and I can churn if you'd like."

"We'll see how things go. I may need your help with the washing later."

Nathan opened the back door and came in with a can of milk. "Smells good in here."

"You can eat any time you're ready. Shall I put on the eggs?" Molly asked.

"Aye. I'll tell Grandpa and Joe." Nathan left the milk on the work counter and went out the way he'd come in.

Molly put the cast-iron skillet on the stove and plopped a generous blob of butter into it. She glanced out the window toward the road before she took the eggs from the icebox.

"Looking for word from Government House this early?" Mum asked.

"Silly, isn't it? If someone does come, it will probably be in the afternoon. I'm sure there are a lot of women closer to town that they'll go to first."

Mum smiled at her, weary before her day's work had begun. "To be truthful, I don't know how I'll get on without you if you're hired. But we're dreadfully low on cash. Anything you bring in will be welcome."

"I know." Molly went to her mother and gave her a quick hug.

"Do you mind so very much?" Mum asked.

"No. At least not yet." Molly smiled. "Ask me again when I know what I'm getting into."

She cracked a dozen eggs into a bowl, stirred them, and poured them into the sizzling skillet. Grandpa and the boys came in, and she sat down to pray with the family while the eggs cooked.

A half hour later, while she washed the breakfast dishes, Molly was surprised by a knock at the front door. She hurried to open it, thinking that perhaps Dr. Trann was making his rounds early.

On the doorstep stood Eustace, the footman from Government House, in his green-and-gold uniform.

"Good morning, Miss Orland." His bright smile left her no doubt of his errand, and her pulse quickened.

"Good morning. May I help you?" She determined not to give him any encouragement in his notion that the maids would flirt with him.

"I've come to you first, miss. You're the farthest out, but I wanted to be sure you knew, and I was certain farm folk would be about early."

"You're correct in that," Molly said.

He smiled even broader. "Well, then, you'll come to Government House between one and three this afternoon for your kit, and they'll tell you when you'll begin work. Sound pretty good?"

"Yes, thank you."

He winked at her. "Right. So I'll be seeing more of you, Miss Orland."

*****

"Molly! Molly!" Allison's voice reached the kitchen at the Orland farm before she did.

Molly threw down her dish towel. By the time she'd gotten to the back entrance, Allison had given a peremptory knock and flung the door open.

"They've given me a job! That footman from Government House—Eustace—just came to our house and told me I was chosen. I'm to go in this afternoon for my outfit."

Molly smiled and drew Allison into a quick embrace. "Wonderful! He came here too, and I was going to stop in after lunch and tell you and see if you'd heard."

"We can go together."

"Yes, let's," Molly said. "Was Fanny Dalton hired?"

"No. I saw her father on my way here, and he said she hadn't heard a word. Since she lives closer to Charlottetown than you do and we've both heard, I expect she wasn't picked."

"That's too bad, though I believe he started with the farthest houses first. Perhaps we'll see her after all." Molly sent a swift prayer of thanks for the relief of having Allison accepted too. It would have been much scarier to begin service alone.

That afternoon, a score of women arrived at the back entrance of the governor's grand mansion. Molly and Allison went with the rest, in through the laundry as they had a few days earlier, to a large room beside the kitchen.

"This is the servants' hall," Mrs. Bolton informed them.

Molly looked down the long table and wondered if extra chairs had been added for the newly hired staff. She'd had no idea so many servants worked at the governor's house.

"You will eat your lunch here on the days that you work. Cook will provide your meal after the family and guests have been served upstairs. Most of the staff eats lunch about two o'clock. If you work into the evening to serve the late dinner upstairs, you'll have tea at six."

The housekeeper called each new employee's name and told her to report either to the first parlor maid or the cook the next morning.

"Molly Orland."

Molly stepped forward.

"You will work under Roberts, the first parlor maid."

Molly curtsied. When each woman had been assigned her duties, she went out to the laundry and received her clothing. The laundress looked Molly over and handed her a plain black cotton dress and apron, black stockings, a kerchief, and a white apron and cap.

"You'll wear the kerchief when you're cleaning these next few weeks. If you serve or go where the family's present, you'll put on the cap. When the royal visitors are in residence, you will wear the white cap and apron. You are expected to look clean and fresh each morning."

Molly nodded. Allison came behind her and received the same wardrobe for the job. Allison had been told to report to the cook in the morning.

As they headed for home carrying their bundles of new clothing, Molly waited for Allison to speak. Her friend was quiet for a while, but after several minutes, she said, "Well then, we shall start something new tomorrow."

"Indeed." Molly eyed her cautiously. "Are you disappointed? That you're assigned to the kitchen, I mean."

"Not really. I'm just delighted to have the job." Allison gave her a weak smile. "Of course I'd rather be where you are, but in all honesty, if I hadn't been hired, we'd have been in dire straits this summer."

"Us too, with Papa laid up."

"I'm sorry. I know it's been hard since he broke his leg."

"Yes. I've been out milking with Nathan and Grandpa every day. It's just too much for the two of them. Mum will have to help them now. Joseph isn't big enough to handle the cattle, but he's learning. Everything is harder without Papa." Tears filled Molly's eyes, and she wished her friend hadn't mentioned their families' situations.

"All this rain too," Allison said. "It's like to ruin the hay crop. Oh dear. I'm so sorry. I didn't mean to upset you."

Molly shifted her bundle to her other arm and patted Allison's shoulder. "Don't be sorry. Things are hard now, but they'll get better." She smiled. "We both have work, and the prince is coming to the island."

"Just think. We'll be washing the dishes he's eaten from." Allison's eyes glistened. "I'll find a way to see him. Somehow I will."

*****

Saturday, August 4

Peter rose at dawn and packed his luggage. He shaved carefully and dressed in the suit he'd reserved for traveling by boat. It wasn't his best, but it was finer than any his family could have afforded. His master, Lord Washburn, provided well for him, and while traveling, Peter dressed better than he had in England when working at the Washburn estate. He now performed a valet's duties and often served the earl while the other aristocrats in the prince's party were present, and so he had a trunkful of new clothes and dressed like a gentleman. Peter found that ironic.

His visit to America was only beginning, though his journey had already lasted nearly a month. After crossing the Atlantic, they'd spent nearly two weeks cruising about Newfoundland,

Nova Scotia, and New Brunswick with the Prince of Wales. Today the prince would head off by railcar for Fredericton, New Brunswick, while Peter would sail in the opposite direction, for Prince Edward Island.

He looked out the window of his hotel room. Once again, it was raining. That shouldn't matter, though the trip across the strait would have been more pleasant on a bright day. Lord Washburn had given him particular instructions. Be sure the people of the island know that the prince will arrive the ninth or the tenth, most likely the ninth. Make certain the ceremonies are appropriate. And if this incessant rain continues, make sure they've provided for the prince's comfort and a way for him to stay dry.

The rain had plagued them since their arrival in British North America, and several in the party were beginning to sniffle. So far the prince had avoided the nuisance and seemed to enjoy every moment of mixing with his public.

Lord Washburn often complained in private—never before the prince or the Duke of Newcastle—that he was wrinkling up like a raisin and his stockings never truly dried out. Peter did his best each night to make sure his lordship's clothing was fully clean and dry—even if it meant sitting up half the night by a fire and holding the earl's smallclothes in careful reach of the flames' heat without scorching them. But it was all for naught. By midmorning, Lord Washburn's feet had gotten wet again and his toes were puckering.

When he had finished getting dressed, Peter went to the hotel's dining room. He didn't expect to see his master so early, as he knew for a fact that Washburn had stayed up to have a glass or two of brandy with the prince and the Duke of Newcastle the previous evening.

The hotel's owner met him at the entrance to the dining room. "Good morning, Mr. Stark."

Peter nodded.

"I understand you are leaving us this morning. I hope you'll enjoy your breakfast, sir."

"Thank you. And could you get a man to take my trunk to the ship?"

"Of course."

Peter gave him a coin generous enough to pay the man who did the work and reward the man sent to summon him. "I'm sailing on the *Valorous*. And I thank you."

The hotelier hurried away. Peter entered the dining room and filled a plate at the sideboard with broiled fish, scones and jam, and a boiled egg. As soon as he sat down, a steward appeared at his elbow with a silver coffeepot.

"Coffee this morning, sir? Or would you prefer tea?"

"Thank you, that's fine. A little cream in it, if you please." He looked up as another man entered the dining room.

"Good morning, Stark."

Peter jumped to his feet and bowed to the Earl of Washburn. "I didn't expect to see you this morning, my lord."

"I wanted to have a final word with you before we part."

"Very good, my lord. Can I serve you breakfast?"

"Nay. I'll take some coffee, and we'll talk. I'll eat later with the prince and Newcastle."

Peter nodded and waited until his master had taken a seat.

"Sit, lad," said the earl.

Peter sat, feeling a bit odd and out of place. Sitting down when the earl was in the room violated the rules under which he lived, and eating in his master's presence was unthinkable.

The steward poured coffee for the earl. "Would you like cream and sugar, my lord?"

"Yes, thank you. Just a bit of sugar."

Washburn said no more while the steward cut a small piece from the sugarloaf, placed it in his cup, and poured in a dollop of cream. Peter began to eat, though it was difficult. He took small bites and tried his best to remember every table manner his mother had ever taught him. He simply couldn't enjoy the well-cooked food with the earl sitting across the table from him.

At last the steward left them.

"Now then," said Washburn, "I'm glad we have a moment with no one else present. You will take the utmost pains, my lad, to be certain the people of Charlottetown put a good face on it when the prince arrives."

"Of course, my lord."

The earl pulled a wry face and lifted his coffee cup. "I know this puts a lot of new responsibility on you, but I think you can handle it. The duke insisted we send someone on ahead to make sure the locals do things properly. They weren't prepared when we landed in Saint John, as you know. I hope we can prevent that from happening again."

"Yes. Of course, His Highness was very good about it."

Washburn sipped his coffee and set the cup down. "Yes, he's been very good-tempered throughout the journey so far, but a little more of this rain and a few more provincials full of excuses—well!" He brushed the thought aside with a wave of his hand. "No matter. You will precede us this time, and the lieutenant governor shall be on the alert."

"Absolutely, my lord. I'll see to it that they've got their program in order. With your letter and the one from the Duke of Newcastle, I'm sure I'll be admitted to see the proper authorities." Peter laid down his fork and gave up all pretense of eating. He had inner reservations about his new duties, but he would never express them to his master.

"That is well, then. I know you'll see to all the details. His Grace was a bit perturbed the other day—more so than His Highness, I believe. Of course, the duke reports continually to the prince consort and the prime minister back in England."

"We'll make certain the islanders are prepared," Peter assured him. He reached for his own cooling coffee. If he did not head for the docks soon, he'd miss his ship to Prince Edward Island.

The earl leaned toward him confidentially. "Of course, the queen hopes this tour of her son's will solidify the local feeling and they'll show more support for the monarchy and confederation of the colonies. You're aware of that."

"Well...yes, my lord, I've heard talk."

Washburn grunted and leaned back. "Then you've also heard that the people of Prince Edward Island are among those most resistant to confederation."

"Yes, my lord."

"This trip is very important. And the prince's temper, while even and sweet to this point, could grow less amiable if he's met with disdain."

Peter straightened his shoulders. "Surely the colonists wouldn't—"

"I don't suppose they would, but we can't be certain, can we? I expect the local officials to fawn over the prince. I'm not so sure about the farmers and workmen."

"Ah." Peter tipped up his cup and drained it.

"Well, you must be off, lad, if you hope to catch the tide." The earl stood.

Peter rose as well. "Yes, my lord. I shall look forward to seeing you in a few days."

"I'll anticipate the reunion as well. Oh, and Peter—"

"Yes, my lord?" His master rarely addressed him by his Christian name, and Peter felt the earl's concern behind his words.

Washburn reached into his waistcoat and brought out a small pouch. "You may have some unexpected expenses."

"You've been most liberal with me."

"Take it. You may have need. They might even send you to a hotel."

"Yes, my lord. Thank you." Peter accepted the pouch and tucked it into the pocket of his jacket. To his surprise, the earl extended his hand.

"And take care, Peter."

"I will."

The earl nodded and looked him over as their hands clasped with a wistfulness that bespoke the loss of his family more than ten years ago. Peter wished he could fill the empty spot in Washburn's lonely life, but in his station, he could be no more than a servant to the earl. And so he released his master's hand and turned to the hall, where he'd left his bags. He only hoped he could fulfill the earl's expectations. When he'd been invited to accompany Lord Washburn on this journey, he'd never expected the prince's reception—and perhaps the loyalty of North American British subjects—to require his personal attention.

He shouldered the small bag that held his personal items and the leather case containing the top hat that wouldn't fit in his trunk and quickened his steps toward the dock. He could not fail his master or his prince.

Chapter Four

Monday, August 6

Peter stepped off the *Valorous* onto the wharf at Charlottetown and looked about. He didn't expect anyone to meet him, and he'd need to find his way to the lieutenant governor's house and present his letters of recommendation. He'd shared the ship with the military band traveling with the prince. They would set up tents in one of the city's larger parks and enjoy a few days of relaxation before the aristocrats caught up with them.

Peter picked up his bags and left the band to unload their gear under Captain Aldham's supervision. The air was moist from recent rain, making the grass of nearby fields glitter and the leaves of poplar trees overhanging the street to shimmer. The beauty of the place struck him—the red cliffs that had welcomed him as he stood on the ship's deck and the verdant fields and farms on the distant hillsides. Only eighty thousand souls called Prince Edward Island home. The rich soil and picturesque views wherever one looked made him long for some land of his own. In a place like this, a man could build his own life and take advantage of all sorts of possibilities.

He strode down the wharf. Charlottetown—what he could see of it from here—seemed a graceful and quiet town. A man in a drooping hat and the rough clothes of a laborer was supervising the unloading of a smaller vessel. Peter paused to watch, and the man waved. "Morning."

"Good morning," Peter said. "Could you tell me the way to the governor's house?"

"Not far—up there, turn left at the corner. Walk to the end and turn right, then left." The man grinned. "Sounds complicated but it's not. Keep toward the shore, sir, and you'll find it." He eyed Peter's satchel. "Or you might want to hail a wagon."

"Thank you."

Rather than deal with the luggage and the unfamiliar streets, he followed the man's advice and hailed a carter. He soon found himself deposited before a fine Georgian house facing the water, with wide lawns in front and gardens and trees behind.

"Please wait while I go to the door," he told the driver. "I may wish you to take me to a hotel afterward."

"Aye, sir."

The willingness of the colonial people to speak to strangers surprised Peter. Everyone seemed more relaxed here—less conscious of the differences between them. Surely this would be the perfect place for a man who wanted to farm and forget the political furor and class distinctions that were so much a part of life in England. Peter seldom dared to think that way at home.

A very grave gentleman dressed in black answered his knock, and Peter gave his name and handed over his letters of introduction.

"Won't you step into the morning room, sir?" said the man, whom Peter pegged as the butler.

Peter removed his hat and followed him inside. It amazed him how quickly he gained acceptance using the precious letters. Under ordinary circumstances, he would enter a house like this only through the back door.

The entrance hall was a tastefully decorated room with a curving grand staircase, a gallery above, and a brass and crystal chandelier. The butler showed him into an opulent room to one side of the hall, where Peter admired the paintings of hunting scenes and a militia regiment drawn up in a battle line. The windows opened on the rear garden, which had been tended with care and now exploded with the hues of a dozen varieties of flowers.

Within five minutes, a woman in a fine yellow gown appeared in the doorway. Her dark hair framed her pleasant face, and she had the lithe figure of a young woman, though she must be nearing forty. She advanced with a fetching smile, holding his documents in her hand. Only when she came within three paces did Peter notice the fine lines at the corners of her eyes that bespoke her age.

"Mr. Stark, I am Mrs. Dundas. My husband is at the Colonial Building this afternoon, but he'll be home shortly. Won't you sit down and have a cup of tea with me while we await his return?"

"Thank you, madam." Peter bowed at the waist and took the smooth, white hand she offered. He straightened and added with some hesitation, "I have a driver outside. Is there a hostelry nearby to which I can direct him with my luggage?"

"Oh, sir, you must be our guest here at Government House—or Fanning Bank, as we call it."

"That is most gracious of you."

"We intend for His Royal Highness and the members of his suite to lodge here with us during his visit, so why shouldn't you begin now? It will make things simpler for you to be near my husband as you make arrangements."

"I cannot thank you enough, madam."

"Mr. Reynold can take care of the driver and your luggage."

Mrs. Dundas went into the hall and gave some muted instructions. Clothing, Peter decided, did make the man—provided, of course, that he also had the recommendation of some high-placed aristocrats. People assumed that Peter was also of blue blood, which he found quite amusing.

He heard the front door close, and Mrs. Dundas reappeared in a swirl of yellow silk.

"There. All taken care of. Please sit down, Mr. Stark. I've asked for tea to be sent in. You must tell me about your journey and what it is like to travel with the prince."

Peter sat as she gestured for him to do, on a velvet-covered chair. The tea Mrs. Dundas served warmed him, and the scones and biscuits she offered with it filled a yawning void he'd been feeling since about the time they'd approached the harbor.

"And will the prince arrive here as we've heard, on Thursday?" his hostess asked.

"Yes, that is still the plan. August the ninth, or surely by the tenth if he is delayed. When I left Saint John yesterday, His Highness was off by railway to Rothesay and then by steamer to Fredericton. He's expected to return to Saint John on Tuesday and journey here by steamer."

Mrs. Dundas smiled. "We do so look forward to this visit. It will be the first time any of the royal family has come to the island."

"His Highness has thoroughly enjoyed seeing Newfoundland, Nova Scotia, and New Brunswick. But I'm sure he'll find this island a unique experience. I was struck by its beauty as we crossed the strait and approached the wharf."

"That is kind of you to say so, especially in this weather. We are partial to the island, I must say. My husband has been here only a year, but he is very fond of the colony and its people."

"Oh, that puts me in mind—" Peter sat forward, eager to take care of one detail he'd forgotten. "The prince's table service arrived on the steamer with me, madam. The captain said he would have it unloaded on the wharf within the hour and delivered here. You're aware of this provision?"

"Yes, indeed. I can barely wait to see it. I've heard that the queen had the dishes specially commissioned for this tour."

"That's right. There are two complete sets, bearing the prince's crest surrounded by a wreath of maple leaves. While one is being used, the second is shipped ahead to the next destination."

"Which would be my house." She smiled with evident pleasure in her role as the prince's hostess.

They chatted for several minutes, and Peter found Mrs. Dundas a good conversationalist. He gladly answered her questions about the Atlantic voyage and the prince's tour, but when she inquired about his family, he touched only lightly on the topic.

"My mother was very excited that I was able to come. I'm traveling as an employee of the Earl of Washburn. He's among the prince's suite—with His Grace, the Duke of Newcastle."

"Oh, yes, I'm looking forward to meeting both gentlemen. I must say, Mr. Stark, that despite your youth, you are doing a fine job of representing your employer—and the Crown."

"Thank you, ma'am." Peter's nerves were a little on edge from being in the plush surroundings, and her comments about his station sent his pulse careening. He would give a lot to avoid discussing his family. He cast about his mind for another subject he could broach without seeming rude. They'd covered the weather, but he harked back to it. "I'm sure the rain will pass before His Royal Highness arrives."

"I do hope you are right." She looked toward the doorway. "Ah, Mr. Reynold."

Peter followed her gaze to where the butler now stood.

"Mr. Stark's room is ready, madam."

"Thank you." Mrs. Dundas rose, and Peter also stood. "A footman will take you to your room, Mr. Stark. Once you're settled, please feel free to return to this room. Would you like me to inform you if the lieutenant governor returns in the meantime?"

"Yes, thank you."

Peter followed the liveried young man up the curving staircase to the gallery overlooking the main hall. His room lay on the second floor, along one hallway and then down another into a separate wing.

They passed several closed doors, and one of them opened just ahead of the footman, causing him to check his pace momentarily. Peter glanced into the open doorway. A lovely young woman, wearing the black dress and apron of a maid and holding an armful of linens, stepped back, her face flushing.

"Oh, excuse me." Her gaze caught Peter's for a split second, and then she looked down. "I beg your pardon, sir."

"Think nothing of it," Peter said. A lock of her golden hair had escaped her black kerchief and lay against the dark cotton of her dress. She presented a charming picture, though she obviously regretted having opened the door when she did.

The footman said hastily, "This way, sir."

41

Peter followed him down the hall. When they neared the end of the passageway, the footman opened the door to a cozy room with windows on two sides. Peter stepped in and looked about. He could barely keep from protesting that the place was too fine for him. The cherry furniture included a wardrobe, a dresser, a large cheval mirror, and a four-poster bed with embroidered brown-and-gold hangings. A mound of brown, red, gold, and purple pillows on the bed reminded Peter of how little sleep he'd caught the night before on the ship.

"Is everything satisfactory, sir?"

"Yes, it's perfect."

The footman gave a nod that was almost a bow. "May I assist you in dressing for dinner, sir?"

Peter reined in his impulse to stare at the man. No manservant had ever before offered to help him dress. "No, thank you. I'll be fine."

The man gave a full bow then. "My name is Milton. If there is anything else I can do for you, sir, just ring the bell." As he straightened, he nodded toward a tapestry bell pull on the wall near the bed.

"Thank you very much, Milton." Peter was tempted to tell him that, in reality, their stations were much the same, but he held back. The earl had trusted him to perform a duty that required authority, and he would erode that authority if he began making friends with the staff at Government House.

*****

Molly watched the gentleman retreat down the hall behind Milton then scurried to the back staircase and down into the kitchen, carrying her burden of soiled linens. She hoped Milton wouldn't tell any of the other staff that she'd opened a door practically in the face of a distinguished guest.

The afternoon waned as she waxed the floors of the guest chambers in the south wing, and soon it was time for her to leave for the day. She took the floor polish and rags to the cupboard in the laundry then peered into the pantry in search of Allison. Her friend sat at a small worktable, polishing silver.

"Ready to go?" Molly asked.

"Nearly. I have to finish this."

"Can I help you?"

Allison smiled. "I don't see why not."

Molly took the cloth her friend handed her and set to work while Allison fetched another.

"Did you hear that there's a dinner guest?" Allison asked. "Very unexpected."

"That must be the gentleman I saw in the hall upstairs. Who is he?"

"Someone to do with the royal tour. Making arrangements for the prince, I suppose, making sure we've cleaned and shined everything. He's probably a stuffy old bureaucrat."

Molly chuckled. "That's not how I'd describe the gentleman I saw a few minutes ago."

"Oh? Tell me more."

"He was quite handsome."

Allison's eyes grew round. "Really? Is he old?"

"Nay, I'd guess not more than five-and-twenty. Certainly no older than thirty."

"Oh my."

The two gazed at each other and laughed. "Aren't we silly?" Molly asked.

"I don't know. Are we? I think it's warranted, when we so seldom get to meet a handsome new man."

"Well, this one is beyond our reach, to be sure."

"What was he wearing?" Allison asked.

"A frock coat and trousers, dark cloth—perhaps because of the damp—but I think they were deep gray."

"A waistcoat?" Allison paused her polishing and squinted into the distance as though picturing the man.

"To be sure." Molly had kept her eyes down during most of the encounter and found herself staring at the gentleman's waistcoat, which she remembered well. "A pearl-gray figured silk. And…I believe a snow-white shirt."

"Ah. Mustaches?"

"No. Nor a beard. He must have shaved this morning."

"If he arrived by ship, that must have been a trying exercise." Molly laughed.

"What are you two hens cackling about?" asked a strident voice.

Molly jumped and looked up at the undercook. "Beg pardon, ma'am."

"We're trying to prepare a company dinner. Is that silver ready?"

"Yes, ma'am." Allison leaped up and knocked a knife off the table as she did so.

Mrs. Randolph—called simply "Randolph" while at work—was nearly as somber as the housekeeper. Molly wondered if she aspired to take Mrs. Bolton's place one day.

The undercook sighed. "Wash that one." She looked over her shoulder. "Here, Jane. Take the flatware to the dining room and set it up proper-like. And do put an extra spoon on for dessert. Cook's made two puddings, besides the cake."

"Do you want me to stay and help?" Allison shot a longing glance at Molly as she spoke.

"Nay," said Randolph. "Just be back bright and early. There'll be extra work in the morning too, with the gentleman here for breakfast. Like as not we'll be making coffee *and* tea, though the governor doesn't like coffee."

*****

"The lieutenant governor just came in. He's gone to freshen up." Mrs. Dundas drew Peter into the morning room. "You'll want to discuss the arrangements for the levee and ball with him, no doubt."

"Yes, thank you."

"Ah, there he is now." She stepped forward to meet the tall, handsome Scotsman in the doorway. Lieutenant Governor George Dundas, with his luxuriant side whiskers, looked to be an open and likable gentleman.

"Mr. Stark, this is my husband," Mrs. Dundas said with an expectant smile. "George, Mr. Stark is here in advance of the royal party. I've put him in the gold room upstairs, and he'll stay with us for the next few days. He says we can expect the prince and his suite by Thursday."

"Wonderful," Dundas said, shaking Peter's hand with enthusiasm. "Has all gone well on the tour thus far?"

"Marvelously, Your Honour. His Highness received a warm welcome in Newfoundland, and again at Nova Scotia and New Brunswick. I heard him remark that each of the colonies is different, but all are intriguing."

"I trust he'll be intrigued by our island as well."

"My dear, I shall leave you now and go dress for dinner," Mrs. Dundas said.

"Oh, yes, indeed. Is it that late?" Dundas glanced at the tall clock in the corner. "I shan't keep you long, Stark, but I would like to have a word with you."

"Of course, Your Honour."

After his wife left, Dundas took a seat and gestured for Peter to sit down. "Now, let me tell you what we have planned for Thursday and Friday. We have it all set up for a warning to be sent when the prince's steamer is spotted. Guns from the battery will fire a salute as they enter the harbor. That will give us at least a half hour to assemble. A contingent of local dignitaries will meet him at the wharf. We'll have a carriage, specially furbished and decorated, waiting to take His Highness from the ship to this house. Other carriages will be available for his suite. I assure you, every detail has been attended to."

"I'm sure you've been hard at work with your advisors to make certain of it," Peter said. "Is there to be a levee, where the prince will receive the local gentlemen?"

"Oh, yes, that will take place here. Have you seen the drawing room?"

"No, not yet."

"You must see it. It's a lovely room, and quite large. Too big for a small gathering, which is why we use this parlor more. But I'm sure it will do for the levee. Now, the ball is another story."

"You are planning a ball as well?"

"Yes, if you don't think it will overtax the prince." Dundas's thick eyebrows drew together. "I understand his visit will be brief."

"Yes." Peter thought the flurry of events might rather overtax the older gentlemen accompanying His Highness, but he would never say so, and neither would they—except to each other. Of course the provincial folk wanted to entertain their royal visitor and show him the best of their colony—in two short days. "The Prince of Wales loves to dance. I'm sure he'll be enthralled."

"Good, good. The ball will be held over at the Colonial Building, in the legislative chamber. I was there this afternoon to speak to the assembly. We'll move their furniture out, of course. It's a well-proportioned room, with a gallery above where the musicians can sit."

"It sounds well suited to the event."

"Perhaps you and I can go over there tomorrow, when the decorations are being placed, and you can view the room."

"I should be happy to do that."

Dundas nodded his shaggy head. "Excellent. And the flower of the island's young womanhood shall be on hand to keep His Highness in partners."

"He will be delighted, I'm sure."

"During the day, of course, we'll provide a mount for the prince, if he wishes to ride. I only hope this dismal weather lifts by his arrival."

"His Highness is used to riding in inclement weather. Riding is one of his favorite diversions. I'm sure that if you provide horses for him and two or three of his companions, he'll be very pleased."

"Good. We have some excellent horseflesh on loan in the stable. And the lanes and country roads about Charlottetown give one a pleasant ride, I must say. Our farmland is unmatched."

"I'm eager to see it myself, sir."

"Ah! Perhaps we can take a ride tomorrow morning, or Wednesday. I'd love to show you some of the best views of the island. The cliffs, the lighthouses, the waves on the red shore…it's impressive, I must say."

Dundas soon excused himself to prepare for dinner, and Peter returned to his room. He had only two other coats besides the one he'd worn on shipboard. The most formal was the one he'd been wearing for state occasions during the tour. That would stay in the wardrobe until the Prince of Wales arrived. He took out his second-best and changed his cravat to a less casual one. He tied Lord Washburn's for him on occasion, and though he did it backward, Peter fancied he did a fair job of it.

Someone tapped on his door.

"Yes?" Peter called, giving his reflection in the mirror a final check.

The door opened, and Milton, the footman, bowed to him. "The governor and Mrs. Dundas are in the small drawing room, sir."

"Ah. Waiting for me?"

Milton lifted his shoulders noncommittally.

"I believe I'm ready," Peter said a bit uncertainly. Should he ask Milton to look him over and see if he'd forgotten anything? He decided against that and strode past the footman, the way his master would have, wondering all the while at his own audacity.

When they reached the grand hall below, Peter stood back and let Milton precede him to the door of the room where he'd met with his hosts earlier.

"Mr. Stark," Milton said gravely.

Peter nodded at him and walked into the room. Mrs. Dundas had donned a blue-and-silver dinner dress with a wide hoopskirt, while her husband was dressed in a short black dinner jacket, a snowy shirt and cravat, and black trousers.

"Ah, Mr. Stark." His hostess met him beneath the chandelier. "Would you like some wine before dinner?"

"No, thank you."

"Well, then, if you don't mind, we'll go right in to dine."

"Of course," Peter said.

Mrs. Dundas bowed her head in acknowledgment. "Cook says everything is ready, and we are a little later than usual."

"That's entirely my fault," her husband said. "I stayed overlong at the Colonial Building this afternoon to go over the arrangements for Thursday with the party leaders. Must have equal representation from all organizations when the prince arrives, you understand."

"Oh, I do, sir." Peter well knew the rivalry of the locals for the prince's attention. Deciding who got to stand closer to His Highness during the welcoming ceremonies would give any man a headache.

Mrs. Dundas waited expectantly. Since he was the only guest, it was up to Peter to escort her to the dining room. He'd never done such a thing, but he stepped up and tried his best to emulate Washburn's manner when offering a lady his arm.

"If you are ready, then, madam?"

"Yes, thank you very much." She slid her hand into the crook of his arm and smiled again. She was quite pretty, and Peter could see the appreciation in her husband's eyes. From the limited accounts Peter had heard, she was an accomplished hostess and well liked by the islanders. He only hoped he could succeed at this masquerade and hold up his end of the dinner conversation.

Chapter Five

Tuesday, August 7

"You will work in the guest apartments this morning." Roberts, the first parlor maid, gave assignments each morning to the four maids working under her. She nodded severely at Molly and the three others who stood before her in the servants' hall. "Remember, the royal party's representative is staying in the house already, so mind you're discreet when you go through the passageways. Make yourselves scarce if you see the gentleman. We do our cleaning while the guests are not about."

Molly nodded, wondering how difficult it would be to tidy up the guests' rooms when the entire royal entourage was in the house.

"With that said, let us prepare all the rooms for the guests today, on the chance that they arrive earlier than expected. I'm told the carpentry work and repainting is finished. We must go over the sitting room, bedchamber, and dressing room for His Royal Highness, a bedchamber and sitting room for the Duke of Newcastle in the north wing, and bedchambers for General Bruce, the Earl of St. Germains, and the Earl of Washburn. The other distinguished visitors will stay at the city's best hotel."

Deborah, who stood beside Molly, stirred.

"You have a question?" Roberts asked.

"Yes, ma'am. It's been said downstairs that some of the prince's people will stay in the servants' quarters."

"I believe we will house two valets, but I shall ask Mrs. Bolton to check with Mr. Stark about that. Mr. Stark, I assume, will stay in his present quarters through the end of the prince's visit, unless His Highness sends him on ahead to the next venue—but for now we'll plan on maintaining the gold room for him as well as those others I mentioned. All clear?"

Molly nodded with the others.

"Fine, then. This morning, fill the wood boxes in case it is cold during the visit and our guests want a fire. Then do a thorough job of dusting and sweeping the apartments. The builders who modified the prince's rooms left some sawdust behind. You'll also need to clean all windows, mirrors, and woodwork. When everything is spotless, you may make up the beds and put fresh sachets in the wardrobes. On Thursday morning, we will place fresh flowers and water in each room."

"Yes, ma'am," Molly and the others murmured.

"Dismissed to your duties."

As they hurried to the laundry to retrieve their cleaning supplies, Deborah said, "Two valets. British, too. This week will be interesting in more ways than one."

"Here, now," said Rosaleen, who was the wife of a farmer and had worked at Government House for several months. "You young things had better watch your step and concentrate on your work, not the visiting gentlemen and their servants."

"Surely we'll have to mix with the gentlemen's gentlemen." Deborah giggled. "I wouldn't mind marrying an Englishman."

Rosaleen clucked in disapproval. "All I know is, if you disgrace yourself with Mrs. Bolton, you'll be out of here in an instant."

Molly opened the cupboard that held the mops, broom, and cleaning buckets and forced a smile. "Well then, shall we begin, ladies?" Deborah's wistful words drew her memory to the handsome young gentleman she'd encountered yesterday. This Peter Stark—where did he fall on the scale of aristocracy and domestic help? She'd had the impression he was a gentleman, perhaps with a title, but Roberts and Mrs. Bolton had referred to him as "Mr. Stark," so he couldn't be a lord. If he were a lower servant, they wouldn't call him "Mr." He carried himself with a confidence and ease that most servants would not exhibit. She found it very confusing.

Of course, her parents—and especially Grandpa Anson—had taught her that she was as good as anyone on the island. But by taking the job at Government House, she'd relegated herself to a lower class. If not for this job, she would have been able to go with her family and neighbors to watch the procession when the prince arrived. Instead, she had to remember to which of the Dundases' domestic staff she was expected to curtsy and which ones she could smile at and greet as an equal.

"We'll probably be scrubbing the bath while the prince is making his address to the public," Deborah said, as if echoing her thoughts.

Molly handed her a feather duster. "Perhaps we'll get a glimpse of him as he dines, or as he walks through the grand hall."

"Now there's a thought." Deborah beamed at her. "Maybe we could hide in the gallery when he comes and take a peek at him."

"We're not supposed to be seen. You're just asking to be sent home without pay." Rosaleen snatched a bucket and a rag and strode back to the kitchen and the pitcher pump where they got the water for scrubbing.

It wasn't really important that she see Prince Albert Edward. *As long as Grandpa Anson gets a chance to speak his piece to the Earl of Washburn, I won't care if I never lay eyes on the prince,* Molly thought. *Well, not excessively.*

*****

Peter and Governor Dundas stole an hour before breakfast to ride out into the countryside. They trotted out through the fields near the governor's house and down a country lane. The bay gelding he rode stepped along smoothly. Peter reveled in the freedom he seldom found—and the privilege of riding a good horse. The island glistened in the heavy dew of a damp morning, but the moisture couldn't disguise the rich farmland and rolling fields. It was land such as Peter often envisioned owning—but he had little chance of achieving that dream.

The governor talked to him as he would any man—with his Scottish accent and a ready laugh. Peter found talking to Dundas easy, and his host soon launched a discussion of the various crops grown on the island.

They swung onto a narrow trail where the horses had to go single file. Peter's mind drifted back to the moment they'd left the stable yard. He'd caught a glimpse of two women in black approaching the rear entrance of the mansion. One of them had blond hair that gleamed in a ray of early sunlight. The girl he'd seen after his arrival?

He wasn't sure why, but the maid's poignant face had stuck in his memory. Something about her demeanor as well—she'd reacted to their sudden meeting courteously, but he had a feeling she hadn't always been subservient. She belonged out here in the countryside, free and active, not cooped up in a rich man's house doing menial labor. The sight of her arriving at the mansion shortly after daybreak suggested that she lived at home somewhere with her family, not in a cramped berth in the servants' quarters. That thought heartened him.

The governor called to him, and he urged his horse up next to Dundas's as they came out on the road again. They trotted back into the stable yard just as rain began to fall in earnest, turning the earth in the yard to sticky red muck. The horses slogged through it, and Peter reluctantly handed his mount over to a groom. He ought to clean up the horse himself.

"Thank you," he told the groom. "I can tell you've been taking good care of him." He ran a hand over the gelding's warm flank and gave silent thanks for the morning's entertainment.

He and Dundas proceeded across the yard on foot, which resulted in Peter sinking to his ankles and having to draw his feet slowly from the mud or lose his boots.

"Would you show me the back stairs, sir?" he asked his host as they neared the house and gained firmer ground. He held up one booted foot covered in mud. "I should hate to leave any of this good red dirt on the carpet."

Dundas gave a hearty chuckle. "I often take the rear stairs myself on such occasions. Come."

They slipped in through the kitchen. The cook and her helpers looked up and curtsied. Dundas nodded cheerfully at them and hurried around a wall that shielded the narrow staircase the servants often used.

"Here we go, Stark. Wipe your feet again on this mat, and we're up one flight."

Mr. Dundas appeared to find the entire morning's activities a lark. He led the way up to the second-floor landing, where Peter again cringed at the thought of setting his boots on the plush rugs that lined the hallways.

"I believe I'll slip my boots off." Peter sat down on a chair next to the stairway door.

"Very conscientious. Leave them at your chamber door, and the footman will take them away to polish them for you."

Peter smiled. While he didn't normally black boots anymore, he had done that chore at Washburn's estate and would not disdain doing it again. He nodded at Dundas. "Thank you, sir."

"I enjoyed it, Stark. Always a pleasure to have a decent horseman as a riding companion."

His Honour ambled down the hallway, leaving evidence of his passing in little clumps of red mud on the rug. Peter smiled at the casual compliment, picked up his boots, and stood. Now if he could only make it to his room without dropping them. He set out cautiously, hoping he didn't meet anyone on the way. He threw a glance over the railing as he passed through the gallery over the main hall. One of the footmen was crossing below in the direction of the dining room.

Peter turned the corner into the hall of the north wing and stopped suddenly, face-to-face with a girl. No, not a girl—a young woman. A very pretty young woman, with golden hair and blue eyes. As he took in the shocked expression that drew her lips into an O, he realized she was the same maid he'd encountered the previous afternoon when under Milton's guidance.

"I beg your pardon." He held his mud-caked boots well away from their clothes and turned sideways to keep them even farther from her dress. Her gaze traveled from his face along the length of his outstretched arm to the boots and then down to his feet. Peter's face heated as he considered that she now regarded his stocking feet. "I…er…riding…"

She looked up with a quick smile. "To be sure. Would you like me to take those boots for you, sir?"

"Oh no, I couldn't ask you to do that."

"Why not? It's our job to make your stay comfortable."

"Oh, it is. I am. I mean…" Peter gave up with a shrug and a tentative smile. "Sorry. I'm Peter Stark."

"Yes, sir."

"And you are…?"

She hesitated, and her cheeks flushed prettily. "I'm Molly, but I don't think…"

Of course. She was forbidden to speak to guests unless they asked for some service. He should have known better. "I'm sorry, Molly. I didn't mean to put you in an awkward position." His own awkward position, with the heavy boots held out at arm's length, struck him suddenly, and he laughed.

Molly laughed too and reached out. "There now, sir. Let me take those. You must have other shoes you'll be wearing today. Breakfast will be waiting for you and the master, I'm sure."

Still Peter hated to give over the boots. He didn't begrudge Molly earning her living, but this seemed too grubby a task for a woman like her. "They'll get your dress dirty."

"That's what my apron is for."

"All right." Slowly he lowered the offensive boots and let her take them by the comparatively clean tops.

"There! We'll get these cleaned and oiled for you and back in your room before your next ride."

"I doubt I'll get to ride again before His Highness arrives." Her eyes flickered. All the young women must be aflutter over the impending visit. Peter asked, "Are you eager to see the Prince of Wales?"

"I admit I am. Curious, you might say. But I'm much more interested in seeing Lord Washburn."

Peter eyed her carefully. Surely he had misunderstood. "You wish to see Lord Washburn?"

The young woman's face flushed, and she looked away. "I beg your pardon, sir. I shouldn't have spoken up."

"Yes, you should have. Tell me, what is your interest in the Earl of Washburn?"

"Oh, I don't think..." She refused to meet his gaze. "I should go and tend to these boots, sir." She stirred as though to flee.

"Please, don't be alarmed. I'm employed by his lordship, and if there's anything I can help you with..."

"You?" Her eyes flew wide open. "Oh no, sir. I shouldn't have said what I did. It's really my grandfather who would like to see him, not me personally. My family..." She stopped again, and Peter sensed great reluctance on her part.

"Yes?" he asked gently. "Your family would like to petition the earl?"

"Not exactly." She shrugged. "We have a connection, that's all, and my grandfather hopes for a chance to meet him. Now, if you will excuse me."

Stunned, Peter stepped aside and watched her walk swiftly down the hall toward the corner. This lovely young maiden living in the colony and holding a menial job had a family connection to his master? The earl had said nothing during their voyage together of having relatives in the colonies. Peter was certain he would remember something like that. But if she was truly related to Washburn, what was she doing cleaning muddy boots at Government House? Perhaps she'd simply meant that her grandfather was at one time employed at Washburn's estate. Still, she'd said "a connection." Didn't that mean a relationship? Or could it mean something else? A business connection, perhaps?

"Wait," he called.

She looked over her shoulder at him. "I mustn't. I'm sorry."

Of course she mustn't. Peter turned and walked slowly to his bedchamber. If she was caught talking to him, she would probably lose her job. He should have known better than to try to engage her in conversation—to imagine that they had something in common. He wished social barriers hadn't come between them. If she only knew that he was more on her level than the governor's. Under other circumstances, he'd be taking his meals in the servants' hall with her and the other maids and footmen. But because of his assignment, she assumed he was one of the aristocracy.

That thought brought a mirthless chuckle. Even if it were possible for Peter to better himself and attain a higher station, he wasn't sure he'd want to. Why on earth would anyone wish to climb the social ladder to gentility when such a winsome young woman belonged to the working class?

*****

Molly took the muddy boots down the back stairs and entered the kitchen, heading toward the laundry. Allison, who was washing dishes, caught her eye and smiled. The cook also spotted her.

"Ack! Get those filthy things out of my kitchen!"

"Yes, ma'am. That's what I'm doing." Molly quickened her pace.

"Be those from the young master who's staying in the gold room?"

"Aye. He went out riding with the governor this morning."

"You'd think it would be the horse with the muddy shoes, now, wouldn't you?"

Molly stared at her. Had the severe cook made a jest?

"Uh...yes, ma'am, you would."

"Set them in the laundry. One of the footmen will tend to it."

"I could do it, ma'am."

"Oh, no. Mrs. Bolton says we must have everything spit-spot today, for we've no idea what time the royal folks will arrive, now do we? Supposing they came a mite early and arrived at the dock tomorrow?"

Molly rid herself of the boots and scrambled back up the stairs to the second floor. She would rather stay below and clean Mr. Stark's boots than make up the chambers of the duke. She had a feeling about Mr. Stark—that he wouldn't lay blame on the servant if a spot were missed on his fine leather boots. Now, the Duke of Newcastle she wasn't so sure about.

At the top of the grand staircase she met Mrs. Bolton. The housekeeper's starched black dress crinkled as she walked, and the keys hanging from her chatelaine clinked.

"What are you about, girl?"

"The gentleman had dirty boots from his ride, ma'am. I took them below to be cleaned."

"Ah. Well, I've just inspected His Royal Highness's chambers, and I believe they are in order. Are the duke's rooms ready?"

"All but the fresh flowers and water. The fire is laid and ready for a match."

"Good. And the general's?"

"I believe they're nearly ready. Rosaleen is doing the last of the dusting."

"Go and help her finish. And when Mr. Stark goes down for breakfast, you must tidy his room while he's gone."

"Yes, ma'am."

Molly hurried to the bedchamber Mrs. Dundas had assigned to General Bruce, who had been designated the prince's governor. Molly wasn't quite sure what that meant. Was he some sort of tutor or companion? The title almost sounded like a male governess. But the prince was eighteen years old. Did he still need close supervision?

"Ah, there you are." Rosaleen turned as Molly entered the general's room. "I believe we're about finished in here."

"I'm sorry I was delayed. I had to take some muddy footwear below stairs."

"Well, no harm done." Rosaleen peeked out the window toward the wooded park behind the house. "If it dries up enough, perhaps we'll be allowed to go out and pick bouquets tomorrow."

"Really?" Molly couldn't help but cheer up at that prospect. "The gardener won't do that?"

"He might. But I've been allowed to help him do it before. It's a pleasant task."

"Yes, I should think so."

"And if it does brighten up, the gardener will be busy catching up on the work he couldn't do while it was wet and muddy. Now, Mrs. Bolton wants us to put fresh water in the pitchers in each of the guest chambers today and to change it in the morning if they haven't arrived. Whenever they get here, we must hurry and put hot water there as well, so that the prince and the other gentlemen can wash and shave before dinner if they wish."

"Oh, I just saw Mrs. Bolton on my way here, and she said we must straighten Mr. Stark's room while he's downstairs for breakfast."

"Right. Maybe I'd better go do that while you fill the pitchers."

Molly nodded, a trifle disappointed that Rosaleen would be the one to clean Mr. Stark's chamber. But that was silly. She had so much to do as it was, she shouldn't wish for more work. Still, her curiosity about him had burgeoned since their second meeting. He'd said he worked for the Earl of Washburn. He could tell her what sort of man the present earl was, if she had occasion to ask him. But Molly found her interest more focused on Peter Stark himself. He seemed a bit mysterious, and she wished she knew more about his background.

She took the pitcher from the washstand and headed for the chamber next door. So many details to remember. Her mind kept jumping back to her encounter with Mr. Stark, which didn't help her concentrate on her work. Just thinking about his smile and his slight embarrassment when she'd caught him tiptoeing stocking-footed through the halls made her pulse accelerate and her cheeks heat. Had she made a mistake in telling him that she had a connection to the earl? Would Grandpa Anson be angry if she told him?

Telling Mr. Stark might turn out to be a good thing, she reasoned. The gentleman might be able to help her grandfather gain an audience with his master. She threw that thought aside. She was unlikely to speak with Mr. Stark again, and even if she did, she could hardly ask him for a favor for her grandfather.

Chapter Six

"And is this a fair sampling of the population?" Peter skimmed down the list of more than two hundred names. "The prince will want to meet dignitaries and businessmen but also plain, upstanding citizens."

"Yes," said Dundas. "We've included farmers, merchants, and shipbuilders. We've tried to make Friday's levee accessible to any of the male islanders who wish to take part. Of course there won't be time for more than a couple hundred to be presented to His Royal Highness. After the list was filled, the rest were told to come to the afternoon party in the garden. They can at least get a glimpse of the prince then."

Peter nodded, knowing it was probably the best arrangement they could make—unless it poured rain and washed out the garden party. The more people who saw the prince up close, the better. So far this tour was proving good public relations for the Crown.

He and Dundas faced each other across the desk in the lieutenant governor's office, on the first floor of his home. Peter's mind reeled at the thought of receiving so many guests in an hour, and yet the prince had done so—with good humor—in Newfoundland, Nova Scotia, and New Brunswick. The Duke of Newcastle had insisted that the levee in Charlottetown be limited to an hour. Peter wondered if the Earl of St. Germains would be able to read that many names in the limited time.

"And St. Germains will stand on the prince's right?" Peter asked.

"Yes, and the Duke of Newcastle on his left. When the gentlemen enter the drawing room from the hall, they will give their cards to Captain Lea—a most reliable man—and he will give them to St. Germains. After the men have been announced and they've bowed to the prince, they will retire through the folding doors at the end of the room."

Peter nodded. "That sounds reasonable. I shall probably be on hand to help keep the line moving. Oh, and if you've any questions whatsoever about royal etiquette, St. Germains is your man. He is Lord High Steward of Her Majesty's Household, and he knows simply everything about proper conduct in these situations and the correct address of the aristocracy."

"Good to know. Now, for His Royal Highness's entertainment..." Dundas shuffled some papers on the top of his desk. "We've planned a carriage ride into the country on Thursday afternoon if he lands in time and the weather cooperates. And as you've seen, we have excellent horses waiting, if he's able to get a ride in either before dinner on Thursday or the next morning. Whenever he wishes, actually."

"He does love to ride. What about hunting?"

"Yes, I think there is time for a shooting party after the levee. It's all very closely planned, of course. The public is invited to the lawn party at half past three on Friday, and the prince can make as long an appearance as he likes. There will be a band and so forth. And at dusk, before he goes over to the ball, he'll view the illumination of the ships of war with my wife and me. The lanterns and fireworks should be spectacular, provided it's not pouring rain. Such a bother, this rain."

"It must be a trial for you, with so much planned for the prince's short visit. Now, about the guests at His Royal Highness's meals..."

"Here are the lists. Local dignitaries at Thursday's dinner in plain clothes, in case the royal party arrives later than expected."

Peter nodded. Without the notes given to him in New Brunswick by the prince's steward and Mr. Dundas's explanations, he was sure he couldn't have kept everything straight.

"Other guests, including several ladies, have been invited to enjoy the evening's entertainment after dinner. Then a small party at luncheon on Friday, after the levee—with a short carriage drive in between if possible, so the prince can see more of the countryside. And at Friday's dinner, we've invited the same number of guests as on Thursday evening, but different people, so more can have contact with the prince. Ladies will also be included in that party."

"Good. And I see that a generous supper is planned for the ball."

"Indeed. We've been informed that the caterer should arrive on the same ship as the prince." Dundas grinned sheepishly. "I'm afraid our cook is a bit put out that the government hired a New York chef to accompany the royal party."

"Oh, yes, the chef is going with the prince wherever he goes and will cook whenever members of the royal suite stay in private homes."

"I understand perfectly. It's our cook whose nose is out of joint." Dundas laughed. "Personally, I'm looking forward to a change of cuisine, but you mustn't tell any of our staff that I said so. It was dreadfully hard to find as good a cook as we have."

Peter laid down the papers he'd been studying. "I think, Governor Dundas, that you and your people have prepared very well. Better than some, in fact, though you mustn't let out that I said so."

Dundas laughed. "Excellent, my boy. You warm my heart, and we shall keep counsel together. My wife was in a dither about the fireworks, but I told her that we cannot control the weather, not even for His Royal Highness. If it is wet, she and I will view the illuminations with the prince from the balcony. That will have to suffice."

"I'm sure it's the best plan, with all the activities scheduled for that evening."

After meeting several local officials who would take part in the welcoming ceremonies, Peter left his host for an hour's stroll about the grounds before luncheon. Afterward, they were due to inspect the site of Friday evening's ball, which was to be held in the legislative chambers of the Colonial Building. They'd already viewed the prince's specially prepared rooms, which were grand indeed for the colonies. Peter's head swam with numbers and details. He appreciated the chance to get away by himself and relax in the wooded area, where he could imagine he was miles removed from the city.

The reluctant sun slid out from behind wispy gray curtains, and the woodland path he followed was nearly dry underfoot. This would be a good place for the prince to walk to get away from the crowds, he thought—though "Bertie" might find it rather tame. The young Prince of Wales enjoyed bustle and activity. He'd be pleased that shooting and riding had been squeezed into his itinerary.

Peter found himself eager to see the Earl of Washburn again. His master was a steady, levelheaded man. So far Peter had managed to stay calm while dealing with the lieutenant governor, the mayor, and others responsible for bits of the presentations, addresses, and entertainments, but the minutiae threatened to overwhelm him. He had never before assumed responsibility for anything so large or so public. His usual duties for the earl consisted of much smaller and more personal matters.

In England, Peter tended to details such as making certain the tenant farmers had the supplies they needed and that transportation was provided for any new livestock the earl bought at auction, while Washburn's steward took care of such concerns as rents and plans for the estate. Overseeing the farmer tenants on Washburn's country estate was Peter's favorite part of his duties. The four months or so spent in London each spring for "the season"—that is, the social season of the upper class—were, in Peter's mind, wasted. He would much rather be riding about to different tenancies and watching the farmers plant their crops. Not only did he enjoy that position of trust, but Peter realized how blessed he was to have a job he liked so well.

Still, he wished he could forget the old scandal that had led the earl to seek him out and the stigma it brought. He didn't expect lavish patronage from the earl—Washburn had his own family to think about and leave his wealth to, and his estate was bound by strict and complicated laws that did not include the likes of Peter Stark. But this job had meant a world of difference to Peter and his mother. With his small salary, they lived without fear of hunger, and he could walk with his chin up and not feel shame.

But here, on this island, in this colony, *here* he believed he could become a man of good standing. He might even someday be able to own a small farm and be his own master, to raise animals and till the soil he loved. This rich, red soil that made such a mess. He smiled to himself. If he were a farmer, he wouldn't care whether his boots were muddy. He wouldn't worry about soiling Mrs. Dundas's fine carpets—only about getting his work done on his own bit of land. If the governor should ride by one day, he'd invite him in for a cool drink and a discussion of crops and livestock.

And would he think about finding a wife, perhaps? A wholesome young woman of the island like… He quickened his steps and determined not to follow that line of thought. He would only be in the colony a few days, and nothing could come of it. But still, Molly's intent blue eyes and neat golden bun would not leave his mind.

Who was Molly, really? Did she speak truthfully about her family? She hadn't the demeanor of someone trying to impress a visitor. He yearned to know more. A connection with Lord Washburn. The earl's father had been a known womanizer—that went undisputed in London circles, and Peter suffered no delusions. While the present earl lived a circumspect life so far as Peter knew, perhaps his father had other rejected children that Peter didn't know about. And perhaps one of them now lived on Prince Edward Island.

*****

At suppertime, Molly walked home bone-weary. Her mother and Kate had the table set. Her father sat in the most comfortable chair in the kitchen, reading a newspaper with his foot propped up on two pillows atop a footstool.

"How are you tonight, Papa?" She stooped to kiss his cheek.

"Not bad." He let his paper fall across his lap and patted her shoulder. "Dr. Trann came by this afternoon. He said I can begin walking with crutches in a few more days."

"Really? Are you sure it's not too soon?"

"Soon? I've been off my feet more than a month."

"Now, David," Mum said gently as she carried a dish of baked potatoes to the table. "It was a bad break, and you know that."

Papa picked up the newspaper. "Have you seen what this week's *Islander* says about your place of employment, Molly?"

Molly eyed him cautiously, not sure she wanted to know. Some of their neighbors seemed to think less of her for taking the job, while others had congratulated her on getting it. The island's newspapers had fumed and fussed about the preparations for the royal visit. Rival editors seemed to relish criticizing the government. One ran multiple editorials chastising the politicians for not doing enough to get ready for the prince's welcome, while the other complained in each issue that too much had been spent.

Her father held up the paper to read from the inside columns. "It says, 'The Government House has been prepared for a reception of the royal party, and the suites of rooms intended for the use of His Royal Highness—the windows of which command a fine view of the entrance of our harbor and the fertile fields adjoining—'"

"And so they do," Molly said.

He smiled and read on, "—are commodious and have been fitted up with every regard to comfort and elegance and do credit to the correct taste of Mrs. Dundas, who has been indefatigable in her endeavors to provide for the comfort of the heir apparent, who in a few days will be her guest."

"My, that's quite a sentence," Mum said.

Molly chuckled. "Yes, it is. But the reporter is absolutely right. Mrs. Dundas has done a marvelous job. I've never seen anything so tasteful and elegant in my life. The prince's chambers are magnificent. New carved woodwork and fitted closets…oh, and the wallpaper! The government must be spending a fortune on the decorating bills."

"Meaning that *we* are paying." Her father folded the paper and laid it aside.

"Supper all ready?" Grandpa Anson called from the doorway to the dairy.

"Come in, Da. Are the boys washed?" Mum quickly brought the rest of the food as the family gathered around the table. Nathan helped ease his father's chair closer to them, and Papa offered the blessing for their meal.

When he had finished, Molly cleared her throat. "Mum, Papa…Grandpa…" She looked at them in turn. "Today I met the gentleman who came to arrange the events for the prince."

"What?" Her mother stared at her with a fork suspended over the dish of baked potatoes.

"Mr. Stark. That's his name."

"How did you happen to meet this gentleman?" her grandfather asked.

"In the hall. He came in from his ride with Governor Dundas, and he was carrying his filthy boots. It was very unexpected. Meeting him like that, I mean. I told him I'd take the boots down to be cleaned."

"And?" her mother asked gently.

"And he hemmed and hawed and said he didn't like to be a bother, that sort of thing. And he asked me my name."

Silence hung over the table.

"That's not good," her father said at last.

"Why not?" Kate asked.

Mum shot her a troubled glance and looked back at Molly. "It draws attention to our Molly, that's why."

"What did you say?" Nathan asked.

"I told him my name was Molly, and I ended the conversation as quickly as I could, but…"

"Did you say 'Orland'?" her grandfather asked.

67

"No, I don't think I did."

Grandpa exhaled. "And did you think he was eyeing you in an unseemly fashion?"

"Da!" Mum frowned at him.

"No, I honestly didn't." Molly reached for the bowl of turnips and put a spoonful on her plate. She wished her face wouldn't go crimson and betray her. Whenever she thought of Peter Stark, her heart galloped. She drew a measured breath. "He's very nice and not pretentious. He told me his name, as if I wouldn't know who he was."

"Everyone in Charlottetown knows who he is, I'm guessing," Nathan muttered.

Molly scrunched up her face at him. "He asked me if I was anxious to see the prince. And then—" She stopped, feeling wary and excited at the same time as she remembered the next part.

"And then?" Mum prompted.

"I said I'd rather meet the Earl of Washburn."

"Oh, Molly." Her mother shook her head. "What must he have thought—to prefer to meet an earl over the prince?"

Molly looked down at her plate.

"Why on earth did you say that?" Grandpa asked.

"I—I don't know. Because we've talked about it so much, I guess. I'm sorry." A lump of lead settled in her chest, and she knew she'd have trouble choking down any dinner. "Grandpa, I didn't mean to say anything wrong. After that, he said that Lord Washburn was his employer, and if there was something I wanted to petition him for, he could help."

"Did he, now?" Grandpa Anson's eyes narrowed.

"Yes." Molly shot a glance at her father. "And I—I said I had no petitions, but—oh, Papa, I'm sorry. Was it wrong of me? I said I was connected to the earl."

Grandpa sucked in a breath, but her father shrugged.

"I doubt anything will come of it."

"I don't know why I said it," Molly hurried on. "I could have bitten my tongue afterward."

"Well, now," said Grandpa.

"David?" Mum said anxiously. "What does all this mean for us?"

"Nothing, most likely. Unless Mr. Stark should tell someone at Government House what she said."

Grandpa looked around at them with a defiant set to his chin. "And if he does tell someone, what of it? She only spoke the truth."

Nathan's eyebrows drew together as he considered his grandfather's words. "Do you think they'd discharge Molly?"

Grandpa hesitated. "Perhaps, if they thought she was claiming a relationship to an aristocrat."

"But—"

Papa waved his hand. "Enough. What's done is done. Your grandfather and I have tickets to the levee. If Washburn is there, Da will have a chance to meet him face-to-face and speak to him in person."

"You won't try to go, will you, Papa?" Molly hadn't considered that he would make the attempt. His injury had kept him in bed for weeks.

"I don't think so. I'll ride into town along with Da if I'm feeling up to it, but I shall probably wait outside."

"It's not until Friday," Grandpa said. "If you begin practicing tomorrow with the crutches, you might be able to work up to where you can go in and be presented."

"I doubt I shall wish to stand in line for half an hour by then, even for the chance to bow to the Prince of Wales." Papa turned in his chair and stretched out his left leg, rubbing his thigh thoughtfully. "Well, we shall see how this old leg is doing by Friday."

Mum's eyes darted from her husband to her father-in-law and back again. "David, you mustn't. The doctor didn't say—"

"Joe can go for him tomorrow. It's time I was on my feet again."

"That's the spirit." Grandpa smiled and gave a firm nod. "If Trann allows it, you can hobble about with the best of the islanders and go in with me."

Mum gazed at her husband with troubled eyes. "But if you fall…"

"Hush now, Liza. No talk of me falling. It's time, that's all." Papa glanced around at the children. He seemed to have changed his mind, and Molly wasn't sure why. His gaze landed last on his father, and she thought she had an answer. Something in his eyes implied that he didn't want his father to be alone when he met the earl.

Grandpa raised his cup of tea to his lips. "Yes, I believe it is time, son. Oh, we'll let the doctor tell you that for certain. But if he declares you're fit, we'll go together to meet the aristocrats." He sipped the strong brew.

After a moment's silence, Mum speared a plump potato and dropped it onto her plate. "I don't know where we'll ever find proper suits for the both of you."

"Our Sunday attire should do," Grandpa said.

"To meet the prince?" Mum seemed to be scandalized at the thought.

Molly swallowed hard. "Papa, what if they won't let you in? What if Mr. Stark tells the earl what I said and they won't let you and Grandpa go to the levee?"

"If they slam the door in our faces, so be it."

Grandpa shook his head. "I've waited a long time for this, and I've abided by the terms of my sentence. I believe the Lord has brought the earl here for a reason and that I *will* have a chance to speak to him."

"You say you didn't give him your surname?" Papa eyed Molly keenly.

"N–no. I only said Molly. I should have included Orland, I suppose, but Mrs. Bolton and Mr. Reynold call us all by our Christian names."

"There, you see?" Grandpa's jaw stuck out as he looked at David. "The earl has no idea he'll come face-to-face with me on Friday."

Papa frowned. "And should he? Da, I'm not so sure it's a good idea for you to confront this man."

"Confront? I'll do no confronting. Now, if it were his father coming to visit our fair island, that might be different. But the present earl? No, there's no point in that. I hold nothing against him. I shall merely make myself known to him."

"To what purpose, Da?"

"You know why. It's not right for us all to be forbidden to set foot in England. Look at the children. They've done nothing to deserve exile."

Mum said gently, "This is their home, Anson. It's the only home we know."

Papa grimaced. "You're right, Liza. None of us plans to visit England, and I doubt this pageantry will make a whit of difference in our lives. What Molly said to the gentleman probably won't matter, either. But Da is right too. He ought to have his chance to speak with Washburn. I'm not saying I like it or that I approve. If it were me…"

"It's not you," said his father.

Papa bowed his head. "I love you, Da. If I were not forbidden to go to England to plead your cause, I'd have done it years ago."

"I know, lad. And now we have this chance. When will we ever have a better opportunity to right an old wrong?"

Papa said nothing but shook his head. Grandpa reached over and laid his hand on his shoulder.

"I would not have wanted you to spend the time and money on such a journey, David, though it warms my heart to hear you say you would do that for me. God has preserved me forty-five years since I last encountered Lord Washburn—that being the sire of this present earl. The life I've had in Prince Edward Island hasn't been so bad, now has it?" He looked around at the family expectantly.

"You're right, Da. We've been blessed," Mum said.

Papa smiled at her. "Yes, we have been."

Molly gathered her courage and spoke. "I'd still like to see things set right for you, Grandpa, and have the ban lifted even if you never wish to return to England."

Grandpa raised his shoulders. "Bless you, child. I'll never go back now. I'd like to have better news of my family there, you know, but this family here is my delight. And I do not plan to do anything that will shame you when I meet his lordship."

Molly wondered if Grandpa would be able to keep his word on that score. Sometimes his mouth ran away with him and things came out that were better left unsaid. There was no use thinking about it, though. She had no control over him—none of them did.

"This levee." Mum frowned as she passed the plate of biscuits. "Finding suitable attire for the two of you will be the difficult part. I'm not sure they'll admit you if you look like—"

"Like farmers?" said Grandpa.

Papa laughed. "Indeed. There are only so many top hats on this island."

Chapter Seven

Wednesday, August 8

The next day, Molly and Rosaleen were allowed to go out and pick flowers for the bouquets to be placed in all the guest rooms. To Molly's delight, Allison received permission to join them in the task for an hour after finishing the breakfast dishes.

As they carried armloads of lilies, flags, and roses toward the back entrance to the kitchen, the lieutenant governor rounded the house, accompanied by Peter Stark.

"Good morning, ladies," Dundas said cheerfully. "Don't those flowers look lovely!"

"Thank you, Your Honour," Rosaleen said with a curtsy. "I believe Mrs. Dundas will arrange them herself."

"Yes, it's one of her favorite pastimes."

Molly was surprised that Mr. Dundas addressed the maids so cheerfully and casually.

"Hello, Molly."

When Mr. Stark spoke directly to her, she nearly jumped out of her skin. She caught her breath and gave him a quick nod.

"Thank you again for taking care of my boots yesterday," he said.

"Oh, you're welcome, sir." She looked anywhere but at him, blushing to her hairline. She edged toward the house. "Excuse us, please. Come, Allison."

Inside the kitchen, Allison hissed, "Why did you cut him short? He wanted to *converse* with you!"

Molly glared at her. "Are you out of your mind?"

"I don't think so." Allison turned to enlist Rosaleen's support. "What do you think? I mean, what girl wouldn't want to talk to such a handsome, polite gentleman?"

Molly didn't wait for Rosaleen to answer. "I want to keep my job."

"It will only last a few more days," Allison pointed out.

Rosaleen smiled and shook her head. "Come on, girls, let's get these into some water. One of you go and tell Mrs. Dundas that we have a nice selection for her to arrange."

"Here, you Allison girl," the cook called across the room. "It's time for Mrs. Bolton's tea. Take her tray to her rooms."

Allison threw Molly a glance of regret and hurried to do as she'd been told.

Molly was relieved that Cook hadn't scolded them for engaging in idle chatter. She carefully laid her bundle of cut flowers on the worktable. "I'll go and tell Mrs. Dundas."

She hurried upstairs to the lady's sitting room, still thinking about Mr. Stark's brilliant smile and cheerful manner, not to mention the stubborn wisp of hair that had stuck out off the crown of his head. She'd wanted to smooth it down. Had she been rude to him? She certainly hoped not, but with the governor standing right there, not to mention the other two maids, overfriendliness might have cost her dearly. She knocked on the mistress's door.

"Enter," came Mrs. Dundas's lilting voice.

Molly stepped inside and curtsied. Mrs. Dundas sat at her secretary, writing on a sheet of snowy white paper. In her blue silk morning dress, with her dark hair beautifully arranged, she appeared to Molly as the model lady of the house.

"The flowers for the guest chambers are ready to be arranged, ma'am."

"Thank you, Molly." As she stood, Mrs. Dundas looked her over and smiled.

Molly felt as though she should have scurried away, but her instructions said that, unless she was dismissed first, she should wait for Mrs. Dundas to pass her and then follow discreetly, disappearing as quickly as possible into the back stairway. She lowered her gaze and stood still against the wall as her mistress rose.

To her surprise, the lady paused beside her.

"You look very presentable, Molly. We need to replace one of the serving maids. Would you be able to do that job?"

Molly's mouth went dry. She'd never expected to be noticed by the mistress or given a higher position. "Serving, ma'am? At table?"

"Yes. With a little special training, could you handle that task?"

Her lungs felt squeezed. Women were not usually allowed to serve the gentry. "I...I believe so, ma'am."

"Very good. With so many guests coming to the levee, we'll need more staff to help, and I'd as soon use some of our diligent maids as to hastily try to train more footmen." Her brow furrowed, and she nodded. "Yes, the footmen can serve the beverages, and maids can replenish the refreshment trays. I'll speak to Mrs. Bolton about it. Perhaps you could serve the family at luncheon today, for practice."

Molly's heart raced as she watched Mrs. Dundas walk toward the grand staircase with her hoopskirt swaying gracefully. This meant she might be serving meals to the lieutenant governor and his wife. And to the royal party? And...to Mr. Stark?

*****

An hour under the butler's tutelage did more to shatter Molly's composure than the prospect of serving royalty. Mr. Reynold's piercing gaze and demands that she adhere strictly to a plethora of rules had Molly shaking within minutes. She doubted she could ever keep straight the order of the courses and the correct manner of serving dozens of dishes.

At noon, she helped set up the dining room, assisting Mr. Reynold and the two footmen who would also serve at luncheon. Only four would sit down at the table—Mr. and Mrs. Dundas,

Mr. Stark, and the mayor of Charlottetown, who was coming by to discuss business with the lieutenant governor. The small party would be less nerve-racking in some ways than a larger one—fewer people would see Molly's mistakes. But with so few diners, Mr. Stark would be difficult to ignore.

Molly wasn't sure when he noticed her presence, as she forced herself not to look his way when he and the others entered. He chatted genially with the Dundases and the mayor, and every time she sneaked a look at him, she intercepted his smile. In fact, he didn't seem to stop smiling throughout the meal. She determined not to glance his way too often, as her stomach did odd contortions each time that she knew weren't caused by her hunger—she wouldn't get to eat her own lunch until she was finished serving. Instead of thinking about Mr. Stark, she made herself concentrate on following Milton's lead as the head footman flawlessly performed his duties. It fell to Molly to serve the mayor his soup, and it took every ounce of calm she could muster not to spill any.

Course by course, they went through luncheon. Mr. Reynold had assured her that this meal would be much simpler than the late dinners served in the evenings. Molly was not to serve that night, but she would certainly help with the levee, and the butler had said she should be prepared to serve at either luncheon or dinner on Thursday if needed. Of course, that depended on how well she performed today. Mr. Reynold did not at all approve of the arrangement. Never before, he'd sputtered, had he seen maids serving at table. It just wasn't done. But Mrs. Dundas was a progressive sort, and all the staff liked her. And so Molly was here, trying her best not to embarrass either Mrs. Dundas or the proud butler.

When at last the time arrived for the dessert course, Milton kindly allowed her to pass plates of sweets rather than expecting her to pour coffee. While Eustace, the second footman, whisked away the dishes from the previous course, Molly carried the confections to Mrs. Dundas first, then to the mayor, and then around the table to Mr. Stark. She kept her gaze downcast, on the tray that she held precisely level.

"I'll have the strawberry compote, please."

She set the cut-glass dish carefully on the table before him.

"Thank you very much, Molly."

She caught her breath. His gentle, intimate tone startled her. Unable to keep her gaze from him any longer, she glanced upward for an instant. The intensity of his brown eyes made her look away at once. She bobbed her head in acknowledgment of his comment and went on around to Mr. Dundas, her pulse hammering.

The lieutenant governor looked over the selection of desserts, an amused smile playing at his lips. "The chocolate cake looks good."

"It's a torte, my dear," his wife murmured.

"Is it? I'll say it again—that looks good. Consider that a 'retort.'"

Mrs. Dundas smiled indulgently, but the mayor let out a huge guffaw and Mr. Stark chuckled. But Molly knew he was watching her, not his host.

Servants must never, ever react to the conversation among the family and their guests. That was one of Mr. Reynold's top rules. Molly clenched her jaw so tightly it ached to keep from laughing. If only she could leave the room—but that would be a horrible blunder. She stood holding the tray until she'd quelled the shaking in her stomach. Carefully she set a plate with a generous slice of torte before the master of the house.

"Thank you," Dundas said. "Molly, is it?"

"Aye, sir." It came out so low, she cleared her throat, lest he speak to her again and she had to answer.

He nodded, and she turned away, relieved to step back out of his notice. Eustace winked at her, and that helped her overcome her urge to laugh. Eustace did not amuse her, though he'd tried once or twice to impress her over the last few weeks and often attempted to flirt with the unmarried maids. He held no interest for Molly, however, and she was able to smooth her features into neutrality. As she carried the tray toward the sideboard, she couldn't help being very aware of Peter Stark's constant gaze and gleaming brown eyes.

*****

August 9

The prince's ship arrived in the rain on Thursday. A salute of twenty-one guns fired from St. George's Battery by the Volunteer Artillery alerted the city. Lieutenant Governor Dundas and the members of the legislature hurried down to the wharf, where they stood in formation, tolerating the drizzle that beaded on their fine hats, as the ship anchored. The mayor of Charlottetown was also present, along with the members of the city corporation, the judges, the high sheriff, the colonial secretary, the attorney general, the archdeacon, the postmaster, and so many other dignitaries and businessmen that Peter could hardly believe they'd all squeezed onto the wharf. If the pier's supports should give way, all of the city's highbrow citizens would be dumped into the saltwater below.

In addition to this collection of welcomers, a troop of Queens County Volunteer Cavalry was on hand to lead the procession of carriages. A company of the Prince of Wales's Volunteers and the 162nd Regiment's band formed a guard of honor at the end of the wharf, prepared to march along to Government House as an escort to His Royal Highness.

Peter hung back at the edge of the crowd and watched the royal party disembark. A barge brought them from the steamer to the pier. The prince made the landing unaided and waved to the people, who responded with cheering. Albert Edward, though young, with a still-boyish face, carried himself with military bearing. His scarlet uniform tunic of the British Army was set off with a blue sash and black trousers with a narrow red stripe down each leg, glinting black leather boots, white gloves, and a black cocked hat that sported a tuft of white plumes, signifying the

Prince of Wales. His regimental sword hung at his side. The crowd grew more boisterous as their distinguished visitor waved and smiled, yelling until they were hoarse in welcome to their future ruler, the beloved Queen Victoria's eldest son.

Among the other aristocrats, Lord Washburn climbed the ladder to the wharf. Peter couldn't hope to get near his master yet, but he saw the earl scan the throng as the initial welcome addresses were given. Washburn nodded in satisfaction when his gaze picked out Peter, and Peter gave a smile and a quick nod in acknowledgment.

After Dundas's formal greeting, the presentations were cut short so that the prince could retire to Government House, where he could dry off. Even in the drizzle, thousands of people lined the streets and cheered as the cavalry preceded the royal carriage from the waterfront and under several decorative arches sporting patriotic sayings and designs made of flowers. GOD SAVE THE QUEEN, one triumphal arch made of spruce bows declaimed. Another shouted, RULE BRITANNIA. However, THE HEIR APPARENT was one that had been hastily modified after some citizens protested the original saying on the arch—OUR FUTURE KING. Some folks had taken umbrage with that, as it seemed to show a mild disloyalty to Queen Victoria and imply that the folks in the colony anticipated the end of her reign. It took several public meetings, but the flowers had been ripped off that morning and replaced in a pattern that formed the new accolade for the prince.

Peter followed along in the wake of the carriages. He could have ridden in the fourth carriage with the prince's physician and the attorney general, but when Governor Dundas had suggested it, he'd declined. He preferred to walk with the crowd and remain in the background.

The walk to Government House, where Mrs. Dundas awaited her regal guests, was less than a mile, and the clouds overhead so far held back their fury. Everyone seemed to be in a cheerful mood as they followed along behind the prince, many walking in step to the band's lively tunes. Peter had no trouble keeping pace as the vehicles moved slowly up Queen Street, giving the people a good view of the man who, despite the nuances of the mottoes on the arches, might one day rule them, and allowing the prince ample time to face his public and respond to their exuberance.

    The Masonic Body had turned out in force, as had the Highland Society, the Benevolent Irish Society, the Sons of Temperance, and several other civic groups. Admirers tossed bouquets of roses and wildflowers at the carriage—so many that the street was carpeted with those that missed the mark. Ladies stood at open windows overlooking the route and showered posies upon the prince and his companions. The shouting assaulted Peter's ears worse than the cannons firing the official salutes had. The local newspaper editors could relax and forget their worries that the islanders would not turn out to show their support of the monarchy. To Peter's way of thinking, the Prince Edward Islanders were giving one of the best welcomes he had yet seen on the tour.

    As the carriages turned in at the driveway to the governor's residence, the honor guard of the Prince of Wales's Rifle Corps formed a line and held the crowds back outside the grounds. Peter quickened his pace and slipped through the gate beside the carriage in which his master rode. He managed to be the one who opened the door for the earl as the carriage came to rest before the pillared front of Government House.

    "Peter! This is a splendid turnout." Washburn laid his hand on Peter's shoulder as he got out.

    "Yes, my lord." Peter held the door for the others as his master moved off.

    The prince was already climbing down from the royal conveyance ahead, immediately before the front steps of the lovely mansion. Mrs. Dundas stood in the shadow of its graceful columns, waiting to greet him.

    His Royal Highness mounted the steps and allowed the lieutenant governor to present his wife. Prince Albert Edward took Mrs. Dundas's hand and bowed over it. Many a lady might have swooned, but Mary Dundas was of sturdy stock. She gave the crown prince a charming smile and welcomed him to her home and the island. They retreated inside, and the other members of the prince's retinue followed.

Peter kept an eye on his master, in case Lord Washburn needed anything. The earl fell in behind the Duke of Newcastle and entered the house. Peter followed the distinguished guests up the steps. The local officials who had been invited were stopped at the door. Their names and calling cards were presented to Captain Lea, who put the cards into the hands of Lord St. Germains, who had the duty of presenting the gentlemen to the prince a few minutes hence, in Mrs. Dundas's drawing room.

When Peter reached the door at last, Captain Lea blinked at him. "Oh, Mr. Stark, it's you. Is this the last of them, then?" He peered about the portico as if expecting more people to pop out at him.

Peter grinned, realizing the captain was treating him as he would one of the young equerries who traveled with Prince Albert Edward. "I believe it is, sir."

Lea let him in and said to St. Germains, "This is Mr. Stark. Perhaps he is known to you?"

"Indeed. He traveled with us from London as far as New Brunswick. Well met again, Stark."

"Thank you, my lord." Peter headed across the now-familiar hall. As he approached the doorway to the large drawing room, he noticed a line of servants, drawn up in their livery and best work dress. Nearly a score had been permitted to stand beneath the gallery to observe the prince and his retinue as they arrived.

Quickly he scanned the line and was rewarded to see Molly's glowing face. Despite the bland black uniform and white apron and cap, she stood out among the others. Her eyes were vibrant with excitement, though she stood perfectly still with the others. Only a hint of her golden hair showed beneath the edge of her cap. Peter realized how little he knew about her, other than her wholesome demeanor, her frankness, and her winsome looks. If only he had time to learn more.

81

As the last of the visitors entered the drawing room, the butler spoke quietly to the row of staff and they dispersed, ready to serve the dignitaries. To serve their betters, Peter's thoroughly trained mind told him. And yet, why should those men in the drawing room be labeled "betters"? Molly's father probably owned a farm. What made Newcastle and Dundas and Washburn "better" than an honest, hardworking farmer?

He didn't question that they were better than himself. None of those men was the child of a woman born on the wrong side of the blanket. No matter how dignified and genteel his mother, she and her offspring would never, ever be admitted to the upper social class.

But Molly? Why was she a servant while her neighbor down the road most likely went in to meet the prince? Dundas had told him that some of the local legislators were farmers. Others owned businesses. One or two had studied the law. Molly might just as easily have been one of their daughters, and then he would rub elbows with her father this afternoon. She would have received a ticket to the ball, along with the daughters of the local gentry. Instead, she would now carry trays of food and wash dishes and wipe up the spills made by the upper crust vying for the prince's attention.

The dust covers had been removed from the furniture in the drawing room, the windows shined, and the mirrors polished. Fresh flowers spilled from vases at strategic points, and the woodwork gleamed. Mrs. Dundas and her housekeeper had done a commendable job—not to mention the bevy of maids who'd worked so hard this week.

Peter edged his way around the room until he stood a few feet from Washburn. Once, in Nova Scotia, the earl had drawn him into a very interesting conversation with a local agriculturalist. But it wasn't up to Peter to initiate such a thing; if his master wished to speak to him, he would. Otherwise, Peter would stand quietly at hand, ready to assist if called upon. Like Molly, he knew his place.

*****

Mrs. Bolton startled Molly when she called her aside with Allison, Deborah, and the first parlor maid, Roberts. "You four will help Mr. Reynold in the drawing room. He and the footmen will serve the gentlemen wine, and you will carry in the trays of sweets and scones that Mr. Sanderson and Cook have prepared."

The scrubbing of floors and making of beds was over. Molly hadn't considered what duties would be assigned her while the royal party was in residence. Certainly not serving dainties in the drawing room.

"Allison!"

Her friend started guiltily. "Yes, ma'am?"

"Straighten your cap."

Allison's hands flew to her head in obedience. Molly looked straight ahead so as not to distract her.

Mrs. Bolton eyed them all critically. Not being reprimanded meant that Molly's uniform and appearance were correct, but she still had to force herself not to flinch under the housekeeper's inspection.

"Yes. Now, mind you, those of you who are new maids, Roberts has been with us for six years, and she knows what is what. If she tells you to do something or if Mr. Reynold should speak to you, do exactly what they tell you. And you are under no circumstances to engage in conversation with the guests."

"Yes, ma'am," Molly murmured with the others.

Mrs. Bolton nodded, still frowning as though she had some misgivings. "All right, then. Go into the pantry and pick up your trays. And remember, you are in the presence of your future king."

They followed Roberts quickly through the kitchen, where Cook was showing the fancy New York chef where her pans were stored.

The undercook, Mrs. Randolph, watched the maids lift the trays of refreshments and shook her head. "Imagine. New girls, green as grass, going into the drawing room to serve royalty."

"They're ornamental," Roberts replied.

Molly felt her cheeks flush. Was that the reason she'd been chosen for this task? Did Mrs. Dundas find her and Allison prettier than the other maids who might have served the refreshments? They'd been chosen over Rosaleen and some of the other, older women. Though it wasn't fair, it presented an opportunity, and Molly knew she must seize it. She determined not to make any mistakes so that the housekeeper would have no regrets and Roberts would not be blamed for her ineptitude. Perhaps Mrs. Bolton would ask her to stay on after the royal visitors left. But Molly didn't want to obtain a job simply because she wasn't stone-ugly. She wanted it because she would work hard and do the job well.

As they slipped into the drawing room, her attention was drawn immediately to the prince. Though she'd claimed otherwise, she found herself eager for a closer look at him. He was so young! In his uniform, he put her in mind of Nathan in fancy dress. At eighteen, the Prince of Wales was a lieutenant colonel in the Royal Army. She supposed they kept him away from battle lines and that the rank was purely ceremonial.

The other gentlemen stood in clusters, talking and laughing together. Which one was Washburn? Her grandfather would want to know if she'd seen him. She ruled out all the men younger than thirty. Was the earl the older gentleman with the luxuriant whiskers? Or the shorter, clean-shaven man with gray hair?

She realized Allison was half a dozen steps ahead of her. Molly focused her attention on her task and carried her tray to the sideboard. Allison took a quick glance about and swished over to Molly. Leaning close, she hissed, "Look. In the corner, under the portrait of the prince consort. It's Mr. Stark, dressed to the nines. And he's looking at you."

Molly nearly dropped her tray.

*****

Molly's blue eyes gleamed as she watched Prince Albert Edward. She made a charming picture. Peter didn't doubt her wonder and innocence as he gazed at her.

He studied her features as she unobtrusively went about her duties, now and then sneaking glances at the party of aristocrats. After a few minutes, she took a nearly empty tray from the sideboard and disappeared. When she returned a short time later, she looked in his direction but not at him. Peter zeroed in on her eyes. Her features remained calm, yet she kept looking toward one person. After a minute, he was certain. Her attention was focused, not on the prince, not on her tray of pastries, but on the Earl of Washburn.

A sudden need to protect Washburn swept over Peter. He eased a few steps closer to his master until he stood almost directly behind him. Perhaps he reacted too strongly. She had no malice in her nature—did she? How could he be sure?

As Molly approached, she glanced past the earl, and for an instant Peter caught her eye. She hesitated and looked down at the tray she held. Her cheeks went a deeper rose. Before the earl, she dipped a tiny curtsy. Washburn barely noticed her. He reached for a scone and kept on talking with one of the local officials—a judge, Peter thought.

Would Molly speak? He didn't want to think she'd make a scene in the prince's presence. After all, who was she? He'd asked himself that question before and concluded that she was a charming, modest farmer's daughter. But this mysterious family matter to which she'd alluded could spell trouble, and his job included keeping trouble away from the Earl of Washburn. Far away.

She held out her tray of puff pastries and petit fours before the Duke of Newcastle and the colony's attorney general. After the gentlemen had helped themselves to her offerings, she backed away and moved on to where Dr. Henry Acland, the prince's physician, was speaking to Mrs. Dundas.

Peter relaxed only slightly. He forbade himself to stare at her but stayed aware of her position. He smiled and spoke to the men who wandered his way. Most of them left him alone and clustered around the aristocracy. Molly and the other maids served the light refreshments and then left the drawing room. The butler continued to make the rounds with a tray of glasses. Milton, the footman, collected the empties. Peter imagined himself in the green-and-gold livery of Government House, standing next to Milton and serving wine to the royal guests—a plausible vision. Around him, the elite of the island continued their attempts to impress the visitors.

The pomp and confusion surrounding the prince was not to Peter's liking. He preferred the peacefulness of the last two days. But he couldn't live that way, not and earn a living. In fact, few opportunities would come his way to make the money he now earned. He recognized that and was thankful, though it meant living among men who disdained him. He had no illusions of being able to climb out of his class. But he wouldn't mind that in the least if he could live away from this hubbub, in a quiet place where class didn't matter.

His thoughts veered back to Molly. The room seemed less inviting since she'd left, the chatter more inane. He'd been foolish to think she could wish the earl harm. She'd only wanted a look at him, and she'd had her chance. He hoped she was content now. If only he had a chance to talk to her again, maybe she would tell him what her burning interest was in the earl.

*****

That evening Molly donned a fresh cap—starched by the laundress at Government House to a stiffness she could never have provided at home. She had done well that afternoon *and* at the previous day's luncheon, or so Mr. Reynold and Mrs. Bolton had judged. She was among the eight servants chosen to help serve dinner to the royal party that evening.

Word had come downstairs that two of the prince's personal servants had caught a chill and were ill. Mr. Reynold and the other more experienced staff—those who regularly served

Governor Dundas and his wife—would take care of the prince and the higher-ranking guests. The other footmen would serve those at the lower end of the table, and maids would help and receive extra wages for their trouble. The women would not do the actual serving, but would carry up trays of food and hold them if needed for the footmen while they distributed food.

Molly's nerves rioted and her stomach fluttered as she scurried about the dining room, helping to put the finishing touches on the long table. Everything had to be perfect.

When the guests took their seats, she was surprised to the see that, while the eight servants accompanying the aristocracy on the tour would eat below stairs with the Government House servants this evening, Peter Stark would dine with the other guests in the grand dining room. True, he sat at the far end of the table from the Prince of Wales and the Dundases, but he was among the chosen—the British guests and the highest of the local officials. His "employment" for the earl must be higher than that of a butler, which was the highest house servant. He must be a steward at the very least. That, or Governor Dundas had taken a particular liking to him over the course of the week. Perhaps that was it. He'd invited his new riding companion as a friend. Molly liked that idea—that Peter was charming and astute enough to make friends with the lieutenant governor.

The meal began with a soup course. Dundas presided, with his wife sitting to his left and the Prince of Wales in the seat of honor to his right.

Molly watched Joseph, the footman who had been assigned to the six guests at the lower end of the table. She was glad it would be Joseph dipping out hot soup. The idea of doing the actual serving still frightened her—what if she scalded a guest? She held the tureen while he scooped out the onion soup and placed individual dishes before the diners. When they reached Peter, his warm gaze met Molly's, completely unnerving her. With difficulty she kept her hands steady, though she could feel her face going scarlet.

Joseph managed to serve all the diners at their end of the table without spilling a drop. Molly then took up a waiting post against the wall behind Peter, where he could not see her. She stood a few steps from where the butler had told her to stand during the meal, but she knew she couldn't remain calm if Peter, with those rich, dark eyes, continually gazed at her.

A few minutes into the meal, she went to refill the pitcher of ice water so that Joseph could offer more to those drinking water, Peter among them. Most of the guests were drinking wine, but Peter had only the crystal water glass before him. It pleased her to know that even though he lived among the rich and decadent, he did not imbibe in strong drink—even when the government paid for it.

She glanced down the table to keep track of Mr. Reynold. He was pouring more wine for the Duke of Newcastle, who had turned out to be the bearded older man. Next to the prince, Newcastle held the highest rank of any man in the party, and Mr. Dundas treated him with great deference. Molly had learned that afternoon that the duke served as Queen Victoria's colonial secretary. His impressions of the colonies were perhaps even more important than those of the prince.

Suddenly Molly realized that the guest of honor was looking down the length of the room. She caught her breath. The Prince of Wales was staring at her.

Chapter Eight

At last the dinner was over. Molly was free to leave the dining room when Mrs. Dundas quitted the room. Since she was the only woman seated at the meal that evening, the governor's wife withdrew alone while the men had their brandy and cigars.

Other people, including the wives and daughters of several of the local gentry, had been invited to come to the evening entertainment, but only Mr. Reynold, a couple of footmen, and one ladies' maid were needed for that. The military band accompanying the prince on his tour would play several selections, and Mrs. MacReady, an American artiste, would recite for the gathering. Molly wished she could stay and hear the lady's recitation, but without an invitation, she could not.

"You may go home now," Mrs. Bolton told her and the other serving maids when they reached the kitchen. "Be back early."

Molly hung up her apron and turned toward the door. She had better hurry home and get as much sleep as she could before dawn. Tomorrow would be another long and tiring day.

"Oh, Molly."

She stiffened at the sound of her name on Mrs. Bolton's lips. Had she unwittingly made a mistake?

"Yes, ma'am?"

"We do need one maid on hand to lay away the ladies' wraps as they arrive and show them the powder room. I had planned for Roberts to have that task, but she fell ill and I sent her home."

Molly hesitated. She was tired, but this extra work would mean more pay, which would help the family. And perhaps she would get to hear the recitation after all. "I...could stay."

"Very good. If your parents won't object."

Though she had no way to let her parents know of the change in plans, Molly accepted the assignment with a curtsy and a thankful heart.

"Your apron," Mrs. Bolton said sharply.

"Yes, ma'am." Molly leaped to get it.

"Oh, here, put on a fresh one. It looks as though you smeared a bit of gravy on that one as you removed the dishes."

Molly took the clean apron and tied it on. Somehow she felt incompetent because she'd soiled the first one, and yet, wasn't that what aprons were for?

"There. You look presentable now. Go out to the hall and do as Mr. Reynold instructs you. Mrs. Dundas's lady's maid will also be in the party, but she will attend as a guest and to attend to her mistress's needs. If any of the other ladies asks for assistance or stands looking about the hall as though lost, ask if you may help her."

"Yes, ma'am."

"While they are in the drawing room, you may sit on the bench in the great hall if no guests are within sight." Mrs. Bolton detailed which powder rooms the ladies were to use and to which bedroom a visiting lady could retire if she felt ill or had some other reason to need a moment's privacy. Wash water, clean handkerchiefs, and a sewing box waited there in case of a minor crisis.

Molly bobbed another quick curtsy and hurried out the door. At that moment, the grand hall was empty. She paused only for an instant to view it in the splendor of the light falling from the crystal chandelier. The decorations of flowers, ribbon streamers, and bunting made the room more awe-inspiring than usual. If she never entered another fine house again in her lifetime, Molly would remember the beautiful rooms of this mansion.

*****

The air of the dining room became hazy blue with smoke, and Peter feared he would choke and disturb the distinguished party with his coughing. He rose and slipped around toward the door as unobtrusively as he could. A short walk in the garden would clear his lungs. When the men joined Mrs. Dundas and her later-arriving guests in the drawing room, the others would have finished smoking.

He'd watched Molly whenever he could during the meal but had been careful not to embarrass her by staring. He'd taken note of the fact that the beautiful maid had captured the prince's attention as well as his own. While Prince Albert Edward hadn't said anything about Molly, it was obvious that he was taken with her appearance and grace.

As he gained the fresher atmosphere of the great hall, Peter noticed Molly coming from the kitchen. He paused, uncertain whether to speak to her. He didn't wish to upset her again, but his longing to know more about her propelled him toward her.

"Good evening, Molly."

She jumped and backed off several steps. "I—good evening, sir. I hope you enjoyed your dinner." She didn't quite meet his gaze and stood clutching handfuls of her white apron.

"Thank you. I did. You performed your duties extremely well."

"Thank you, sir. It was my first time helping serve at a formal dinner."

"I'd never have known it. Um…"

Her gaze flickered to him and away.

"I wondered if any of your family will attend the levee tomorrow."

She relaxed a bit, blinked, and managed to look at him. "My father and grandfather are invited. Grandpa is quite anxious to come, but Papa is recovering from a broken leg, and he may not be able."

"Oh, dear. I hope he's healing well. A pity if he has to miss this occasion."

Her eyes were huge as she nodded. "It depends on how he's feeling, and whether he can get into his Sunday suit. Still, I'm not sure he should. And besides that, he and Grandpa don't have—" She stopped abruptly.

"What is it?" Peter asked softly.

Molly gulped and glanced about. A footman came out of the drawing room and took up a post near the front door.

"It's not something I should tell you, I'm sure, sir," she whispered, "but…well, after seeing the way you gentlemen dress, I doubt they have suitable clothing for the occasion. I hear a man can't come if he hasn't a top hat."

Peter almost laughed aloud, but her sober expression helped him contain his mirth. "Molly, there are two things I'd like to tell you."

She eyed him uncertainly, and he noticed how her thick, feathery eyelashes shielded her gaze. Some of the ladies in the queen's court would puff up with envy if they could view this young woman's lashes and complexion.

He went on before she could object. "First of all, I am not what most people would call a 'gentleman,' regardless of the way Mr. and Mrs. Dundas have treated me this week. I'm a commoner, and one of the commonest sort at that."

A trace of a smile formed on her lips. "You certainly don't act like one, sir."

He chuckled. "Ah, if you could see me at home, in my mother's little cottage, you would not think me very illustrious then. But second, and perhaps more important"—he lowered his voice—"I'd be honored to scour up a top hat for your grandfather to wear to the levee."

"Oh, I couldn't let you do that." She drew back in alarm.

"And why not?" Peter glanced at the footman, but he appeared to be fascinated by the lamp on the table near the door. "My duties will keep me inside during the levee, and the top hat I've been given for when I must attend state occasions with the earl shall remain solitary and morose in my chamber."

She quaked, and a little laugh escaped her lips. "Ah, your hat is very sensitive, sir."

"Yes, and very sociable." Peter warmed to the lighthearted topic, glad he'd been able to chase away her nervousness and engage her in banter as he would a friend. "As a matter of fact, I expect my hat shall feel terribly neglected if forced to miss the levee. I'd be honored if your grandfather—or your father, for that matter—would give that hat a little outing."

"I'm sure I shouldn't accept, sir."

"You've no good reason not to. I assure you, my offer is made with the purest of motives. I'd only like to help you and your family—and my hat, of course."

Her shy smile revealed a dimple he hadn't noticed before. "All right. For Grandpa. Papa wouldn't mind so much, but Grandpa is determined to see the Earl of Washburn face-to-face, and the earl wouldn't think much of him if he came without a proper hat."

"Oh, the earl may not be such a stickler as you imagine, but yes, your grandfather must be properly dressed when they meet, if only to give him confidence. I've learned that when one must take on a duty that's a little frightening—such as speaking to a person he fears may turn him away—why, the proper clothes can make all the difference, both in the speaker's courage to speak and in the listener's attitude."

"Very astute, sir. Er...do you think the earl would turn him away? Or have him tossed out?"

"Not if he behaves like a gentleman."

"I'm sure he will, especially if carrying a gentleman's hat."

Peter nodded. "How shall I get it to you?"

"Well, I..." She looked about again, and slight apprehension crept back into her eyes. "You mustn't take it to the kitchen. If the cook or Mrs. Bolton got wind of it..."

"Mrs. Bolton being the dour housekeeper?"

"Yes, sir—that is—" She halted and winced.

Peter chuckled. Of course she wouldn't describe the housekeeper as "dour," but she was in the awkward position of having agreed with him.

"I'll look for you in the morning, shall I, and pass it to you discreetly?"

"Yes, sir. Thank you. I shall arrive early."

The door knocker thudded and the footman swung open the heavy door, revealing a party of two gentlemen and several brilliantly gowned ladies.

"I must go now," Molly whispered. "I'm to assist the ladies."

She darted off to stand near the footman, ready to serve at the merest suggestion of a need. Peter watched her for a moment. Her jaw had a determined set to it, but that could not mar her striking features. She gathered the ladies' evening cloaks and carried them off without a flicker of a glance his way. A stir to his right brought him back to the moment. The gentlemen were leaving the dining room.

Peter hurried across the hall to another door that led out on the back garden. In a moment, he would go station himself behind his master's chair in the drawing room. But for this one minute, he wanted to look up at the stars peering between the brooding clouds and think about Molly.

*****

The next fifteen minutes passed in a whirl of bright hoopskirts and repartee among the guests. While Milton collected top hats and walking sticks, Molly accepted the women's wraps, trying hard to remember which one belonged to each lady. Less than a dozen ladies were among the new arrivals, and she knew a few of them by sight. She carried their cloaks and shawls to the cloakroom and hung them in the order she received them.

When she returned to the hall after the third batch was hung, Milton had admitted another party of guests. Molly glanced at them and stopped short. Emmet Price and his mother stood just inside the front door, along with one of the partners in Emmet's law firm and his wife.

Molly set her jaw and stepped forward. "Good evening, Mrs. Price."

Emmet's mother whirled and looked at her at the same moment Emmet discovered her presence.

"Molly?" His tone reeked of disapproval as he surveyed her black dress and apron.

She bowed her head. "Good evening, Mr. Price." Turning back to his mother, she did her best to speak sweetly. "May I take your shawl?"

"No, thank you. I believe I'll keep it by me." Mrs. Price peered at her for a moment, gave a little cough, and turned toward the drawing room door.

Knowing Emmet still watched her, Molly gave her attention to the other lady. "May I take your cloak, ma'am?"

"Yes, thank you."

The solicitor helped his wife remove her evening cloak and handed it to Molly. Glad for a reason to escape, Molly hurried away with it. When she returned, Emmet and the rest of his party had left the hall.

"There's only four more expected," Milton told her in low tones. "Once they're all here, we're to go in and discreetly stand in the back of the room until the entertainment begins. Watch for a sign from any of the ladies, and be ready to help them if they want it."

Molly felt almost invisible as she stood against the wall, scanning the women's faces. Emmet was seated where he wouldn't see her unless he craned his neck. Molly did notice his mother turning her sweeping gaze on her once, and she tensed until Mrs. Price's attention moved on.

"Hsst. The lady in green," Milton whispered.

Molly searched for the woman in question. She was looking toward them and beckoned with one finger when she caught Molly's eye.

Molly hurried around the edge of the room to her side. "May I assist you, madam?"

"It seems my husband stepped on my hem out on the steps. Have you anything—?"

"Yes, ma'am, I've a needle and thread in the other room. Would you like to come with me?"

She led the lady to the retiring room and opened the sewing box. It took Molly only a few minutes to fix the stitching in the hem of the lady's gown. Strains of a stirring march came from the drawing room.

Molly knotted her thread and cut it off. "There, I believe that will hold until you are able to tend to it more thoroughly."

"You've been very helpful." The woman slipped a coin into Molly's hand.

Molly's cheeks flushed warm. "Oh, there's no need—"

"You earned it." The lady stood and examined her reflection in the looking glass beside the door. "I can't even tell where the repair is. Thank you." She bustled out into the hall.

Molly turned down the lamp and followed. The band was playing another number when she slid back into the room and stood against the wall. A gentleman sitting near the back raised an empty glass, and Milton stepped to his side to take it away. The Earl of Washburn, Molly noted. Milton apparently asked if he wanted another drink, but the earl shook his head and turned his attention to the band. Molly noticed Peter sitting on the other side of the earl. He glanced at Milton and then beyond to where Molly stood. Molly's stomach flipped. Peter gave her a slight nod and what might have been the tiniest smile.

She looked away quickly lest anyone else should notice, but throughout the music and Mrs. MacReady's stirring performance, she felt a glow of contentment. While she wasn't a member of the elite party, Molly thoroughly enjoyed her evening. She managed to avoid Emmet and his mother during their departure.

When she left the governor's house just before midnight, the stars gleamed overhead. For a while at least, the clouds had parted. Since Allison, her usual companion, had not stayed to help serve, Molly walked alone through the shadowy streets. She pulled her shawl close about her, against the cool breeze wafting off the bay. Turning onto the next street, she spotted a lone figure leaning against a lamppost.

Her neck prickled, and she hesitated. Although this was the most direct route home, it might be better to retrace her steps and take another way—but that would involve walking through a more isolated area.

As she faltered, the man detached himself from the lamppost and walked toward her.

"Molly?"

"Nathan!" Relief coursed through her. She hurried to her brother and seized his arm. "What are you doing here?"

"Mama was worried about you."

"I told her I'd be late."

"Yes, but she didn't think you meant *this* late."

Molly's legs felt as if they'd melted, but she slid her hand into the crook of Nathan's arm and kept pace as he led her rapidly toward the road leading out of town. The strain of the long day had brought on a wobbly fatigue. She could picture Mum watching out the kitchen window for her and growing more and more uneasy.

"I'm sorry. I thought I could leave after dinner was served, but one of the other maids was ill. Mrs. Bolton asked me at the last minute to take her place and tend to the ladies who came for the evening."

"Ah. I'm sorry you had to do that."

"Well, I'm not." Molly grinned up at him. "I'll get extra wages, and I got to hear Mrs. MacReady recite."

"Who is Mrs. MacReady?"

Molly's laugh tumbled out over the dark bushes on the side of the road. "She's a very famous woman who gives readings and recitations for the rich and indolent."

"Well, now. An actress, you mean?"

"No, no! She's quite a lady, and well respected. And the band, Nathan! The prince's regimental band goes everywhere with him. Did you know that?"

"I can't say I did."

"They're marvelous musicians."

"I've heard his entire regiment is camping on the outskirts of town."

"Yes, one hundred men. They form his honor guard."

"I hope they aren't making trouble in town."

"I doubt it. They were kept late at Government House too. But I heard the Earl of Washburn remark that it's sometimes hard to find transport for them all."

"You saw the earl?" Nathan stopped for a moment, staring down at her.

"Well, yes. I didn't speak to him, of course, but he was in the gathering in the drawing room this afternoon. That's when I heard him talking. He was at the dinner tonight too, but I wasn't stationed near him then."

"What's he like?"

"He seems a proper gentleman. And Mr. Stark—that's his man—seems to think highly of him."

"Hmm."

Molly squinted at him in the starlight. "It wasn't him, you know."

"What wasn't who?"

"The one Grandpa Anson had his quarrel with."

"Oh, I know. But still…"

Molly began walking again. "So anyway, they had to engage an entire steamship just to bring the soldiers and all their equipment and the band instruments over from New Brunswick."

Nathan shook his head. "What a lot of money we're spending."

"We? The Crown is paying for the regimental escort, I think. Or perhaps the provincial government is paying part."

"Ah, yes, the government pays for everything—but as Papa says, we are the government. That is, Papa and Grandpa and all the other taxpayers."

"I suppose so, but it's much more pleasant not to think of that."

He squeezed her hand. "Well, I'm glad they're paying your wages. You don't have to be back at six o'clock in the morning, I hope?"

"I thought so, but on my way out, I was told to arrive by nine."

"Well, good. They realize you need some sleep."

"Yes, but…"

"But what?"

"Nothing." Molly didn't want to reveal her conversation with Peter Stark to Nathan, but she did wish they'd hit upon a better plan. How would she get the top hat from Mr. Stark, and how she would get it to her grandfather in time for the levee at eleven the next morning?

"So what does the prince look like?" Nathan asked.

A much safer topic. Molly launched into a glowing report of the young heir to the throne, for the most part repeating what she'd heard other people say about him. But as they strode along the North River Road, the problem that still badgered her was that of the sociable hat and the handsome young man who owned it.

Finally, when they turned in at the farm lane, she stopped and tugged Nathan's arm so that he stopped, too, and peered down at her in the meager moonlight.

"What is it?"

"I've something to tell Papa and Mum, and I'm not sure how to explain it to them. Perhaps if I tell you first, you'll know what to do."

"Now, that sounds ominous. What's it all about?" Nathan tipped his head toward his shoulder and waited.

Molly pulled in a deep breath. "It's about a hat."

Chapter Nine

"What's this about you borrowing clothing from a tony gentleman?"

Molly paused on the bottom step and drew a deep breath before stepping into the farmhouse kitchen. She hadn't expected to face her father's inquisition as soon as she got up in the morning. Nathan must have shared their midnight conversation with her parents before he went out to milk the cows.

Papa sat at the table with a bowl of porridge and a cup of tea before him. Mum was busy at the worktable already, rolling out a pastry crust, but she glanced Molly's way with a frown.

"It's only a hat, Papa," Molly said. "Mr. Stark won't be wearing it this morning, and he offered—"

"How is it you're so friendly with this man that he would offer the use of his personal belongings?"

Molly's cheeks began to burn. She stepped down onto the bare boards of the kitchen floor and walked slowly to the stove, where the teakettle steamed. "I had to serve last night, you know, Papa. After dinner, when Mrs. Bolton had asked me to tend to the ladies, I was going to the drawing room and Mr. Stark was out in the hall. He spoke to me and asked if my family were attending the levee."

Her father grunted. "So you volunteered that we were too poor to own a proper hat."

"Not exactly, but... Oh, Papa, no matter what I say, you won't be pleased, I'm afraid. You don't approve of Mr. Stark, but that's because you don't know him."

"And you do?"

Molly sighed. She seemed to be digging her rut deeper and deeper. "No. I don't know him well at all. He's spoken to me a

101

couple of times. His inquiry was polite, as a guest might ask a servant at the end of a long day—'Do you enjoy working here?' 'How is your family?'"

"It sounds to me as though you gave him overmuch detail about your family."

"David," her mother said softly.

He swung around and arched his eyebrows at her. "What, Liza? You don't want our daughter forming a connection with some Englishman we know nothing about."

"No, of course not. But our Molly is a sensible girl. She wouldn't throw her heart about willy-nilly. She must be kind and polite to the governor's guests, though."

"Well, I don't like it."

As Papa spoke, the door to the dairy opened and Grandpa walked in carrying a pail half full of milk. "Don't like what, lad?"

"This business of Mr. Stark telling Molly he'll lend her his top hat for you to wear."

Grandpa set his bucket down and straightened, putting his hands to the small of his back. "Well, now, I wouldn't look a gift horse in the mouth if I were you."

Molly donned a calico apron over the black dress she would wear to Government House and poured herself a cup of tea. "Papa, I promise you, I shall behave decorously."

He grunted and lifted his cup to his lips.

"And how am I supposed to get this fabled hat, lass?" Grandpa asked.

Molly frowned. "I'm not certain. He didn't say exactly how he would get it to me. I told him I would arrive early today, but that was before I knew how late I'd be getting home or that Mrs. Bolton would tell me to go in later than my usual hour."

"Nathan could walk in with you and wait outside the grounds," her mother said.

Molly gave her a grateful smile. "That might be best. But if I can't get it straightaway, he might have to wait a long time."

Grandpa shrugged. "If he waits until eleven o'clock and you haven't brought it to him, we'll be there waiting to go in and be presented to His Royal Highness, won't we, David?"

Papa set his cup down. "I suppose we shall, Da. If you think we dare to go in our rustic attire."

Grandpa scowled and scratched his chin through his white beard. "We'll have to wear our regular hats. And if they won't let us in, I shall have to devise another way to see the earl, that's all."

*****

Peter set down his satchel and leaned against one of the columns in the front portico of the governor's mansion, looking out toward the sea. He hadn't spotted Molly among the scurrying maids this morning, and he hated to ask for her. He was well aware of the problems a person from "upstairs" could bring on by showing particular interest in a servant.

Still, barely two hours remained before the levee. He'd gone over the arrangements with St. Germains and Newcastle this morning, and already farmers and shopkeepers were collecting outside the gates. He'd seen it before—people would stand in line for hours for a glimpse of Queen Victoria or a member of her family. The show of loyalty and devotion to the Crown would be gratifying to the royal family, but Peter couldn't help pitying the islanders. The sky was again clouding up.

He picked up the satchel, walked down the front steps, and strolled around the side of the house. Perhaps he could catch Molly at the back entrance that led to the kitchen and the laundry.

He wandered about the rear gardens, taking his time admiring the flower beds, the shrubbery, and even the kitchen garden. Soon he would have to go inside and change his clothes for the levee and see if the earl needed his assistance. He hoped he'd made the right decision when he put one of the earl's coats in the satchel along with his own formal hat. If Washburn asked for that particular coat, he'd have to explain that it wasn't available—but he had already laid out a different one. The one he'd chosen for Molly's grandfather was an older, less fashionable cutaway coat His Lordship rarely wore. Peter felt quite secure in borrowing it for Molly. At least he had an hour ago. Now he wondered if everything would fly to pieces.

He paced toward the house and back out to the flower beds again. The gardener, the fellow the Dundases called the "useful man," and two young boys were setting up an awning for Mrs. Dundas's afternoon party. He eyed the gray sky and hoped they had several awnings. If not for his quest, he'd have gone to help them, but then he might miss his chance to see Molly. With any luck, no one would question his hovering about the back garden.

At last his patience was rewarded. One of the maids came out the door lugging a large basket. He dropped the leather bag and hurried to her.

"Let me help you with that, miss."

She glanced up at him, wide-eyed. "Oh no, sir. I'll be fine."

"That wet laundry in your basket must be heavy. I don't mind. Just tell me where you'd like it." He reached for the handles, and she surrendered the burden to him.

"Well then…thank you, sir. 'Tis yonder, through that trellis arch."

He followed her into a prosaic portion of the grounds he hadn't seen before. Here were the clotheslines and a compost pile. Peter set the basket down beneath the nearest clothesline. The young woman looked familiar—Peter had seen her laying out breakfast this morning.

"Are you Molly's friend, by any chance?"

She stared at him. "Yes, sir. I'm Allison. We've known each other since we were tykes."

Peter smiled. "Ah. Then perhaps you can help me."

Allison smiled back. "Why, yes, sir, I expect I can."

*****

"Psst."

Molly looked about, startled. From behind a large vase holding a potted plant, Allison beckoned to her. As Molly started toward her, Allison darted down the hallway and turned toward the laundry. Just outside the door to the busy room where scrubbing went on nearly all day, she stopped. Molly hurried closer to her.

"What's going on?"

"That gentleman is looking for you."

"Mr. Stark?"

Allison nodded, her eyes glittering. "He said he has something for you. You can find him in the small breakfast room."

Molly squeezed her friend's arm. "Thank you so much!"

She hurried off, knowing Allison would be frustrated that she didn't explain, but she needed to see him as quickly as possible. The levee would begin in an hour. She still felt accepting Mr. Stark's offer a bit daring and somehow improper, but Grandpa had been so pleased that she couldn't refuse now.

She ducked through the grand hall, where Mrs. Dundas was speaking to the butler about the exact manner in which he was to keep the vast array of company under control—with help from a couple of visiting gentlemen. No one looked her way, and she scurried around the corner and out of their sight.

At the doorway to the breakfast room, she hesitated. She heard no voices within, and she peeked cautiously around the jamb.

"Molly! At last. I was afraid I wouldn't be able to find you in time." Peter's crooked smile sent a telling blow to her heart. He was more handsome than she'd remembered, and he had a boyish enthusiasm she was sure would charm anyone—even her parents, should they ever have the chance to meet him.

"Allison told me." She stepped into the room.

Peter held out a leather satchel. "I'm most grateful to her. I've been shuffling this about for an hour and a half."

"I'm sorry. They had me come in late, and when I arrived I was put right to work at setting up the drawing room."

"Not your fault, and it's no matter. But I wanted to be certain you got this and your granddad could feel himself well-turned-out when he's presented."

"I know he will. Thank you, Mr. Stark."

"There's a coat in there too. If he can't use it—"

"I'm sure he can. How very kind of you. My brother was to wait outside, to one side on the street, to see if I was successful in getting the hat. I must run out and give this to Nathan so he can take it to Grandpa."

"Make sure you get back quickly so you won't be missed."

Odd, that a gentleman would think of that. He seemed almost as concerned about her as her family would be.

"I will. Pardon me for being so hasty."

"Go."

His smile warmed her as she dashed back down the passageway, along the edge of the great hall beneath the gallery—praying that no one in authority would notice her and call her name—and down the hall leading to the laundry again. She would be less conspicuous if she went out through the kitchen garden. It would take her longer to go the back way, but she ought to be able to reach the street without being seen.

Her heart pounded, more from the giver's smile than from her exertion. Mr. Stark had joined the conspiracy almost as if they were friends—as if he genuinely liked her and cared about her grandpa and his quest, though he knew nothing about her or her family.

What would happen if he did know? What if he learned why Grandpa Anson wanted to see the Earl of Washburn? Would he be as friendly then? She gulped and ran along a path through the wood behind the mansion to a small gate in the wall.

Nathan stood at the appointed place, leaning against the wall and watching the island's men flock toward Government House in their best clothes.

As Molly pulled the gate open, he whirled toward her. "You got it!"

"Yes." She placed the satchel in his hands and stood panting. "A top hat *and* a coat. I do hope they fit. Where are Papa and Grandpa?"

"They said they'd come in the wagon and leave it at Donald Manden's house."

"Can Papa walk from there to Government House with his bum leg?"

"He says he can. He's got the crutches. If he doesn't want to take them in, I'll go with him as far as the gate and he can leave them with me."

Molly frowned. "I wish I could help."

"You have." Nathan unclasped the satchel and peeked inside. He gave a nod of satisfaction. "Perfect."

He turned, but Molly grabbed his jacket's hem. "Wait! How do I get it back?"

"Hmm. Are you getting off at suppertime?"

"I don't know. And Mr. Stark might need it tonight, for the ball at the Colonial Building."

"What do you suggest I do, then?"

"Bring it to the back door this afternoon—the laundry entrance. But don't ask for me. Ask for Allison."

"Allison? Why don't I just ask for Mr. Stark?"

"No, wait. I have a better idea. There's a public gathering on the grounds this afternoon. The prince is supposed to make an appearance for all the people who couldn't attend the levee. They expect a couple of thousand to attend. Bring it then. No one will notice you in the crush. I'll meet you right here."

Nathan closed the satchel and hurried off down the crowded street. Molly watched only for a moment then turned back and closed the small gate, latching it securely from the inside.

Her father had been suspicious of Peter's intentions when he'd heard the young man was loaning her a top hat. What would Papa say when he learned that the loan also included a formal jacket? Molly hadn't been able to explain why she trusted Peter, but she did, as completely as she trusted Nathan—perhaps more.

She hurried back to the house and decided to slip in through a side door, rather than risk Cook or Mrs. Bolton's seeing her come in the back entrance. She hoped no one had missed her while she took the bag to Nathan.

Too late, she realized the route she had chosen would take her into the grand hall. Several gentlemen were just descending the staircase. She leaped back and ducked into the nearest doorway, the one to the breakfast room where she'd met Peter a short time before. She prayed the men on the stairs would head straight for the drawing room and not come around this way and see her. Leaning forward, she peeked out toward the stairs and was relieved that they had turned away from her hiding place.

"Well, now," said a deep voice behind her. "What have we here?"

Chapter Ten

Molly swallowed with difficulty. Someone was behind her, in the room where she'd taken refuge. Her first thought was to run, but another voice spoke.

"Come now, miss. We're eager to see your face."

It couldn't be. But if it was…one couldn't disobey a request from the Prince of Wales.

Slowly she turned, her cheeks flaming. The prince and the Duke of Newcastle sat on delicate, upholstered chairs, dressed in their finery. She guessed they were waiting until the last minute when they would go and stand in the drawing room to meet the hundreds of guests. She didn't blame them for seeking a moment's quiet before the storm.

"Ah, it's the pretty maid from last night's dinner party. How fortunate we are, Duke."

Molly veiled her eyes with her lashes, unable to speak.

Newcastle smiled. "You're scaring her, Your Highness. Let the poor thing go. I expect she's only trying to escape notice, and we've rather botched her plans."

Molly managed to gather fistfuls of her skirt and curtsy, though her knees shook. "I—I beg your pardon, Your Highness. Your Grace. Please forgive my intrusion."

Prince Albert Edward chuckled. "She speaks as prettily as she looks."

"Now, Bertie," the duke said. His bushy beard and eyebrows gave him a rather fierce look, but his low tone was quite gentle.

"I shan't bite her head off." The prince raised his chin. "What's your name, girl?"

She gulped. "Orland, Your Highness."

"Orland? Have you a Christian name?"

"Aye. It's…Molly."

"Molly Orland," the prince said.

She nodded. Her ears were likely to burst into flame, they burned so.

"Not hiding from your mistress, are you?" A mischievous twinkle gleamed in his eyes.

"Oh no, Your Highness. Some of the gentlemen were coming into the hall. I only meant to wait until they were gone and then go back to the kitchen."

"Get on your way, then, girl," said Newcastle.

Molly took a step backward, toward the hall.

"No, wait, Molly Orland," called the prince.

"What are you about?" The duke's frown sent a warning to the young prince.

"I should like to dance with her at the ball this evening. She's the prettiest young woman I've met here and closer to my age than any of the ladies who joined us last evening. I don't mind dancing with the dowagers and the wives of the local dignitaries, but it would be nice to have one woman under thirty at the ball."

"You needn't worry about that." Newcastle's voice sharpened. "Those locals have daughters, too, and I'm assured that the cream of the island's beauty has been invited to provide you with partners this evening."

Molly kept her gaze on the carpet, but the warmth of a flush crept into her cheeks. Of course the likes of her would not be invited to dance with royalty. The prince was poking fun at her.

Newcastle looked over at her. "You may go back to your duties, miss."

Obviously the duke agreed with her assessment. Inviting a parlor maid to a royal ball would be most unseemly.

Her face still heated, Molly dipped another curtsy and backed out of the room. As soon as she'd stepped beyond the threshold, she turned and fled.

*****

"You've checked all the footmen's attire?" the Earl of Washburn asked. "I'm sure Dundas's household servants are competent, but sometimes these colonists aren't quite up to scratch."

"Yes, sir. They're all putting forth their best effort for us. Captain Lea has the complete list of guests."

"Good. You'll keep things moving, Stark. I'll pass folks to you, and you get them out the door. You understand."

"Yes, my lord."

The earl nodded and clapped him on the shoulder. "I know we can depend on you." He went to stand slightly between Peter and where the prince would preside as the local gentlemen were presented to him. For once, the earl was part of the window dressing as much as Peter was—there to lend a hand if the prince or the Duke of Newcastle needed anything and to add to the elegance and pageantry of the occasion. The two young army officers—equerries, they were called—traveling with the prince as friends and companions, stood behind the prince's position, as did Dr. Acland and General Bruce. When the prince entered, he would be the focus of attention, flanked by Governor Dundas and the Duke of Newcastle.

Peter headed for the set of folding doors at the far end of the room, where men who had been presented to the prince would make their exit. He stood beneath a painting of a ship of the line under full sail and reminded himself that this event would last only an hour and he had one of the best jobs in the world, even though this part was not his favorite. The crowds of admirers who came to gawk at the prince made him feel hemmed in, sometimes almost to the point of suffocation. The more events he saw the prince endure with grace, the more he appreciated the young man. His training and natural good temper stood the Prince of Wales well under these circumstances. Peter was sure that if he were in Albert Edward's place, he would lose patience and refuse to be constantly put on display.

As he admired the intricate molding and plastered ceiling of the room, two figures came through the doors just to his left. He straightened, surprised that the prince and Newcastle had come in the back way. It made sense, though, for them to avoid the throng in the front hall. All of the prince's retinue was gathering, and the steward, Dundas's butler, and General Bruce were nearly ready to admit the first callers to the drawing room.

"What was her name again?" the prince asked as they walked past Peter.

"Whose name?" asked the duke.

"The maid who burst into the morning room, of course."

"I didn't bother to remember it."

"Molly something. I want her at the ball tonight."

Peter's heart lurched and he clenched his teeth, determined not to reveal that he'd heard.

"You're joking, of course." The duke stopped short and eyed the prince reproachfully.

"No, I'm not. I was serious about that."

Peter stared straight ahead in his best "invisible footman" manner. Though his heart hammered, the prince and duke ignored him.

"Look, Bertie, you'll cause a scandal if you ask for a serving girl by name. Let it drop."

Lord St. Germains advanced down the room toward them. "Are you ready, Your Highness? It is eleven o'clock."

"Yes, yes." The prince pulled in his lower lip and straightened his shoulders. "See to it, Newcastle."

Peter watched as Albert Edward began to greet the gentlemen of the island. Again he admired the prince's ability to step into the role of public figure and benefactor. He presented a cheerful exterior and seemed to enjoy himself to the hilt as he was introduced to tradesmen, farmers, shipbuilders, and lawyers. One of the local journalists had described the heir apparent as having a strikingly handsome, intelligent countenance and a "large and beautiful eye." He was not far off. The young man did carry himself as the son of Queen Victoria ought—as the heir apparent to the throne of the British Empire. If his mother were present, she could be proud of him. Even his father would be pleased if he could view his eldest son's behavior today.

And yet it had not always been that way. Peter had heard rumors that the prince consort—Bertie's father, Prince Albert—had spoken sharply to the young man about his performance at school last term. Already, it seemed, the heir apparent was showing a bit of a wild streak. Indeed, General Bruce and the Earl of Washburn were included in this tour largely to advise and keep an eye on the prince—and make sure he behaved in a suitable manner.

The overheard snatch of conversation niggled at Peter. *That maid. I want her at the ball tonight.*

In his four days at Government House, Peter had seen diligent servants everywhere attending to their duties. The maids were, for the most part, plain and sturdy young women. He hadn't seen one beautiful enough to catch the prince's eye—other than Molly. No doubt Mrs. Dundas and her housekeeper had put the girl in the dining room for that very reason. Besides being quick to learn and steady of hand, Molly had a pretty face, which would please the guests more than if a homely woman served their dinner.

He shoved the troubling thought aside as men began filing past the visiting dignitaries toward the exit. Of all people, he knew the havoc that could result when an aristocrat decided to pursue a pretty girl of the working class. Peter bowed and smiled, bowed and smiled, helped an elderly man retrieve the gloves he dropped, and bowed and smiled.

Captain Lea and Lord St. Germains held up admirably with the presentations. St. Germains's loud, clear voice carried each name down the long room. Peter kept an ear open and an eye cocked for his sociable hat.

As the guests passed on down the room beyond the prince, they were greeted by the other members of the royal suite. The Earl of Washburn was especially good at this. He spoke a few words to each man, easing them down from the nervous moment of coming face-to-face with the Prince of Wales and perhaps making them feel, just for a few seconds, a part of the great British Empire—a part that mattered.

By halfway into the hour, Peter had stopped hearing the names as the steward called them out. His mind was numb from the swirl of men, scrubbed and brushed, wearing their best. Only the pronouncement of a familiar name in St. Germains's stentorian voice jerked him back to attention.

"Mr. Anson Orland."

Orland.

Peter leaned forward to see the man advancing toward the prince. A white-haired gentleman with a jovial face and magnificent beard stood upright, tall and distinguished-looking, wearing a rather fine tailcoat and carrying a top hat perhaps not quite as elegant as his coat. Peter swallowed hard. This had to be Molly's grandfather. He hoped Washburn wouldn't recognize the man's wardrobe.

Anson Orland murmured something and bowed to Prince Albert Edward. The prince nodded a proper, regal response.

However, from the moment Orland was announced, Washburn stood stiff as a poker. As the elderly man stepped over to bow to the Duke of Newcastle, Washburn strode to Peter and gripped his shoulder.

"Did you hear that gentleman's name?"

Peter glanced toward the old man speaking to the duke. "Yes, my lord."

"His name is Orland." The earl's facial muscles tensed. He reached into his pocket then tucked something into Peter's hand—a coin, by the feel of it. The earl's teeth clenched, his amiable manner gone. "Get rid of him."

Chapter Eleven

Peter stared after Washburn as he strode through the folding doors. He looked down at the gold piece the earl had passed him. His mind swirled with suppositions. The man carrying his hat had to be Molly's grandfather. But the man carrying his hat was named Orland. Therefore, Molly's grandfather was named Orland, and Molly must be a member of the Orland family. The earl had blanched and fled the room when he heard the name.

Peter drew a steadying breath and turned toward a tradesman who had just come through the line.

"How do you do, sir? You may exit right through here." Even as he spoke, Peter watched the next visitor, Anson Orland, who had been presented to the governor and the prince and now greeted the duke.

The old man turned away from Newcastle smiling but then looked about, seemingly confused. Slowly he approached Peter.

"Good afternoon, sir," Peter said. "You may exit through these doors."

Mr. Orland stopped and surveyed him. With a start, Peter realized that Orland's vivid blue eyes—very like Molly's—were on a level with his own. The old man must have been a giant in his youth.

"Young man, is the Earl of Washburn present? I understood he was to be here today."

Peter strove to keep his features calm and betray nothing. "He was, sir, but he had to leave suddenly."

"Ah. Too bad." The white-haired man frowned and shook his head.

Peter's mind raced as he tried to recall every word Molly had spoken about her grandfather. "Is there anything I can do for you, sir?"

"No. No, I just wished to meet the earl. I met his father once, back in England. Before I emigrated." His face had gone a dull red, and he looked about once more as though hoping to spy the earl behind one of the vases of cut flowers.

"Ah, I see. A pity that you missed him. I apologize on behalf of his lordship." Peter began to walk slowly, and the old man accompanied him to the exit. That made the job the earl had given him easier. Molly had mentioned her grandfather's hopes to see the earl, but given the elderly farmer's agitation and the earl's reaction to hearing his name, perhaps it was best that the two did not meet.

Orland paused by the door and turned Peter's hat round and round by its brim. At last he nodded. "Thank you, young man."

As the old gentlemen left, Peter let out a sigh. Several others had been presented and were hanging back, waiting for Orland to clear the doorway. Peter stepped back.

"Thank you for coming, gentlemen. You may exit here."

Not five minutes later Washburn returned and resumed his place beside the duke, a few yards from where Peter stood. He seemed to have collected himself—and perhaps a glass of sherry. He greeted the next guest with warmth, and Peter began to relax. His pulse slowly returned to normal…until another thought struck him.

I've met Molly's grandfather.

He smiled to himself. It wasn't the way he'd have preferred to meet a member of her family. But with the earl so on edge when he learned a man named Orland was present, it was probably best that Molly's grandpa Anson didn't know his identity. If he'd realized that Peter worked directly for Washburn, he might have asked for a favor, especially if he knew that his granddaughter had stolen Peter's heart.

There, he admitted it, if only to himself. Molly's shy, modest manner, her diligence and ingenuity, along with her wholesome beauty, had smitten him. If only he lived another life, held a different station…but that was a silly wish. If his life were different, he'd never have met her.

Another more disturbing thought wrestled for his attention. The name Orland had entered the conversation on that occasion, four years ago now, when the Earl of Washburn had called him into his study. Peter hadn't untangled the threads yet, but he had begun to understand Molly's words and Anson Orland's desire to see the earl. There was a connection indeed, and Peter determined to sort it out. He wouldn't bring up the topic, but if his master did, he would learn all he could. If Washburn didn't broach the subject, perhaps a discreet inquiry to Dundas about the farming family could shed some light on the Orlands' situation.

"Mr. David Orland."

Peter's heart kicked at the Lord High Steward's words. He whirled to stare at the tall man hobbling toward the prince, using two canes to support himself. He was a younger version of Anson Orland, very tall but hunched over the canes, with the same shimmering golden hair that Molly had. Peter tensed. In addition to one of his canes, in his left hand the man held Peter's hat by the edge of its brim. So they had both come, but separately. What did it mean?

David Orland face's was creased in lines of pain as he shuffled forward. Molly had said her father was recovering from an accident—a broken leg. Yet he'd gone to great effort to come and meet the prince. Or was it Washburn he'd come to see as well? Peter held his breath. That was likely it. The earl was turned to one side, speaking to General Bruce and smiling. Had he not heard the name St. Germains had just given?

David Orland placed his canes carefully and bowed with precision before his prince.

Peter couldn't hear any words—perhaps none were spoken. Albert Edward nodded, and his expressive eyes filled with sympathy.

As usual in a public gathering, the prince exuded a modest and caring attitude toward the people. Peter didn't think it was a ruse. The young man had been trained since birth to know that without the people there would be no empire. As his mother did, he truly cared about his subjects—in so far as he was able to understand their needs. Peter had no doubt that the Orland men had needs of which the prince had no inkling.

Should he warn the earl that a second member of the Orland family had entered the room? Peter took a step toward his master. Too late—David Orland was now leaving the governor and the prince and speaking to the duke. It would be too conspicuous to grab the earl—the next person in line—and yank him aside.

Before Peter had closed half the distance between them, Washburn had turned with his smile still in place and surveyed David Orland.

"Well, now, sir. It's an honor that you've made the effort to be here today." Washburn extended his hand.

"Mr. Orland," said the footman beside the earl.

Washburn froze for a moment. Then he laughed. "Well, now, that's an excellent coat you're wearing, sir. I believe we must have the same tailor."

Peter caught his breath. How big a blunder had he made, out of sympathy for a pretty girl?

David flushed but braced one cane under his arm and took the earl's hand. "Thank you, my lord. My daughter claims it's in good taste for the occasion."

"Your daughter is right."

Peter exhaled. Thanks to Molly's father's ready wits, he might get by with his caper.

David Orland fixed the earl with his gaze, and for a moment silence hung in the room. "You are the Earl of Washburn, sir?"

"I am."

"Then I believe we have a connection."

Peter winced. He couldn't turn away, though something told him he'd regret witnessing the meeting.

Warily, the earl looked Orland over. "Oh?"

"Yes." David lowered the cane's tip to the floor again and leaned on the two sticks with a slight grimace. "My father has lived on this island for the last forty-five years because of a wrong done by your father."

*****

As Molly entered the kitchen from the rear passageway, Allison rushed toward her carrying an armful of table linen. "Hurry. Mrs. Bolton came in here and asked for you by name. Take these into the dining room and help set up for the luncheon. They're serving twenty-four after the levee."

Molly clutched the embroidered table napkins to her chest and scurried for the passage between the kitchen and dining room.

Mrs. Bolton was just emerging. Molly hesitated, but there was no avoiding the stern housekeeper.

"And where have you been, Molly?"

"I'm sorry, ma'am. I was held up for a moment."

Mrs. Bolton's creased forehead grew even more furrowed. "Get those serviettes laid out and fill the finger bowls. Quickly now. The guests are being admitted to the levee, and His Royal Highness is receiving them. You are not to be in evidence in the great hall or the passageways the guests use. Do you understand?"

"Yes, ma'am." Molly dipped a curtsy and dove for the dining room door.

Rosaleen was holding a vase of flowers, while Mrs. Dundas arranged another just so on the table. Another maid, Pauline, was setting up chafing dishes on the sideboard. Molly hurried to lay out the linens. Mrs. Dundas smiled at her, and Molly felt undeserving of her confidence.

When the formal dining room was ready, she was sent to prepare the servants' dining hall. No telling what time the staff would eat today, since the luncheon for the Dundases and their guests would be served late. She prayed silently as she laid out the pewter flatware and thick ironstone plates.

"Molly."

She jerked toward the door. The first parlor maid, Roberts, stood there.

"Yes, ma'am?"

"As soon as you are done here, report to me. The footmen will be setting up in the back gardens for Mrs. Dundas's lawn party, and we need to arrange the decorations and refreshment tables."

"Yes, ma'am." The rain must have stopped, at least temporarily, or they wouldn't dare begin to set out tables and benches.

"Though why they want to let everyone and his brother trample those lawns and gardens is beyond me." Roberts looked at the clock above the breakfront that held the servants' dishes. "Are you serving at the state luncheon?"

"I don't know, ma'am. I've not been told."

Roberts clucked her tongue in disapproval. "I'll find out. If you are, you'll need to be back in the dining room soon. I've never seen such disorganization."

She turned away with a swish of her skirts. Considering the short time the staff had between events, Molly thought they were doing quite well. So far they'd stayed one step ahead of the aristocrats. Quickly she laid the plates and went back to the shelves for cups and saucers.

*****

The earl's eyes narrowed and he hesitated. He looked around with an air of impending disaster, his face turning an odd shade of mauve. His gaze settled on Peter.

"Stark." It came out like the caw of a crow calling a warning.

"How may I help you, my lord?" Peter stepped up beside him so that the earl would feel the support of his physical presence.

Washburn drew an unsteady breath. "I fear I'm indisposed. Would you please make my excuses to Mrs. Dundas at the luncheon?"

"Certainly. Would you like me to help you to your chamber?"

"No. No, thank you." Washburn nodded curtly in David Orland's direction. "Forgive me, sir. I'm not well. Perhaps we shall meet again."

He walked unsteadily toward the folding doors. Peter longed to run after him and assist him. Perhaps he could ask Dr. Acland to go and take a look at his master, to be sure he was all right.

He inhaled and extended his hand to David. "I'm sorry, sir. My apologies for his lordship. We're delighted that you came today."

Orland eyed him keenly as he took his hand. "You're Stark—the earl's man?"

"Yes, sir."

"I'm thinking my family owes you a word of thanks."

"Think nothing of it, sir. I was happy to lend my aid, although"—Peter cast a glance toward the doorway through which his master had disappeared—"I fear my impulse may have done more harm than good in this matter."

"How much did our Molly tell you?"

"Nothing except that your father wished to speak to the earl."

David nodded, leaning heavily on his canes while holding on to the hat's brim. Other gentlemen moved around him toward the exit. Peter knew he neglected his duty, but one of the equerries stepped up in his place and guided the visitors toward the door.

"It's just as well," David said. "I wasn't coming in today. My leg frets me, so I was going to stay in the wagon. But then Da came out and said the earl wasn't in here. So I—" His eyes twinkled. "You may laugh, sir, but I borrowed his finery and took my turn, hoping to see if I could learn what happened to Washburn. My father has waited many years for this, you see."

Peter lowered his voice. "For what, sir? Surely he doesn't mean to harm the earl?"

"No, never. Only to ask for justice. It wasn't this earl who wronged him, but his father, what's now dead."

"I understand that. Perhaps I understand more than you think. But why is your father so adamant about seeing *this* Lord Washburn? You must realize, sir, that part of my job is to protect him."

"You like your master?"

"He's a good man."

"I'm glad to hear it. His father was a rascal, by all accounts I've heard." David glanced behind him. "Well, I'm in the way. I'll go tell my da I managed to see his lordship. But I can't say I got very far with him."

Peter walked with him toward the folding doors. "Sir, no matter what's passed between the Orlands and the Washburns, I'm pleased to meet you."

David looked him full in the eyes. "And I to meet you, Mr. Stark. You're one man I've heard nothing but good about." He nodded. "Good day."

Chapter Twelve

Molly helped carry the hot dishes up for the luncheon without making a single mistake. She wasn't as nervous as she had been the evening before, but part of that might have been due to the fact that neither Peter nor the Earl of Washburn was present in the dining room.

Once or twice she saw the prince looking at her down the length of the room, but she pretended she didn't notice and gave extra attention to the trays she carried and people she helped Milton serve. The guests ignored her most of the time, but one of the equerries thanked her when she refilled his water glass, and the local magistrate asked if she wasn't David Orland's girl.

"Yes, sir, I am," she replied with a smile.

"And you're in service here?"

"Temporarily, sir. For the royal tour."

"Of course." He went back to his meal and his conversation with the legislator on his right and ignored her from then on.

The next time she glanced toward the head of the table, the prince was speaking to Mrs. Dundas. Molly relaxed. He was still hardly more than a boy. Perhaps he was looking for people his age among all these middle-aged denizens of high society.

Later, as she went to have her own meal in the servants' hall, Molly made a conscious decision not to inquire about Peter and his master among the other staff—that would be unseemly. But she kept her ears open to see if she could learn anything.

"I took lunch up to that fancy earl," Rosaleen told her in a low voice as they began passing the dishes around the table.

"I noticed he didn't come to lunch," Molly said. "Is he ill?"

"I'm not sure. Mr. Stark was in his chamber with him when I carried the tray up, and he took it from me at the door. Such a well-mannered young man! But I saw the earl pacing about by the windows, so he can't be too sick."

Molly thought about that as she ate. She enjoyed the food at Government House, and Cook seemed to be making a special effort in her meals for the staff while the New York chef was in residence and cooking for the family and guests. Allison had given her opinion that Cook was trying to show the chef that she was every bit as good a cook as he was…and to keep him from completely taking over her kitchen. Whatever the reason, the staff ate well that week, and they also got a few leftovers from upstairs.

She reported to the first parlor maid after the servants' lunch was over, expecting to be given more to do for the afternoon party, but instead Roberts told her, "Mrs. Bolton wants you in her sitting room."

Molly raised an eyebrow, but Roberts only nodded, so she turned and hurried up to Mrs. Bolton's rooms. As she went, her heart began to pound. This couldn't be the result of their earlier encounter, could it? Was it possible Mrs. Bolton had learned that she'd gone out to meet her brother during work time? Even worse—had the housekeeper somehow heard about the clothing she'd borrowed for her grandfather? Perspiration broke out on Molly's forehead, and she paused on the landing to dab at her face with a handkerchief.

An even more dire possibility struck her—maybe the prince had complained about her barging into the room where he and the duke were sitting that morning. Perhaps she was about to be fired. With all her missteps today it might be justified, but even so, she didn't think she could bear the shame. Breathing was suddenly very difficult. She forced herself to walk down the hall and around the corner to the wing where Mrs. Bolton lived.

The cook and butler had their living quarters on the second floor with Mr. and Mrs. Dundas, while other live-in servants had rooms in the cellar or attic. Molly went to the housekeeper's sitting room and tapped on the door.

"Enter."

She turned the knob and crossed the threshold.

"Ah. Molly Orland."

"Yes, ma'am." She curtsied, angry at herself for allowing her voice to tremble.

Mrs. Bolton's eyes narrowed as she looked Molly up and down. "I received rather an odd request from one of our guests."

"Yes, ma'am?" It came out almost a squeak, and Molly cleared her throat, wishing desperately that she could be elsewhere.

"Yes. The Earl of Washburn has asked me to see that you were invited to this evening's ball."

Molly's chin jerked up involuntarily, and she stared as the housekeeper continued. A heavy weight seemed to have settled on her chest, making it nearly impossible to draw another breath.

"I checked with Mrs. Dundas, of course, and she didn't see any harm in it, since you're not a regular employee and your father was at the levee this morning."

Molly swallowed with difficulty, trying to think what Mrs. Bolton's words meant. The ball? It was impossible. And why her? And especially, why did the Earl of Washburn make the request? Had Grandpa Anson spoken to him at the levee and told him that his granddaughter was temporarily in-service in the house? Added to that, her father had made an appearance at the levee after all.

"I—I don't understand, ma'am." She looked down at her shoe tips as heat rushed into her cheeks.

"Don't let it go to your head, girl. The royal party wants to be sure there will be plenty of pretty young women for the prince to dance with."

Molly gulped. Had the request from Washburn originated with the prince? The humiliating memory of her unexpected encounter with the prince flashed across her mind. But Washburn wasn't with him then—the Duke of Newcastle was. What had he said about wanting dance partners? This request must have come from that suggestion she'd thought was a jest.

"From what I've heard, the prince can be charming," Mrs. Bolton went on. "He'll dance with all the dowagers, but he likes a little fun too. It seems you caught his eye, and he asked for you especially." Mrs. Bolton eyed her keenly. "I spoke to Mr. Reynold, and he assured me that you did nothing while serving at mealtime to draw attention to yourself."

"I hope not, ma'am."

"He tells me you stayed at the lower end of the table and went nowhere near the prince."

"That's true, ma'am."

"Yes. Well, since Mrs. Dundas approves, I suppose we'll have to let you go."

"But…" Molly stared at her, suddenly terrified. "But…I can't!"

"Whyever not, child?" The housekeeper's eyes snapped with disapproval. "The mistress has agreed to fulfill the request. You cannot say no at this point."

"But—but I don't have a suitable gown, ma'am. The ball is tonight, and even if there was time to shop, we don't have enough money. It's impossible."

Mrs. Bolton shook her head. "Don't you fret. Mrs. Dundas's lady's maid is close to your size, and she has dozens of gowns her mistress gave her. She can lend you something. Mrs. Dundas assured me she would see to it." She muttered something under her breath and lifted her arm to a bellpull that dangled near her chair. She tugged it so hard that the keys on the chatelaine at her waist jangled. Molly thought she caught the words "…what we're coming to."

The housekeeper fixed her disapproving gaze on Molly once more. "You mind your manners, young lady. There'll be no one but you to keep your humility and guard your reputation. One slip and you'll disgrace the entire population of this island."

Molly's heart thudded at the thought, and her throat constricted. "Yes, ma'am."

"After your gown is fitted, you'll have to go home and rest this afternoon. It won't do to have you serve dinner and then go to the ball yawning." She shook her head. "I shall have to find another footman or parlor maid to help serve this evening. This is very irregular."

Molly stood still, averting her gaze and trying not to squirm. A moment later a light knock came at the door and it opened.

"You wished to see me, ma'am?" Mrs. Dundas's lady's maid, Thompson, stepped inside.

"Yes. The mistress says you're to outfit this young lady for tonight's ball."

"Yes, ma'am. Mrs. Dundas told me." Though Thompson's features remained impassive, Molly wondered how she really felt about having to lend her personal belongings to a farmer's daughter.

"I see Molly is a wee bit taller than you. Do the best you can."

The maid looked over at Molly and measured her with her eyes, from her face to her feet and back up again. Thompson's mouth drooped for an instant before she collected herself. "Yes, ma'am. I'm sure we'll find something suitable."

"See that she looks wholesome, won't you?" Mrs. Bolton's brows drew down as she peered at the young woman. "Nothing too daring."

"Of course, ma'am." Thompson dipped a small curtsy and looked at Molly. "Won't you come with me, miss? We'll have to hurry, as Mrs. Dundas will need me soon."

Molly nodded to Mrs. Bolton and followed Thompson out into the corridor. The lady's maid strode swiftly along the carpeted hallway, and Molly scurried to keep up. How much resentment was seething beneath the surface? Thompson was in her midtwenties, and ladies' maids served only so long as they remained youthful and pretty. This one probably had five to ten years left to serve her mistress, if all went well. Then she would be put aside for a younger woman. If she had saved enough during her service, Thompson could retire. Ideally, she would find a husband. Otherwise, she would have to take a cut in pay and status to keep working after she reached thirty-five, probably as a parlor maid.

Around a corner they came to Thompson's rooms. She led Molly into her bedchamber. The cherry four-poster bed and huge armoire dwarfed them as they crossed the plush carpet.

"This way." Thompson opened a door and entered another room with Molly on her heels.

Molly caught her breath. The entire room was full of racks of clothing. Dresses, skirts, and crinolines hung on padded hangers on the four long racks. One small window admitted light, and several lanterns hung on pegs on each wall.

Thompson looked back at her and walked to the farthest corner. "There's a dusty rose dress that Madam gave me when they first arrived here. It may be suitable for you. I wore it once, but it's too juvenile for me now."

She lifted a pink gown from the rack and turned, holding it out. "I suppose you need to try it on. I'll get one of the housemaids to help us."

"I think I can do it myself," Molly said quickly.

"Oh no, not these hoopskirts. They have to be worn with a crinoline. You'll need at least two people to help you dress. Here." As she spoke, Thompson first hung the gown back on the rack and then thrust a corset into Molly's hands. "Put that on over your chemise. It ought to fit. I'll lace you up when I get back."

Molly flushed, even though Thompson was walking out the door. She'd not needed assistance to dress since she was a toddler. She stared at the closed door for a moment, trying to take it all in. Not only was she going to the ball tonight, but Thompson was loaning her a dress worthy of a princess—or a governor's wife. Mrs. Dundas must have worn this gown in years past. Thompson had said it was dusty. Molly examined it closely but saw no dust on the pleats and gathers. At last it occurred to her that "dusty rose" was the name of the gown's soft pink color.

As fast as she could, she scrambled out of her black pinafore and dress and wrapped the corset around her. She was able to hook it in front, but it hung too loose on her frame. She tried to pull up the strings in the back, but she couldn't fasten them—Thompson was right about that.

The door swung open.

"Rosaleen will help us." Thompson eyed her critically. "Turn around."

Molly had to stand in her undergarments and withstand the indignities of being dressed by women she barely knew. How did rich women stand it? The corset was followed by an under-petticoat and a camisole for a corset cover. Thompson gave terse instructions to Rosaleen, and they both lifted the crinoline from its hanger and hoisted it over Molly's head. Another petticoat covered the crinoline to protect the gown from the steel hoops. Over this came a decorative embroidered petticoat. At last the gown went on.

Thompson frowned as Rosaleen straightened the folds of pink satin. "Too short, and I'm afraid there's not enough material to lengthen it."

Molly looked at Rosaleen in dismay.

Rosaleen studied the hemline. "It is a bit short for today's style."

Thompson strode to the rack of evening gowns and riffled through them. After a moment, she brought out a gold brocade dress.

Molly didn't like the color. With her fair hair, it would make her look drab, though a dark-haired woman like Mrs. Dundas could carry it off regally. And the material looked heavy and hot—but she mustn't complain.

Rosaleen spoke up. "Begging your pardon, miss, but she can't wear that. Not in August. 'Twill be prodigious warm in that crowded room. His Royal Highness wouldn't like it if one of the ladies swooned."

Thompson's lip curled. "I suppose you're right." She sighed and put the gown back.

Molly glanced at Rosaleen. Perhaps Thompson was offering her only the dresses she disliked or those that didn't fit her well.

Rosaleen gave Molly a nod as if to say, "I'll make sure she treats you well, you'll see."

"Well, there's this. It's certainly a summer dress." Thompson drew out a simple white gown with blue ribbons catching up gathered swags of the bleached muslin skirt. Around the edge at the hemline, embroidery embellished a cutwork design. "It's very simple, not really a formal gown—more of an afternoon dress."

Molly puzzled over that. The dress didn't look simple to her.

Rosaleen's eyes lit. "Ah, but with the right coiffure, miss, and accessories—gloves, perhaps a pin in her hair, and a necklace?"

Thompson's mouth tightened. "I suppose it would do."

Was she thinking she'd have to provide those items too? Molly said, "My mother has a necklace that would work with it, if the dress fits."

"All right, let's get the rose gown off and this one on."

With the hoops pushing out the skirt, the white dress took on a more elegant line. Molly stood before the mirror and stared at her reflection. She couldn't remember ever feeling beautiful before, but the superbly cut dress and her rosy cheeks and bright eyes gave her an undeniably attractive air.

"You'll have your hair up," Rosaleen said, a little breathless.

"Yes." Molly still could barely believe the image in the glass was her. The dress fell away from her waist in a frothy cascade with bunches of bright sky-blue ribbons catching it up at intervals around the skirt. It was perfect—the dress she would have dreamed of if she'd known how.

"Are you done gawking?" Thompson asked.

Molly jumped. "A–are you sure you want to loan me this?"

Thompson shrugged. "It fits you. Anything else would require alterations, and frankly, I don't have time. I have to shorten most of Madam's gowns because she's taller than I am, but this one has that intricate cutwork edging at the hem, and I didn't want to spoil it. And so I've never worn it." A touch of regret tinged her voice as she eyed Molly's form in the mirror.

"If you don't—"

"Tsk. It fits you perfectly. Now get out of it."

Rosaleen helped lift the billows of white over Molly's head. Thompson hung the gown on the end of the nearest rack while Rosaleen helped Molly out of the layers of undergarments.

"Thank you." Molly blushed as she wriggled back into her own shift and petticoat.

"I'll send it around to one of the housemaids' rooms. You can dress there this evening."

"She can dress in Deborah's room," Rosaleen said. "I'll stay and help her."

"Thank you." Molly threw her a shaky smile and pulled on her black dress.

"Let me see your feet," Thompson said. She scowled as Molly up held her skirt. "I fear you won't squeeze those into any of my slippers."

Molly felt the color in her cheeks deepen. She'd always known her feet were too large to be called dainty.

"I can never wear Mrs. Dundas's shoes—they're too large, so I give them to my mother. I'll check the mistress's wardrobe for a pair of slippers she won't be needing. I don't suppose you have silk stockings or long gloves?"

"Er…no. Nor my mother."

"All right, then. I'll make you a bundle and send it up later this afternoon. Now I must see to my mistress."

"Thank you," Molly called.

Thompson went out of the wardrobe room without looking back.

Rosaleen held out Molly's apron. "Tonight's your dream night, eh?"

Molly let out a breath and grasped her wrist. "I can't believe this is happening. Why me?"

"You have to ask? They want pretty young ladies to dance with the prince."

"But I'm a domestic servant."

Rosaleen smiled. "What the Prince of Wales wants, the Prince of Wales gets."

"Oh!" Molly stopped with the apron strings untied in her hands. "Rosaleen! This means I have to dance with him. I have to *touch* him."

She laughed. "Actually, you'll probably touch his glove and his coat. Barely."

"Oh my."

"Here now, child. Don't go all woozy on me. Turn around and let me tie your apron."

"Mrs. Bolton told me to go home and rest."

"And so you should. I'm surprised they're not making you work all day too."

Molly stared at her. "What will my parents say? What if they won't let me go this evening?"

"Don't you worry about that. You've received a singular honor. I should be very surprised if they said no, especially when the request came from the prince himself."

"Mrs. Bolton said the Earl of Washburn was the one who asked Mrs. Dundas."

"But it's because of the young prince. He must have wanted you there."

Molly stared at the beautiful gown she would wear. "I suppose it is." The flush returned to her face as she recalled her bumbling entry to the breakfast room. No one must know about that.

Rosaleen reached for the frothy white dress. "Here, now, I'll take the gown to Deborah's room and you'll know it won't get mussed. Come back this evening, and I'll help you get dressed."

"You're a dear."

"Oh, go on." Rosaleen lifted the hanger and carefully draped the spotless folds over her arm.

Molly took one last look at the gown she would wear that evening. If only, instead of the prince, the man who'd requested her presence was Peter Stark. Now *that* would be a dream come true.

Chapter Thirteen

"That's not the worst of it." The Earl of Washburn strode to the brocade drapes, peered down into the garden, turned, and paced back. "The prince has requested that a certain young woman—one of the housemaids here—be included in the guest list for tonight's ball."

"A servant?" Peter stared at him as the awful truth hit him. The heir apparent had followed through on his whim. Ordinarily Peter would make an effort to control his reaction to anything one of the aristocrats said, but they were alone, and the earl obviously wanted a sympathetic response. "That's highly unusual."

"Yes, my boy." Washburn locked his hands together and squeezed them. "Of course, he's only a young pup—doesn't know what he's doing—but I'd have expected Newcastle and Bruce to put a stop to it."

"They didn't?"

"On the contrary. Just before the levee began, Newcastle appointed me to approach Mrs. Dundas about it. I think he was too yellow to ask her himself."

"And Mrs. Dundas agreed."

"Oh, yes, yes, yes, all too easily if you ask me. But the worst thing is the girl herself."

"What about her?" Peter asked, attempting to keep his tone neutral.

"She's Orland's daughter. The prince has taken notice of the family, Peter. Why did it have to be her? And what am I to do?"

Peter pulled in a deep breath. "I'm not sure."

Washburn ran a hand over his face. "The prince will go to the Colonial Building immediately after luncheon to hear some speeches, and afterward he hopes to ride in the country, if the weather permits. The duke will go along in a carriage with some others, and they expect me to go."

"Would you rather stay here and rest?" Peter asked.

"No. I suppose I must deal with these Orlands sooner or later. Can you find out where they live? If it's close enough to town, perhaps we can pay them a call."

"I…are you sure you want to do that, my lord?"

"Yes, yes. Might as well get it over with." The earl stopped before the window and ran his fingers through his thinning hair. "Speak to the coachman. If he knows where the farm lies, perhaps you can suggest that route to the governor."

*****

Mum dropped her shuttle as Molly entered the kitchen. "Why are you home so early?"

"I'm to rest and then return this evening."

"Oh. I suppose that's a kindness of them, to allow you a nap. You're serving at dinner and attending the ladies afterward?"

"No, not precisely."

"What is it, then?" Her mother stood and left the loom, where she'd been weaving woolen cloth for winter clothing. "Molly…?"

Molly exhaled and raised her chin, determined to get it over with. "I'm to attend the ball."

"What? Will you be waiting on one of the ladies?"

"No."

"Surely you can't mean you'll be a guest." Her mother's expression changed from inquiry to shock. "What's the meaning of this?"

Molly sat down on the nearest chair. "I'm not sure, but they wanted more dancing partners for the prince. At least, I'm told—"

"So Mrs. Dundas felt they hadn't enough young ladies?"

"Well, she did approve it. The housekeeper told me so, but… She said Lord Washburn requested my presence."

"Washburn!" Her mother's face paled. She staggered to a stool and plopped down on it. "Your father claimed he barely said a word to him this morning. He told him who he was and then Washburn stalked out of the levee."

"Really?" Molly swallowed hard. What was she in the middle of? Had Washburn invited her with the intention of humiliating her family in some manner? "Perhaps I shouldn't go."

Her mother took two shaky breaths and shook her head. "We'll ask your father. That's what we'll do." She rose and opened the door of the dairy that adjoined the kitchen. "David!"

A distant voice answered.

"Come in here, please," Mum called. "Bring your father too. There's news."

Molly gritted her teeth and waited. She couldn't very well refuse the invitation, could she?

Her mother turned around, her face wrinkled. "Whatever will you wear?"

"They're loaning me a gown. It belongs to Thompson, Mrs. Dundas's maid."

Her father stumped in, using his canes. Grandpa and the boys followed, and even Kate scampered down the ladder and looked questioningly at Molly. When Molly avoided her gaze, Kate sidled over and took a seat near her.

"What is it?" Papa leaned against the wall near the stove.

"You may as well sit," Mum said. "I've no doubt we'll be chewing this over a bit."

They shuffled to their chairs, taking their usual seats at the table.

"Well?" her father asked.

"Our Molly is going to the prince's ball. She's to dance with His Royal Highness this evening, and 'twas Lord Washburn who inquired about it to Mrs. Dundas."

Grandpa Anson's eyes lit. "Aha. Perhaps the earl wants to tell me something, and he saw our Molly as his best way to get me a message."

"Message? What do you mean?" Molly met her grandfather's gaze.

"Why, he could talk to you on the dance floor, girl. Tell you whatever it is he wants me to know."

"That's silly. Isn't it?" Molly looked to her mother.

"I don't know."

"I don't think Lord Washburn wants to dance with me. He's an old man."

"Easy, girl. He's a lot younger than me," Grandpa replied.

Her mother turned a beseeching look on her husband. "David, what does all of this mean?"

He shook his head. "I don't know either. It seems to me that if the earl wanted to send Da a message, all he had to do was inquire for Anson Orland. We're well-known in these parts."

"Perhaps we'd better send Nathan with Molly tonight, to wait outside the Colonial Building and bring her home after the ball." Anxious lines etched the corners of Mum's mouth.

"Or keep her home."

Molly stared at her father. The silence lengthened.

Grandpa brought his fist down on the table. "Nay. She must go."

Mum nodded slowly. " 'Tis a great honor for them to single out our Molly. The prince is only a lad, and if someone thinks our girl is a proper companion for him, then she ought to accept with grace."

"Of course she'll go," Grandpa said. "One doesn't ignore a royal request."

"The earl's the one who asked." David frowned and shifted his leg. "I wouldn't like to think he had his father's tendencies. I spoke to his man—Stark."

Molly's eyes flew wide and her mouth went dry.

136

Her father looked her way and nodded. "And he says the present earl is an honorable man. I don't think he'd try to besmirch our girl, though he might want to have words with Da."

Molly considered telling them about her mistake in walking into the room where the prince sat that morning but decided against it. Maybe the prince had nothing to do with this. Maybe, as Grandpa said, it was all the earl's doing, and the whole thing came about because of what Papa had said at the levee.

"So...I should go back this evening and do as I'm bid?"

Her father looked at Grandpa. "I suppose there's naught else to do. But Nathan will be in the portico outside the ball, waiting for you."

"I shall be more at ease knowing that."

"Oh, and the clothes." Her mother jumped up. "You must take them back to Mr. Stark."

"Yes. I hope I can find a way to get them to him without anyone noticing."

Grandpa beamed at her. "Now, isn't it a blessed happenstance that your father met Mr. Stark today?"

"I'm sure I don't know. Was it?" Molly turned to appraise her father.

"Aye." Papa absently rubbed the thigh of his injured leg as he spoke. "And I expect your grandpa saw him too, but he didn't realize who he was."

"What exactly happened at the levee?" Molly asked. "Did you go in together?"

"And how should we do that, without the proper clothes?" Grandpa asked with a gentle smile.

"I wasn't going in," her father said. "Da put on the coat and top hat, and I decided to wait for him in the wagon. He came out half an hour later all sputtering and red in the face. Seems the earl wasn't in the room when he was presented to His Royal Highness."

"But seeing the prince was worth it," Grandpa conceded. "He's a likely lad. I'll warrant he's a fine dancer too."

Molly looked back and forth between them. "The earl wasn't there?"

"Nay," her grandfather said. "He'd stepped out or some such tomfoolery. When I told David, he said he would go in and find out what nonsense that was."

"So I put on the coat and top hat and in I went," her father said a bit sheepishly.

"And you met Lord Washburn."

"I did indeed. He remarked on the fine cut of my coat."

Molly's jaw dropped. "He didn't."

"He did."

"Oh, Papa, do you think he recognized it?"

"I'm not certain. 'Tis a plain coat, though well made."

"Oh, I *must* get it back to Peter as soon as possible. To Mr. Stark, that is." Molly felt the heat rush to her face.

"Aye, probably a good idea to return to Fanning Bank a few minutes early," her father said.

Her mother rose and went to the stove. "Perhaps you can ask one of the footmen to deliver it to Mr. Stark's room without telling him what it is or how you came by it. But now, child, you must rest." She turned with a stick of firewood in her hand. "Who will dress your hair? Oh my, this is so unexpected."

"I shall ask Allison, if she's not kept at some other duty," Molly said. "She's very good at hairdressing. If she can't help me, perhaps another of the maids can. Rosaleen has offered to help me get ready, and my dress is waiting in Deborah's room."

"I suppose all shall be well, then."

Molly couldn't help smiling as she remembered the white gown. "Oh, Mum, I wish you could see the dress they've loaned me. It's the loveliest thing, but not at all pretentious." She shot a glance at her father. "Or immodest."

"Well, that at least is a comfort," he said.

Not much else about the situation comforted Molly. She'd never danced in public, though Papa and Grandpa had whirled the children about the kitchen enough that she knew the rudiments of the art. She and Allison had practiced clandestinely a few times in the Johnsons' barn. But she didn't consider herself at all skilled in dancing. What if she tripped over the prince's feet or stepped the wrong way at a critical moment in the quadrille?

The men went back out to the barn, and Mum shooed Molly upstairs to lie down. In the little chamber that she slept in with Kate, Molly removed her apron, dress, and shoes. As she stretched out on her cot, Kate tiptoed in.

"Hello, Katie."

Her little sister sat down on the quilt that covered her cot, opposite Molly's bed. "Are you really going to dance with Prince Bertie?"

Molly smiled. "I don't know. Perhaps not. We shall see tonight."

"Will they have cake and tea?"

"I expect so. I saw the chef put pans of batter in the oven today."

Kate sighed. "Nathan and Joe say there will be fireworks tonight."

"I heard that."

"I wish I could see them."

"I'm sorry you can't. I don't think I'll see them, though, if that's a consolation to you." Deborah's tiny room on the upstairs back of Government House, where Molly would dress for the ball, held no windows.

"It's not." Kate's face was very grave.

"There now, sweetie, let me rest, if you please."

Kate stood and walked to the door. She turned back. "Could you bring me a little cake, do you think?"

"If I'm able."

Her little sister left her, but Molly lay wide awake, hearing the distant lowing of the cattle and the rattle of wagon wheels on the road. So much to think about… Returning the formal clothes she had borrowed from Mr. Stark. Finding someone to do her hair. Dressing in the ethereal white gown that Thompson had never worn. Remembering the proper forms of address for a prince, a duke, an earl, and countless other gentlemen. If need be, she must recall whether to say, "Thank you very much, your grace," or "Thank you, sir," or even "Thank you, Your Highness." And what if a gentleman asked her to dance and she didn't know his rank? How should she address him then?

Despite all the fretful details, one thought stayed uppermost in her mind and kept her from drifting off to sleep. One all-consuming, burning question: would Peter be at the ball?

Chapter Fourteen

Peter fetched his boots from the armoire and sat down in a chair covered with jacquard brocade to pull them on. They gleamed in the afternoon sunlight that spilled in between the heavy gold curtains—fine boots the earl had insisted on buying for him for just such an occasion as this, riding out with the prince.

He finished with the boots, rose, and reached for his hat and gloves. All set for the ride now. Peter looked out the window. The prince and his friends—the two equerries, Captain Grey and Major Teesdale—were heading for the stable while the band carried its instruments to the back garden. They would have only an hour for the ride, after which the prince must put in an appearance at the lawn party. Peter hurried down the stairs and out to the stable yard. Gravel and straw had been strewn in the worst of the muddy spots and made getting to the barns easier.

"Oh, there you are, Stark," the earl called. Peter hastened to his side. Washburn stood with the Duke of Newcastle and a local couple named Mulgrave. "We'll be riding in a carriage behind His Royal Highness and the others."

Peter bowed slightly. "If you'd prefer, I can ride in the carriage, my lord."

"No, no. You go on and enjoy yourself. You young fellows seem to have no end of energy, and I know how much you love riding." Washburn stepped away from the others and lowered his voice. "Newcastle's complaining of a sore throat, and St. Germains has the sniffles. It's this damp. At least the prince is holding up well."

"Yes, he has a strong constitution." Peter looked up at the gray sky. For now, the rain held off, though the soft breeze brought moisture that beaded on every surface and a threat of more showers to come.

Washburn sighed. "Well, he knows he can't get sick before he opens that bridge in Montreal and lays the cornerstone for the parliament building in Ottawa."

Peter repressed a smile. Washburn seemed to believe that royals could control their health until all official duties were completed. Maybe they had a secret the likes of Peter didn't know.

"Yes, sir. I'm sure the prince will perform admirably at those events."

"Hmm, yes, he's done very well so far. Well, go on, lad. Get your horse and have at it. I shall enjoy a good visit with these folks. I believe a couple more carriages are coming along."

Peter hurried to the stable door. The prince's ride was turning into a cavalcade of dignitaries, rather than a peaceful outing with a couple of friends. At least the young man would get some exercise and fresh air. By the time they led out their saddled mounts, the clouds had thinned even more and the sun shot tentative rays between the wisps that remained. Peter began to hope that Mrs. Dundas's party would not be deluged after all.

The horseback party included George Dundas. He was privileged to slip off for some recreation while his wife fussed over the final details of the public lawn party. The two young army officers, Teesdale and Grey, were also going, and Captain Stapleton of the local militia, besides Peter and the prince. The six saddle horses trotted out smartly in the van, quickly outdistancing the carriages that rumbled along behind.

"You'll want to get a view of our racecourse," Dundas told the prince gleefully. "Too bad you can't stay long enough to enjoy a racing meet, Your Highness. You'd like it excessively."

"I'm sure I would—right, Chris?" The prince looked expectantly to his friend, Major Teesdale, who rode beside him.

"We all would, Your Honour," Teesdale said. "I've heard you've some good racing stock on the island."

Dundas smiled. "As good as any in the Canadas."

The prince spurred his mount into a canter through the acreage behind the house, and the others followed. Major Teesdale kept his horse within a few strides of the prince's magnificent black gelding—standing in for General Bruce, Peter assumed. The prince's governor had succumbed to the catarrh many suffered from and had retired for a nap rather than join the riding party.

They rode through the streets of Charlottetown at a sedate trot, but once out away from the busy streets, the riders let their horses again break into a canter until they reached a muddy stretch of road. The prince reined in his horse, and so the rest of the party did the same.

Peter hung back, content to ride last of those on horseback. The equerries laughed and bantered with the prince comfortably, as friends are wont to do…but Peter would never be privy to such a conversation with royalty. He let the military men and the governor enjoy their time with Albert Edward, while he enjoyed the freedom and contentment he always found in the saddle. Peter had never owned a horse—he and his mother couldn't afford to stable an animal. But over the last few years he'd had the privilege of riding the earl's horses often while carrying out his duties. One of his dreams was to have his own horse one day and enough turf to graze it on.

The party turned onto the North River Road—Dundas was taking them on Peter's suggested route. Satisfied, Peter let his mind wander. A couple of miles from town, they rode past fields of lush potato plants, long rows of them stretching to the tree line on the horizon. Almost all the fields sloped along the gentle hillsides, and the damp red earth between the rows of blossoming potato plants, framed against the blue-gray sky, presented a picture worthy of an artist's brush.

A fenced pasture was next, with a score of brown-and-white milk cows grazing placidly. One of the equerries said something to the heir apparent, and the prince pulled up his horse to wait for the governor to come alongside him.

"This is one of the places you said we might stop at? Charlie says it's a nice dairy farm. I believe dairying is a great industry in the colony?"

"Oh, yes, Your Highness," Dundas said. "Potatoes are our biggest export, but dairying is extremely important to the economy, as are fishing and shipbuilding." He pointed to a neat house, whitewashed and tidy, in the distance. "I believe that is the farmhouse that goes with these fields. Would you like to meet the owner?"

The prince surveyed the compact house and the solid barn connected to it. Several other outbuildings dotted the half acre around them.

"Yes, I would, if it's not too much trouble."

"We shall have to make it a short stop," Dundas said. "I don't suppose the farmer would object to a dooryard call, though. As it happens, he is one who was at the levee today. I imagine he'd be delighted to receive you."

Dundas turned and searched the faces of those in the party. His gaze lit on Peter. "Mr. Stark, would you be so kind as to ride ahead to the farmhouse and ask the householder if he'd mind answering a few questions about his dairying for His Royal Highness?"

The prince looked Peter's way. "And ask them if I might beg a cup of water. Riding is thirsty business."

Peter bowed his head and steered his horse around the others, into the short farm lane. The prince was showing a commendable interest in the local people, as well as displaying his amazing energy. Already that day, in addition to the levee and luncheon, he had inspected the regiment of Volunteers, allowed journalists to take photographs, gone by carriage to the Colonial Building—where he received the addresses of the Executive Council—and shot a few birds with the governor and the equerries. Now he was cantering about the farmland near Charlottetown and would soon return to Government House for the lawn party. After mixing with the public there, he would dress for dinner and the formal ball. Somewhere in there, he was expected to view the Illumination of Ships in the harbor. How long could the young man keep up this frenzied pace?

A tall, white-haired man emerged from the barn as Peter approached and stood eyeing him as he rode up. Peter tugged gently on the reins, and the spirited roan halted before the gentleman.

Though he held a rustic cap in his hand rather than a silk top hat and wore homespun trousers and shirt instead of a fine suit, there was no mistaking the elderly man. His blue eyes twinkled as he surveyed Peter.

"Mr. Stark. Imagine that."

Peter nodded. "Mr. Orland. This farm was recommended as one where His Royal Highness could stop while having a ride with the governor and a few others of his suite. I'm sorry we didn't give you advance warning, but the prince is just up at the head of your lane. He asked if he might meet the owner of so well-kept a farm and obtain a glass of water."

"Indeed. I shall have to call out the rest of the family as well, if it's all the same to you. I'm sure my daughter-in-law would like to meet you—and His Royal Highness, of course. And my son and I would be happy to lift a glass with the heir apparent."

Peter laughed. "I'm not sure there's time for that, as he must be back at Government House soon for Mrs. Dundas's fete."

"Too bad. I've a fine local ale inside."

"It might not be remiss to offer a glass. Go and tell your son and any other family members you've got about the place. I shall tell His Royal Highness you will receive him with a good will." Peter lifted the reins.

"Aye. Oh, and Stark—"

"Yes, sir?"

"Is the Earl of Washburn in the party?"

Peter nodded toward the road. "You see the three carriages coming in the wake of the riders? He is in the first of those, with Lord Newcastle and a couple of your local dignitaries."

"Ah. I don't suppose now is the time to try to speak to the earl, then. Too many folk about."

"On the contrary, his lordship is willing to set up an audience with you and your son."

"Is he, now?"

Peter nodded. "He instructed me to tell you so if I had the opportunity."

Orland gazed up the road at the approaching carriages. "Go on. We'll be ready in a moment." He turned and walked toward the barn door.

Peter wheeled his horse about and trotted to meet the other horsemen as they entered the muddy lane.

The prince smiled at him. "What's the word, Stark?"

"Your Highness will be received with pleasure."

"As if they would refuse," said Captain Grey.

The prince laughed. "There now, Charlie, these farm folk are more polite than you are."

Peter watched the other members of the party, but no one seemed to think Grey had acted in an overly familiar manner. Grey and Teesdale, he understood, had been friends with the prince from boyhood. Perhaps when they were alone the Prince of Wales dropped all aloofness and became an ordinary boy. Did he wish he could act with the easy freedom his friends did at other times? Grey and Teesdale could walk about the capital unattended any time they wished, stop in at a pub, or pause to watch a troupe of strolling musicians. The prince could never do that unless accompanied by a retinue of bodyguards.

Thankfulness for his own station in life—and the ensuing liberty it gave him—swept over Peter. The prince had noticed Molly and liked the look of her, so he'd seen that an invitation was issued to her for the ball. They might have one dance together, during which Molly would likely be tongue-tied. Peter, on the other hand, had managed a couple of conversations with her and anticipated getting to know her better at the ball. He could even approach her between dances and, if God favored him, ask her to walk in to supper with him.

Ah, Lord, that would be more blessing than the likes of me deserves.

"Well, come on, Stark," the prince said.

Peter jerked his head up. "Yes, Your Highness." Surprised, he guided his roan back toward the farmhouse in advance of the other riders. He'd expected to follow last in line as usual.

Molly's father, with crutches supporting him, and her grandfather had emerged and stood before the door of their snug little house. A woman in a plain housedress stood beside them. Her cheeks bloomed bright red and her hair was a bit windblown, but she was lovely. Peter couldn't help but smile as he traced the lines of Molly's features in her delicate chin and well-proportioned nose. A lad of about the prince's age and a boy of ten stood beside their grandfather, and a girl somewhere in age between them hovered in her mother's shadow. All the children bore the golden hair and blue eyes he'd found so striking on Molly.

Peter dismounted and held the horse's reins as Anson stepped forward.

"My daughter-in-law is Eliza," Anson said in a stage whisper.

Peter nodded in gratitude and noticed that the old man held a frothing tankard.

The prince, Dundas, and the equerries drew up and remained in the saddle.

Peter gulped. It seemed to be up to him to take on the steward's role. Would the prince recognize the Orland name and connect it with Molly, the maid he'd insisted be invited to the ball? He could do nothing about that.

"Your Highness, may I present the Orland family? We have here Mr. Anson Orland and his son, David, who were presented to you earlier today, and Mrs. Eliza Orland, and…three of their children."

The prince nodded with a smile. The Orland men bowed, and Eliza and her daughter dipped curtsies.

Peter hesitated then cleared his throat. "The queen's representative, Lieutenant-Governor Dundas."

Dundas inclined his head, and Peter went on to name the other gentlemen in the party.

Anson Orland stepped forward, extending the tankard to Peter. "If it pleases His Royal Highness, I would like to offer him a draught of our local ale."

"I shall accept with pleasure," said the prince.

Peter took the tankard and carried it to the near side of the prince's horse. He'd never directly served a member of the royal family, and it was all he could do to keep his hands steady as he raised the drink to the prince. *He's just a lad,* Peter told himself. *I'm handing a mug to a boy.*

The prince raised the tankard to his lips and drank deeply. Teesdale whipped out a handkerchief and handed it to him. Albert Edward blotted his lips and smiled down at Anson.

"Excellent. I must say, this colony has shown us food and drink of fine quality."

Anson bowed. "Thank you, Your Highness. We'd be happy to serve the rest of these gentlemen as well." He shot an anxious glance toward the road. The three carriages had caught up to them, and the first one now turned in at the farm lane. Peter could almost hear Anson's thoughts as he inventoried his stock of ale.

As he spoke, Eliza and the three children scurried to the doorstep, where they'd left a tray of cups and two pitchers, and managed to pour out cups for all the riders before the first carriage gained the dooryard and made a sweeping turn through the mud. The other two carriages paused in the road at the head of the lane. Apparently the coachmen had second thoughts about stuffing all three vehicles into the slick yard.

Mrs. Orland approached Peter. "May I serve you now, Mr. Stark?"

"Oh, no thank you." Though light ale was a common drink among men of nearly any religious persuasion in his culture, Peter never drank it. He didn't want to insult the Orlands, but he'd promised his mother long ago that he would not indulge in alcohol. He intended to keep that promise.

Mrs. Orland looked deeply into his eyes. "Our Molly says some gentlemen only drink water. I've a pitcher of nice, cool, sweet water from our well."

Peter felt the tension flow out of him. "Thank you, ma'am. That would be most welcome."

She brought it to him in a heavy china cup, and he downed it. "Thank you. That was most refreshing."

She smiled at him. "You're very welcome. And it's pleased I am to meet you." Mrs. Orland took the cup and carried her tray around to collect the others from the mounted men. The prince had meantime engaged David and Anson in a lively conversation about the dairy business.

The driver of the first carriage halted his team, apparently waiting for instructions.

The prince looked over at Dundas. "I suppose we must push on, or we'll hold up someone."

"I'd be happy to show you the byre, Your Highness," Anson said with a bow. "We keep our place clean and have the best producing cows on the island."

"Thank you," Dundas said, "but as His Highness indicated, I fear we've overstayed the time we allowed for this outing. It was a pleasure furthering our acquaintance with you gentlemen and your family." He and the prince nodded and smiled and turned their horses toward the road, and the others followed. Peter hastened to mount his roan.

"Mr. Stark."

He bounced into the saddle and looked down at Anson Orland. "Yes, sir?"

"Thank you for bringing us to the prince's notice."

" 'Twas none of my doing."

"Ah. Well, then, thank you for all the small kindnesses you've done us. You are welcome here any time, sir."

Peter nodded and looked over the rest of the family, who stood watching him or gazing toward the carriages in the roadway. "It's been my pleasure." He swung the horse around.

Molly's family. The prince hadn't realized whose fields and cattle he'd admired, of that Peter was certain. It was God's doing. And by it, Peter had gotten a chance to see the rest of Molly's kin and deepen his regard for her family. Molly's mother had looked him over cautiously at first, but he'd felt sure Molly had spoken to her about him. Her expression had changed to welcome and warmth. He hoped the Orlands liked him as well as he liked them.

An elegantly clad arm beckoned to him from the window of the carriage in the yard. A thin drizzle had begun to fall again. Peter's horse minced its way across the mud to where the coachman held the team. The Earl of Washburn leaned out the window.

"How may I help you, sir?" Peter bent down so the earl could see his face without twisting his neck.

"Mr. Mulgrave here tells me this is the Orland farm." The earl gazed out at him innocently, as though he'd not instructed Peter to try to steer them there.

Peter could play along for the sake of the others in the coach. "Yes, sir. The prince asked to stop and meet the husbandman. Mr. Orland offered him a glass of ale."

Washburn's eyes went wide. "I saw that."

Peter smiled. "He said it was an excellent brew."

Washburn flicked a glance beyond Peter. "I believe that's Orland coming toward us. If he asks—"

"Ho, Mr. Stark!"

Washburn drew back from the window.

Peter looked behind him. The rain had increased, and a stream of water trickled off his hat and down the back of his neck.

Anson Orland walked up to stand beside the horse and looked toward the carriage window. "If you've got Lord Washburn in there, sir, I'd like to have a word with him. I missed being able to this morning."

"Well, I…" Peter clamped his lips together, unsure what to say. Washburn seemed to blow hot and cold as to whether he would converse with the Orland men or not. Peter half expected his master to yell, "Drive on!"

Instead, Washburn's grayish face appeared at the window. He glanced at Anson Orland then beckoned to Peter.

Peter jumped down from the horse and stood close to the window. "What would you have me do, my lord?"

Washburn sighed. "I fear I shall have to deal with these people one way or another."

Anson stepped closer. "I'm glad to see that your lordship is feeling better."

The earl looked helplessly at Peter.

Before he could speak, Anson continued. "It's redress I'm seeking, my lord." Despite the rain that was now almost a downpour, the old man pulled the cap from his head. "I'm sure you're aware, sir, of the wrong done to me many years ago by your father, who was then Earl of Washburn."

"What's the meaning of this?" came Newcastle's gruff voice from within the carriage.

Washburn turned away from the window for a moment and spoke to his companion. When he turned back, he said, "Mr. Stark, make an appointment with this gentleman, please. I'll see him later this afternoon at Government House if he can come, or if not, in the morning, before we take ship."

"Yes, my lord."

Peter stepped back from the carriage, tugging the horse's reins so that the animal backed up, and laid a hand on Anson's sleeve. "If you please, Mr. Orland."

Anson hesitated, then nodded and took a step back.

Peter called to the coachman, "His lordship wishes you to drive on."

As the coach left the yard, Peter faced the Orland men in the unrelenting rain. Mrs. Orland and the two younger children had gone inside, he noted, but Anson, David, and Molly's eldest brother remained, all waiting with stony faces for him to speak.

Chapter Fifteen

Molly watched the carriage lumber up the lane to the road. She exhaled and realized she'd held her breath, fearing the wheels would mire and the aristocrats would be stuck at the farm. Peter turned in the saddle for a moment. She ducked behind the curtain but didn't take her eyes from him until he'd trotted up the lane and out of sight, down the road behind the carriages.

The family had taken heroic measures in the three minutes' warning they'd received. Katie had run in from the dairy and told her mother the prince was coming. Mum had called to Molly up the stairs, and she and Katie had dashed about the kitchen to help their mother gather cups and prepare the refreshment—but Molly had begged not to be included when the prince met the family.

"I'll see him tonight," she'd said. "I don't want him to see me now—like this." She looked down at her worn housedress.

Her mother had given in and sent her back upstairs. By then Nathan and Joe had come to carry the tray and pitchers. The rest of the family piled out into the spongy yard to meet the distinguished visitors while Molly hid upstairs and cracked her window open so she could hear what went on.

Now it was time to put on her maid's costume and go back to Government House so she could prepare for the ball.

She put a cloak over her black dress and covered her hair with the hood. Her mother had put her best pairs of stockings and gloves in a bag, along with her marcasite necklace. It wasn't a valuable piece, but it was the finest item of jewelry the Orlands this side of the Atlantic owned. Molly hadn't told her that Thompson had promised to lend her silk stockings. If Rosaleen thought Mum's gloves looked all right with the gown, she would wear those.

She went down to the kitchen. Kate stood before a dishpan of soapy water, holding up Grandpa Anson's favorite tankard, while her mother sat peeling beets.

"The prince drank out of this cup," Kate said dreamily.

"Well, wash it up," her mother said. "Your grandpa will want it at supper."

Kate's eyebrows drew together. "Oh, we can't wash it."

"Whyever not?" Mum asked.

"The prince himself drank from it."

"Don't be silly."

Kate looked into Molly's face. "Isn't the prince handsome?"

"He's a beautiful boy." Molly squeezed Kate. "Best wash the tankard, though. You'll always have the memory."

Mum rose and gave her a hug. "Have a wonderful time tonight."

"Thank you." Molly's unsettled stomach discouraged her from even thinking about eating, and she doubted she would be able to relax and enjoy her surroundings tonight. Perhaps if the prince danced with her early in the evening, she could sit and watch the others dance and memorize the scene. Kate and her mother would want to know all the details tomorrow.

She said good-bye to Mum and her sister and went out to the barn, carrying the small canvas bag with her extra clothing inside her cloak. Her grandfather and Nathan had harnessed Piney, the smartest of their farm horses, to the wagon, and placed Peter's bag in the back.

The rain had slackened, and Nathan drove her to town in a light drizzle. Now and then a ray of sun struggled through the clouds. In town, people thronged the sidewalks, carrying umbrellas toward the governor's mansion.

"I hope Mrs. Dundas's party wasn't drowned out," Molly said as they approached the side gate of Government House. Beyond the fence, hundreds of people pressed together and listened to the regimental band playing a march. Footmen and maids hurried about, carrying trays of refreshments to the serving tables.

"I don't suppose people mind the weather much if they get to see the prince," Nathan told her.

Molly gathered her skirt and hopped down, and Nathan handed her Peter's satchel.

"Now remember," he said. "I'll be waiting in the porch at the Colonial Building from ten o'clock on, no matter how late it gets."

"You're a good brother." Molly smiled up at him. "Thanks. I hope you're not too uncomfortable."

"Ha. Like as not, I'll fall asleep. Maybe I should take a pillow."

Molly laughed and went in through the gate. No one said a word to her as she skirted the crowd and slipped in through the entrance to the laundry with the leather satchel tucked against the folds of her skirt. One of the laundresses looked up and smiled without stopping her work. But in the damp passageway leading to the kitchen, she paused, knowing she couldn't get to the back stairs without being seen. Perhaps she could stash the satchel in a cupboard and retrieve it later.

She tiptoed forward and peered into the kitchen.

"What are you doing?" hissed a voice behind her.

Molly jumped and whirled around, banging the satchel against the door frame.

Allison, in her black dress, white ruffled apron, and cap, eyed her with fascination. "Is that... *his*?" She pointed to the satchel.

"Yes, and I need to get rid of it before I go to prepare for the ball."

"Mrs. Dundas's party is in full swing in the back gardens."

"Yes, I saw the crowds."

"Well..." Allison looked over her shoulder. "Give it to me. I'll run it up the front stairs."

Molly arched her eyebrows. "You're joking."

"No. All the guests are out there. The mistress came in a few minutes ago and walked out on the prince's arm. They're *all* out there, I tell you." She raised her head for a moment. "Listen."

Molly turned back toward the rear entrance. Strains of full, brassy music wended through the passages. "The band is still playing."

"Yes. So give that here."

"Won't you be missed?"

Allison winced. "Maybe. I'm supposed to be getting more tea cakes."

Two other maids hurried in from outside and squeezed past them.

"All right, take it yourself," Allison whispered. "Run right up to the gentleman's room and tuck it in his armoire. No one will be the wiser. If someone does see you on your way, they'll think you've brought a petticoat and some shoes for the ball." She slipped into the kitchen and left Molly alone in the passage.

Her heart pounding, Molly turned and followed the hallway to another door. This one led into another nicer passageway—one with gilt-framed paintings on the walls and deep carpeting on the floor. She tiptoed along it to where it opened on the great hall. Allison was correct. The hall was deserted.

"Just act as though you've been commanded to run this errand for the mistress," she told herself. She threw back her shoulders and skittered across the empty room to the stairs. As she reached them, the door to the dining room opened and Eustace emerged.

"Say, Molly! Haven't seen you all afternoon."

She tossed him a regretful smile. "Sorry, Eustace, I can't stop. I'm on an errand."

She turned away and began mounting the stairs.

Eustace walked over to the newel post at the bottom of the staircase. "I heard you've been invited to the ball. As a guest of the prince."

She hesitated. "Yes, Mrs. Dundas arranged it. I really must be going."

Eustace said no more, and she went on up the stairs hoping he wouldn't ask what was in the satchel. When she reached the landing, she glanced back. He was walking into the passage that led to the kitchen.

She exhaled and quickened her steps, sliding past the family's rooms and the guest chambers. At the end of the main hallway, she turned into the wing where the lesser guests were staying—the doctor and General Bruce, along with Peter Stark.

At Peter's door, she paused and listened. The entire wing was eerily quiet. She tapped softly on the door then opened it and peeked in. As she had expected, the room was empty. She whisked inside and closed the door behind her.

She'd seen the elegant room when she and Rosaleen had cleaned it, but that was before Mr. Stark had taken up residence. Crossing to the armoire, she forced herself not to look about too much at his personal belongings, but she couldn't help noticing a pair of men's dress gloves lying on the dresser—perhaps to be worn to the ball tonight?—and a book bound in green leather on the night table. She glanced over her shoulder again before opening the wardrobe doors. There was just enough room at the bottom to squeeze in the satchel beside his tall riding boots. She smiled at the sight of them. Those boots had played a significant role in their acquaintance.

She closed the armoire and hurried back to the door. She must show up in Deborah's bedchamber on the third story at four o'clock, and she had only ten minutes to spare. Against her better judgment, she paused for a peek at the book's title. He was reading an American author, Oliver Wendell Holmes. Had he chosen the book because he would soon be in America and wanted to be able to discuss their authors with his hosts—or simply for pleasure?

She cracked the door to the hall open and put her eye to the slit. With a gasp, she drew back and closed the door. Mr. Stark was striding down the carpeted hall toward his room. Unfortunately, the door gave a telltale *thud* as it hit the jamb.

She stood still with her hand on the knob, holding her breath.

After what seemed an eternity, a gentle rapping came on the door panel near her face, and the crystal knob turned slightly beneath her grasp.

She gulped and stepped back. The door swung slowly open, and Mr. Stark peered in at her.

"Hello." A smile started in his eyes and drew his lips upward. "What a pleasant surprise."

"I—I—" Molly looked down at the rug. "Forgive me, sir. I was returning the—the—"

"Oh, *that*." His smile took on a conspiratorial air. "I did wonder about it. Your grandfather looked fine today, but I confess I thought your father looked even better."

Molly thought she would choke. "I'm so sorry. They weren't both intending to use it, but Grandpa missed the earl, and…" She let her words trail off and instead gazed into his laughing brown eyes.

"It's all right. May I come in?"

She realized he still stood in the doorway, with her blocking his entrance to his own chamber. "Oh, I'm so sorry. Please—I must—"

She stepped back and he stepped forward. She dodged to her right, but he moved to his left at the same time, and they nearly collided. He grabbed her arm to steady her. A shock of awareness shot through her.

"There we go," he said. "I'm sorry. I'm not usually such a clumsy oaf."

"Oh, please, it's entirely my fault. But I must go. Quickly." Had he ever seen her when her face was not crimson with shame?

"Of course. I won't keep you, but—I heard you'll attend the ball tonight."

Her lips trembled. "Y–yes. I've been told to do so."

"You don't wish to go?" Peter frowned as he spoke, and she wondered if he would be disappointed in her answer.

"I suppose every girl on the island wants to go, but...well, it's not my place, sir."

"Nonsense. This is the colonies. You're not in service for your whole life, are you? I thought this was a temporary job."

"So it is."

"And your father and grandfather are respected men in the community."

She straightened her shoulders. "Indeed they are, sir."

"Well, then, if you've been invited, what's to stop you? I daresay those other young ladies you spoke of had to buy tickets to get in the ballroom. But you're going on the invitation of the prince himself."

She sucked in a breath. "Is it that way? I'd heard it, but I didn't quite believe it, though I feared it was true."

"Why did you fear it?" Mr. Stark cocked his head. "You don't wish to dance with the prince?"

"I was told Lord Washburn made the request. I thought perhaps it had something to do with my family. That perhaps he was...angry because of what my father said to him this morning. But then when folks began saying the prince asked for me, I admit it scared me a little. And when you came to the farm this afternoon..."

"You were there?"

She hesitated then nodded miserably.

"Why didn't you come out?"

"I..." He looked so eager and welcoming. How could she say she'd seen enough of the prince for one day—wouldn't that be disloyal to the Crown?—or that she didn't want His Highness, or Mr. Stark, either one, to see her in her everyday clothes. "I wanted His Royal Highness to see me tonight and remember me in the clothes that are loaned to me. I didn't want him to take home a memory of a poor farm maid."

Mr. Stark's face went very grave. "Some men wouldn't mind holding that picture in their hearts."

She caught her breath. Was he saying he would cherish the memory of her? His eyes looked into hers, past them, and into her soul. Molly couldn't move.

He reached out slowly and paused with his hand not an inch from her sleeve.

Molly stepped back. "Please. You are the earl's man."

"Of course." He drew back his hand.

"And your master is not happy with my family just now. Papa said the earl seemed displeased to see him and Grandpa again when they came to the farm. They couldn't have known it was our land or Lord Washburn never would have come there."

"You're wrong, dear Molly." He spoke softly, watching her intently.

Molly's heart lurched. She had to get away from this man. He made her feel all jumbled inside, and if she stayed, who knew what would happen? His rich brown eyes seemed to be pleading, asking something of her. Was this what Mum had warned her against? She choked out, "He said he would see Papa and Grandpa later today."

"Yes."

"Do you know—does he plan to do something to them? To tell the governor about the past? Grandpa thinks not, but Papa is worried."

"Tell him he needn't be. Molly, Lord Washburn isn't angry with your family. If anything, he's upset with his own. Your father did not insult the earl this morning. The levee was perhaps not the best place to bring up a sensitive family matter, but I understand completely. He took the only chance he had."

"He said the earl walked out. Was the prince upset?" She put her hand to her mouth, covering her trembling lips.

"I don't believe anyone realized what was going on but Lord Washburn. And myself, of course. It's true, my master was shaken at coming face-to-face with your father. I cannot speak for the earl, but I know he regrets the incident that links your family to his. However, it had nothing to do with him, and he cannot change things. That is what he will tell them when he meets with them."

"But is he angry? Angry with my papa and my grandpa for coming to the levee intending to speak about it? Does he think they intended to humiliate him? I'm sure that was not their purpose."

Peter let out a long, slow breath. "I spoke to the earl at length. He's not sure what your family wants. I suggested… " He paused and looked toward the window for a moment, then back at Molly. "Perhaps I shouldn't tell you what he said, but I do believe he wants to help your family if he can. He asked me to find out where the Orland farm lay and seek to guide our party there this afternoon. He knew this matter had to be settled, though it is distasteful to him. But if there's animosity to be shown—"

"No, no! I'm sure there's not."

He nodded. "Then don't worry about the meeting. He is a gentleman, and he will not want to cause you and your loved ones harm. Come to the ball tonight, dear Molly. Perhaps he will ask you to dance and tell you that he doesn't bear any grudges toward the Orlands."

Gazing up at his firm jaw and compassionate eyes, Molly believed it might turn out all right. "W–will you be there?" As soon as she'd asked it, she knew the question was too forward. She looked down at the rug and Peter's gleaming shoes, feeling the fire in her cheeks.

He reached out again. This time he placed one finger beneath her chin, gently easing her head up. His touch jolted her, and she gazed into his eyes once more.

"Yes, I shall, and I hope you will save a dance for me."

She took two quick breaths before she could trust her voice. "Thank you, sir. I shall be honored. Now I must leave."

*****

Peter opened the armoire and smiled when he saw the leather satchel there. He took it out, set it on the bed, and opened it. The earl's cutaway coat looked to be in fine condition. Someone had folded it carefully, and it looked barely wrinkled. He could place it back into Washburn's wardrobe now, and if he had a chance he would press it later, though he doubted the earl would wear it in Charlottetown. Tonight he'd wear his best tailcoat for the ball, and tomorrow they'd be off for Lower Canada—Quebec City, Montreal, and onward for the rest of the tour.

He carried the bag through the door to the adjoining room, where the earl slept. After giving the coat a gentle shaking, he hung it in Washburn's wardrobe. Once that was taken care of, he returned to his own chamber and placed his hat on the high shelf in his armoire.

Peter could not have been more pleased with the way things had worked out. He considered it providential that Molly had chosen to return the borrowed clothing at the exact time he went to change into his dinner clothes. He gave silent thanks for the opportunity.

The family connection batted at the edges of his mind. She was Anson Orland's granddaughter. And he… Some might call him a distant cousin. Others might not. Some would do whatever they could to hide the affiliation. What would Molly do if she learned his true identity? And would he have to leave Prince Edward Island without revealing it?

During his chat with the earl after the levee, Peter had decided to keep quiet for the present. Washburn's agitation had convinced him that opening the subject in public would only cause his master more distress. Although it pained him to keep silent, Peter would do what he believed was best for the man who had helped him so much.

Dressed in his white shirt and cravat, black knee breeches, and dinner jacket, he opened the armoire and reached for his best shoes. He smiled again as he lifted them out past the leather satchel. Dear Molly. How she must have quaked to venture in here with the bag. And he could imagine her horror when the prince showed up at her doorstep this afternoon. Her family must have had a frantic few minutes while he rode back and forth. He couldn't blame her for not wanting to make an appearance then. How prosaic to meet your future dance partners while dressed in an apron and housedress even less attractive than those she wore at Government House. Let her keep the mystique she would radiate when she entered the ballroom tonight.

Chapter Sixteen

Molly tried to sit still while Rosaleen stroked a brush through her tresses. She wasn't used to having someone else dress her hair.

"This is the big night for you." Rosaleen smiled at her in the small mirror propped up on Deborah's dresser.

"I suppose so."

"Listen to you! Why, when I was a girl, I'd have given my eyeteeth for the chance you've got. Will I get to dance with a prince tonight? No. After you're ready, I'll walk home in the rain and get a late dinner for my husband and four children, that's what I'll do."

"Oh, Rosaleen, I'm sorry I'm so glum." Molly turned her head to look at her.

"Uh-uh. Keep your neck straight. Pretend you have a bone in it, my mother used to say."

Molly chuckled and faced forward again. "I do appreciate that you've stayed later than you needed to for this. I hope your family won't mind too much."

"They understand that as long as the prince is here I may be keeping odd hours." Rosaleen tucked a pair of hairpins between her teeth and reached for a comb.

Molly couldn't work up any enthusiasm for the evening. The other maids were jealous of her, especially the young, single girls, but Molly dreaded dancing with the prince. What if she stepped on her gown or said something inappropriate? The thought of coming face-to-face with Lord Washburn frightened her even worse. He was supposed to be talking to her father and grandfather right now. What if he was angry with them? Would he express his displeasure to her at the ball? The only good thing about tonight would be Peter. Now, *that* dance she was looking forward to.

He liked her, she was certain, but she felt she'd botched it with him. He'd reached out to her this afternoon and she'd kept her distance, as was proper. But did Peter want a proper woman? She hoped he did. Still, he was leaving soon, and she was not likely to see him ever again. So what was the point? She ought to have been able to keep her emotions better harnessed and not let them bolt off after a dashing young man who would not be on the island another twenty-four hours.

She sighed and tried not to move her head. Would Peter do more than fulfill his duty and give her the promised dance? She hoped he would want to talk again, but he now knew more about her family than she had ever intended to reveal. Had he learned from his master that her grandfather was in exile for assaulting the earl's father? He must not know that, she concluded, or he wouldn't have treated her so kindly. He loved his master and was loyal to him. He probably wouldn't want to spend time in her presence if he knew her grandfather's transgression. Still, the earl's own family wasn't innocent either. Peter knew that but remained faithful. And what did she know about him, beyond that? She pressed her lips together, mentally ticking off his good qualities. He was charming, handsome, intelligent, and compassionate.

She sighed deeply. What more would any woman ask?

"Now what's the trouble?" Rosaleen asked.

"Nothing, really. It's just that…well, a certain gentleman asked me to save him a dance tonight."

"You mean the Prince of Wales?"

"No, though I suppose I may dance with him too."

"That's the whole reason you're going, or so I've been told."

"Yes." Molly clasped her hands together. How much should she reveal?

"Is this a local gentleman?" Rosaleen asked. "A sweetheart?"

"No. Oh, no." Molly looked up at her, forgetting that Rosaleen had told her to sit still. "It's Mr. Stark."

Rosaleen smiled. "I wondered. He seems like a nice young man."

A brief rap came on the door.

"Come in," Molly and Rosaleen called together. They both laughed.

Allison poked her head in the doorway. "What's so funny?"

"We are," Molly said. "Are you done with work?"

"No, but I have a half hour off. I need to be downstairs after that to assist the ladies when they view the illuminations."

"Are they going to the harbor?" Rosaleen asked.

"No, the rain has begun again, so they're staying here. They'll either go out on the lawn with umbrellas or see what they can from the window." Allison sat down on Deborah's bed. "I heard some things."

"What sort of things?" Molly asked.

"Oh, things like the prince giving Mrs. Dundas the stunning new diamond bracelet she's wearing tonight."

"Oooh." Rosaleen gave a deep sigh. "Isn't that lovely? I wonder if he's brought one to give each of the governors' wives on his tour."

"It boggles the mind to think about it," Allison said. "Do you really suppose he's traveling about with a treasure chest full of jewels?"

"You never know."

Allison leaned toward Molly. "Anyway, there's something else that will probably interest you more."

"Oh? What's that?"

"I heard that Mr. Stark is leaving on the first ferry in the morning for Lower Canada. He'll be checking all the arrangements for the prince and his party in Quebec and Montreal."

Molly's heart sank. The first ferry would leave shortly after sunrise. So whatever time she had with Peter at the ball tonight would be the last she'd see of him.

"And when does the prince leave us?" Rosaleen asked.

"Mrs. Bolton said he'll receive some officials in the morning and have luncheon aboard the *Hero* with Mr. and Mrs. Dundas and a few others before he leaves. The chef is going with them, and Cook is in a blithesome mood."

Molly smiled at that.

Rosaleen patted the back of her hair and then put down the comb and brush. "There, and aren't you the lovely lady, Miss Molly?"

"Are you eating dinner with us?" Allison asked.

"Perhaps you could get her a plate," Rosaleen suggested. "She'll have to get over to the Colonial Building in an hour."

"Oh. How am I to get there?" Molly looked anxiously at her friends. "Am I to walk?"

"I hope not," Rosaleen said. "Mrs. Dundas wouldn't want you to, I'm sure. Why don't I go and see if I can find Thompson and ask her to put the question to the mistress?"

"I can do that when I go to get her supper," Allison said. "You need to get her into that dress. You're lovely in that shift, Molly, but it's not at all the fashion."

Molly looked down at her chemise and homespun petticoat and laughed. "I should think not."

Rosaleen gave a nod. "Go, Allison. I'll get her into the corset and crinoline, and after she's had something to eat, you or Deborah can help us put the gown on her."

"I'll alert Deborah. I'll need to be back on duty soon." Allison hurried out the door.

Molly examined her reflection in the mirror. She didn't know that she'd ever looked so pretty—hadn't imagined she could. "Thank you so much, Rosaleen. You did a wonderful job."

"You're welcome, my dear. Now, would you let me put just a dab of rouge on your lips? I don't think your cheeks will need it. You have a lovely high color when you're excited, and I expect when you walk into the ballroom you'll be flushed with eagerness."

"I'm not sure I'd have called it eagerness." Molly turned the mirror a bit and caught a different view of her coiffure. "Foreboding, perhaps."

"I'm sure the prince will find you a charming partner."

Molly turned her face upward and let Rosaleen apply the slightest bit of color to her lips. What did it matter, a hairpin here, a little lip rouge there? But for some reason, it mattered very much. Not for the prince's approval, or even for Lord Washburn's. But Peter's view of her tonight would be the image of her that he carried for the rest of his life.

*****

Peter tapped softly on the polished door panel between his room and the earl's. No response came, and he hesitated. The man was worn out from all the travel, dampness, and activity, but it stemmed mostly from his turmoil over the business with the Orland family. How odd that when Peter first encountered Molly and lost his heart to her, he had no idea she belonged to the clan that was so entwined with his own past.

He knocked again, louder. Something like a snore issued from within. Peter turned the knob, feeling guilty—like a burglar with a conscience. But this was what servants had to do sometimes, and his master had specifically told him to wake him in time to prepare for the appointment with Anson and David Orland.

He tiptoed to the bed and then shook his head. Why try to be quiet? The earl *wanted* to be wakened. He walked to the window, not trying to soften his steps this time, and pulled back the drapes. The gray late-afternoon light did little to brighten the room.

He turned back toward the bed. In the dim recess beyond the velvet hangings, the earl still slumbered. Such a pity, when the man was obviously worn out. But there was nothing for it.

Washburn lay facing the far side of the bed, and Peter walked around it. He bent over, touched the heavily embroidered coverlet, and shook his master's shoulder.

"My lord, it's time to rise and dress for your meeting."

"What—what?" Washburn threw back the covers, sat up, and flung his legs over the side of the bed in one motion.

"I'm sorry, my lord. You wished to be roused at this time."

"Yes." Washburn yawned and brushed his hair from his forehead. "I fear you see me at my worst on this trip, lad."

"And perhaps at your best, my lord."

"Thank you. I shall try not to betray that trust." He glanced up and met Peter's gaze. "You know this is difficult for me. I didn't expect to have to face it now."

"I think I do understand, my lord."

"Of course you do—better than anyone else could, except perhaps your mother. If I'd known…but I didn't, and now there's nothing to be done about it. The man has a right to speak."

Peter held up his Turkish dressing gown, but the earl waved it away.

"No time for that. I suppose you let me sleep till the last possible minute."

"Well, I… Yes, my lord."

"Then let's get on with it. I shall dress for dinner now and not have to change again after this appointment."

"That was my thought, and I've laid out your smallclothes."

The earl stood slowly and put both hands to the small of his back, grimacing as he stretched. Peter had shaved him that morning, and though he eyed his reflection critically in the mirror, Washburn did not ask to be shaved again. Peter brought over his clothing, item by item, and soon his master was dressed as a gentleman should be for a state dinner and ball. Peter tied his master's flowing cravat, combed his hair, and brushed his clothing for any possible loose hairs or specks of dust.

"You know, I was just a child when it happened," the earl said.

Peter paused with the brush in his hand, unsure how to answer. "Yes, my lord."

"I had no idea what was going on. All I knew was that my father got out of the carriage at the stable and a man jumped him and beat him. It was horrible." He sighed, not focusing on anything in the opulent room. "I was five, and I only knew that a bad man was hurting my father, and Father was bleeding. The coachman and groom hauled Orland off him but…" He turned his head and looked helplessly at Peter. "I've never forgotten."

Peter nodded, unable to imagine Molly's white-haired grandfather brutally attacking another man.

"I'm not saying that what my father did was right." The earl examined his hands closely. "But still…he oughtn't to have been beaten like that in front of his family. Hmm. I believe I have a hangnail, Peter."

As Peter rummaged through the top dresser drawer to take care of the need, the earl paced the carpet. "You'll stay at hand while I meet with them, won't you?"

"Of course, my lord." Was the earl thinking that the Orland men might attack him as Anson had his father? Surely enough communication had passed between them that he was not frightened of the old man, and David was all but incapacitated. "I'll stand just outside the door if you wish, where I can hear you."

"Inside the room, please."

"As you wish, my lord." Peter found the nail scissors and file and quickly tended the offending finger. They left the room together and walked down the grand staircase, only three minutes late.

Washburn paused on the bottom step. "I haven't asked your opinion of this matter. What do you think of the Orlands? You've seen them."

"They're a bit rough-and-tumble, but I like them," Peter said.

"Do you?"

He smiled. "Yes, my lord, I do."

"I suppose that's good." Washburn resumed his pace.

David and Anson Orland were seated in the small parlor, but Anson jumped up as Peter opened the door and David rose slowly, levering himself out of his chair with his canes. Both wore what Peter supposed was their Sunday best—black coats and trousers of plain material, with white linen shirts.

"Good afternoon," Washburn said.

Both the Orlands ducked their heads, but when Anson raised his chin, he looked the earl in the eye.

"Good day, sir. I'm guessing we all know why we're here."

"Not really." The earl sat down on a plush green sofa.

Peter took up his position against the wall just inside the door. What game was Anson playing with the earl? Obviously he couldn't—or wouldn't—bring himself to call Washburn "my lord." But the earl was cagey too. Of course he knew why the meeting had been arranged.

"What exactly is it that you want from me, gentlemen?" Washburn asked.

David cleared his throat, but before he could speak, his father jumped in again.

"Why, to exonerate me, of course."

"Sit down," Washburn said.

Peter wondered if they would obey the curt order. His master might do better to be more courteous to them. However, the two tall farmers resumed their seats without quibbling.

Once they were seated, Washburn inhaled deeply and addressed Anson. "I realize that you've suffered for my father's wrongdoing, Orland, but you may be forgetting that I witnessed the incident. I may have been young, but that perhaps caused the image to be even more deeply etched in my mind. I can never forget that you savagely beat my father, or that you might have killed him had not his retainers been quick to stop you."

David leaned forward and said with cold precision, "My father, here, is brother to a woman who bore your father's child."

Washburn's face went scarlet. "You want to be blunt, do you? Your father could have been hung for what he did. Instead, he was sent over here and allowed to own land and build up a farm that could support his family. He is a free man. I say my father was generous to allow that."

Peter's heart hammered as the two faced off. It was all he could do to keep from springing forward and restraining the men.

"You want to talk about generosity?" David's voice rose. "I'd say Da was generous not to go at your father with a weapon. He seduced my aunt when she was only a girl."

Peter took a step toward them, but Anson reached out and grabbed David's wrist.

"Now then, lad, let's be calm. We didn't come to accuse this man of anything. As he's pointed out, he was barely more than a babe back then. And he's right that I went about it wrong. But I knew the law wouldn't aid my sister." His blue eyes held a glint of steel as he gazed at the earl. "Fifteen, she was. Full of promise. And she didn't know she could refuse such a man as your father. A so-called 'gentleman,' one who was responsible for his tenants' well-being. She thought she had to give the lord what he asked. What he took from our family can never be replaced."

Washburn sank back on the sofa, the high color draining from his face. "I am so sorry. Believe me, if I could do anything to make things right…"

"Lift the stain from my father's name," David said. "You have influence. My father has been forbidden for forty-five years to ever return to England. So have I and my children, though we weren't born when this happened. That isn't right, sir. The sins of the fathers should not be laid on their children's backs. Give us the right to visit our homeland with our heads high if we wish to go there, and to see the faces of loved ones we've never gazed upon."

Anson cleared his throat. "My sister Mary is dead now, God rest her soul. A distant relative informed me of that. But there are others we would wish to know. She had a child that I've never seen. I don't even know if it was a boy or a girl, but the child would now be grown."

Peter felt tears burn his eyes. His shallow breath seared his lungs. Surreptitiously he took out his handkerchief. Turning his head aside, he wiped his eyes.

"Why can we not even write letters to our close kin?" David asked, a hard edge to his voice. "Why was my father forbidden to communicate directly with his mother and sister and brothers? He was not just exiled, he was made anathema. Twenty years passed before a letter reached him from a cousin who dared to address it to him here in the colony, and after that, two more years went by before his letter in response was answered. By then, Mary, for whom my father gave up all that was dear to him, was dead."

"Yes," Washburn said softly. "She has been gone many years now."

Anson eyed him keenly. "You knew her, sir?"

"Nay, I never met her."

Anson grunted.

"We were told," David said carefully, "that she was married within a month of the incident. Married to a shopkeeper."

The earl sighed. "I believe that is correct. I also believe that she had other children later on, and that she was not unhappy. She was taken care of."

"What do you mean by that?" Anson seized on the phrase and glared at Washburn as though he would pierce him with his gaze if he could. "How was she taken care of? You mean that her husband provided for her?"

"I'm sure that he did." Washburn harrumphed. "My family also provided. My father made certain the family wanted nothing—that the child was not in need. He…sent a gift to Mary and her husband each Christmas."

"Oh, that was very kind of him," David said bitterly.

Washburn raised his head and gazed at Anson. "I have often wondered about you. And I confess, I have conjectured what I would have done in your place."

Anson said nothing but sat blinking, his chin high.

"The issue," David said, "is what you can do now."

"I shall look into it."

David leaned forward, belligerence showing again in his snapping blue eyes. "That is not enough. When my Aunt Mary confessed to her family that she was with child, it fell to my father to confront the Earl of Washburn. You see, their own father was dead, and Mary had no one else to protect her, to speak up for her, but her elder brother. And what did His Lordship do? I'll tell you. He denied the child was his."

"Surely you're mistaken."

"Oh, no," Anson said. "There is no mistaking what he said when I confronted him."

Washburn slumped lower on the sofa. "But I was there.... Of course, I was still in the carriage, and my mother restrained me, trying to keep me from peering out the window. There may have been words exchanged that I did not hear."

"Oh, there were words, all right," Anson said. "I knew he was lying. Our Mary wouldn't make up something like that, and besides—she'd not had any sweethearts." He shook his head. "I was so angry, I took a swing at his lordship. He swung back, and the next thing you knew, we were into it and I was getting the best of him."

Washburn's pained expression deepened. "Yes. That I saw. My father's servants pulled you off him and had you arrested."

"So they did," Anson said, "and Lord Washburn refused to listen to my pleas for leniency."

"Can you blame him?" the present earl asked. "I mean—really, sir? Can you? You broke his nose and his jaw and scarred his face for life."

Anson clenched his teeth together and lowered his chin. "Do not forget, sir, what our Mary lost. She was scarred for life as well."

Peter felt his lungs would burst if he had to listen to much more of this. He inhaled slowly and deeply, forcing himself to unclench his fists.

"So he was deported to Prince Edward Island and forbidden to ever set foot on Great Britain again," David said briskly, "or to contact his family."

The earl took out a folded handkerchief and blotted his brow. "I understand that, Mr. Orland. And had your father come peacefully to my father and talked to him civilly, perhaps things would have turned out differently."

"Oh? How?" David tapped the floor sharply with one of his canes. "He would have given the Orlands a farm perhaps, in exchange for their silence? That sort of compensation?"

Washburn put his hand over his eyes for a moment and then lowered it. "Please believe me, I know this was a tragic situation. And I admit that what my father did to that girl was unconscionable. But what would you have had him do afterward? He was married, had children of his own. He couldn't marry your aunt." He turned beseechingly to Anson. "I ask your forgiveness, Mr. Orland, on behalf of my family. I cannot undo the past. Your sister was grievously wronged. And I realize you did what you felt you had to do."

Anson sighed deeply. "I've had forty-five years to mull it over, and in the long run I can see that I'd probably have been better off to go to your father meekly and take his bribes to be silent. Perhaps Mary would have been better off too. I cannot know."

"She never lacked for material things, I assure you," Washburn said. "She didn't live in opulence, nor did she live in abject poverty. I am told that her husband was fond of her and she of him."

"How do you know this?" Anson jumped up. "Who told you?"

"My steward."

Both Orland men eyed him curiously.

After a long moment of silence, Washburn said, "When my father died, I, of course, inherited his title and estate. The steward came to me and asked if I wished to continue the small stipend he gave annually to a couple living in Stratford. I asked who they were and why my father paid the man. The steward replied that it was the woman who received the compensation. And he told me why. But she was recently deceased, and he thought my father had been inclined to stop making the payments. The child was nearly grown, he said." Washburn sat in silence for a moment then stirred himself. "But I thought otherwise."

"What did you do for them, if I may be so bold?" Anson asked.

"I had my steward bring the man to me. He owned a tailor shop in the town, and he did all right. He said he had no complaints. I asked about the young girl—the eldest child in the family. Catherine, her name was."

"Catherine," Anson said softly.

"Yes. Your niece. He said she was a good girl who helped care for her younger brothers and sisters. I—I increased the stipend my father had given Mary, stipulating that it was for the girl now, to be used for her benefit. She could spend it or save it as she wished. I've been given to understand that she used some of it for her siblings but saved a good portion of it as a dowry. She later married a tinker, and I'm told they loved one another and were happy."

"She's gone now?" David asked.

"No. No, she's still living, but her husband died six years ago."

"Are there any children?" Anson asked quickly.

Washburn hesitated. "Yes. They had a son."

"Ah. I should like to know this boy," the old man said. "It will never happen in my lifetime, but David or one of his children might someday wish to go to England and meet him, were the ban lifted—and perhaps they could meet Catherine too. Their cousin. That is something you could make possible, sir."

Washburn stood. "Allow me to think for a moment, gentlemen." He crossed the room and stood at the window. "Stark, glasses of sherry for all of us, if you please."

"Yes, my lord." Peter hurried into the hall and strode toward the kitchen. At last he was able to escape the taut atmosphere.

Was it within the earl's power to grant Anson Orland's request? And beyond that, would Washburn reveal any more to these men? He could do anything while Peter was out of the room. Had his master sent him away to lay bare his secret while he was beyond hearing? Peter's legs shook, and he paused for a moment in the hall to collect himself before entering the busy kitchen.

He found the butler in the pantry preparing the wines for the state dinner.

"Please, Mr. Reynold, the earl wishes sherry for three if you are able to provide it. I will take it to him and his guests."

"Of course, Mr. Stark."

Reynold disappeared, and Peter leaned against the wall with his head bowed, thinking about the three men he'd left in the small parlor. He'd known for some time now about the hasty marriage arranged for Mary Orland forty-five years ago. He also knew that because Anson was not there to work the land, Mrs. Orland—Anson and Mary's widowed mother—had lost the farm tenancy the family had held. Apparently the previous earl's largesse had not extended to old Mrs. Orland. She'd gone into service in another house to earn enough to support herself and her three younger children. Did Anson know that his mother had served until her death as a housemaid?

The butler came back with a bottle of wine and set three glasses on a tray. "I assume you know how to serve wine, Mr. Stark."

It was something Peter seldom did, but he'd learned quickly on the previous stops of this tour, so he nodded. "Thank you." He carried the tray along the hall, half expecting to hear raised voices coming from the parlor, but all was quiet. Dusk was falling, and the room was dim.

"So you see," Washburn was saying as he entered, "I'm not certain I *can* do any more for you. It's a touching tale, and you, sir"—he nodded at Anson—"did commit a crime."

"Oh, yes, yes, I admit as much. Striking an aristocrat. As you said, I could have been hung."

Peter set down the tray and poured three glasses of sherry. He was still the invisible servant, and so his secret was still intact.

"I ask you, sir, is that fair?" David asked.

"Of course not, but it's the way things are." The earl looked at Peter as he offered the tray. "Ah, Stark, thank you very much." He took a glass and frowned at the others. "Only three?"

Peter met his gaze, not knowing what to say. He would never think of drinking with his master and guests except at a meal where he was included, and then he would drink water.

"Ah, of course," Washburn said.

Peter tried to keep his hands steady as he served the Orland men.

Anson took a tentative sip from his glass before setting it on a side table. "Now, you'll not deny, sir, that you could help restore the Orland name."

"Yes, and have the banishment lifted," David added. He downed his sherry in a gulp; then his eyes widened.

Peter used the tray as an excuse to turn away and took his time positioning the bottle on another table.

David coughed, but the earl ignored him.

"Well, now," Washburn said, "so far as I know, there is nothing I can do on that score."

Anson said, "But could you speak to someone—I don't know who—but someone with authority to let me openly contact my kinfolk?"

As they talked, Peter lit a lamp. The shadows it threw on his master's face made the earl look haggard.

"Perhaps a word to the queen's high steward when I return to London," he said at last. "It may help. I will do what I can."

"Thank you." Anson smiled. "That is all I ask, unless there is more you can tell me about Mary's family."

"Only what we've discussed." Washburn gazed at Peter across the room. Peter's pulse tripped. Was the earl inviting him to speak? All his life he'd hidden the secret of his mother's birth. Was this the time to end it? These men seemed kindly disposed toward Mary Orland's progeny and had not used the foul names he'd been called countless times.

The earl looked away, and Peter knew the moment had passed. He turned and removed the chimney from another lamp, but his hands shook.

"Mr. Orland, I am willing to forgive what you did to my father, but that is all I can promise." Washburn stood and extended his hand to Anson.

The old man took his hand. "Thank you, sir."

David positioned his canes and heaved himself forward. Peter hurried to his side.

"Lean on me, sir."

"Thank you." David rose ponderously and gained his balance. He looked at Washburn. "And thank you for seeing us. You've been…most civil. We've wanted for many years to know more about Mary's family and what became of her child. What you've told us will be somewhat of a comfort to Da, I'm sure."

"Yes," said Anson. "Catherine. And she has a son."

"That is correct."

Anson nodded. "I wish the lad well."

David eyed the earl with a sudden inquisitive air. "I wonder, sir. When you make your…annual contribution to Catherine…"

"Yes?" Washburn asked.

"Would it be too much trouble to send us a note—or to have your steward do it—telling us how my cousin and her son are faring?"

"Mr. Orland, it is my hope that by that time you will have received permission to write to her yourself. If I manage to gain that cachet for you, I will personally send your cousin's address. Until then…" Washburn held out his hand.

David took it, and then the earl shook Anson's hand solemnly.

Peter walked over to open the door.

"Good evening, Mr. Stark," Anson said as he passed into the hall.

"Good evening, sir." Peter nodded at David as he shuffled past with his canes.

When the two visitors were out of the room, Washburn said softly, "Close the door please, lad."

Peter shut it and turned to face him.

"I apologize."

"For what, my lord? I thought you handled the situation admirably."

"I didn't know what to do, though—what would be best for you. For although I do care about the Orlands—and in particular, Mary Orland's daughter, Catherine Stark—you must know that most of all, I care about you."

Hot tears seared Peter's eyelids. "Thank you, my lord."

"Ah, my boy." Washburn went to the small table and poured himself another glass of sherry. "If my son had lived, I would wish him to be like you. Not only that, I would wish him to know you and enjoy your company as I have."

A lump formed in Peter's throat.

His master sipped the wine and cocked an eyebrow at him. "Should I have told them tonight? I sensed you weren't ready."

"I don't know. I shall leave at dawn. I suppose I have missed my only chance to spend time with…" He cleared his throat. "With my family here in America."

"Yes. I hope you don't regret it. If we could stay a few more days… But we must go where Prince Albert Edward goes, and you must precede us. Thus the ferry, before the rest of the suite has risen."

Peter bowed his head. What had he just tossed away? He felt like running down the hall and out the carved front door to catch the Orlands as they climbed into their farm wagon.

"Well, there's tonight," Washburn said. "Tonight at the ball."

Chapter Seventeen

Deborah burst into the tiny bedroom panting. "I declare, those stairs get longer and steeper every day."

"Catch your breath and tell us what you think of Miss Orland," Rosaleen said.

Deborah looked her over, and Molly felt vulnerable in her shift.

"Well, your hair looks lovely, and I must say you look sophisticated, but we've got to do something about your wardrobe."

Rosaleen joined Deborah's laughter and indicated the elegant undergarments strewn on the bed. "Her finery awaits, and the two of us shall put it on her, layer by layer."

"How much time do we have?" Molly asked. "Allison said I was to be downstairs by nine to ride over to the Colonial Building with Thompson." Since the ball was not being held at a private residence, the lady's maid had been invited to attend and be ready to wait on Mrs. Dundas if she needed anything.

"An hour, then. Wish I were going." Deborah's lips drooped as she picked up the sateen corset cover. "You and I shall never have fittings so fine as this, Rose."

Rosaleen smiled. "Isn't it wonderful that Molly has a chance to wear them?"

"I was astounded when I saw all the things Thompson sent up," Molly admitted. "If I tear so much as a stitch, I'll be mortified."

"Don't fret," Rosaleen said. "Just try to enjoy the evening."

"Yes, you may never get another chance." Deborah held up the white silk stockings. "I wonder how much these cost."

"Here, now, don't be so cheeky." Rosaleen snatched the stockings from her. "Put these on, Molly, and I shall tie your garters."

Molly laid aside the hand mirror. The stockings were followed by cotton drawers and a thin lawn chemise. Next, Rosaleen took the corset from the bed and smiled at her.

"Raise your arms." She molded the corset to Molly's figure and fastened the hooks. "Now turn around and I'll tighten the laces. Tell me if the stays dig into you—though this is so well made, you'll probably barely know it's there."

"I doubt that." Deborah scowled at the garment. "But I suppose it would be worth it to squeeze yourself into all these clothes to get to go to the ball."

Molly smiled at her. "Believe me, if it were possible, I'd trade places with you."

"Is that so?" Rosaleen eyed her knowingly. "Something tells me you wouldn't really. All right, let's get the camisole next."

"If I had a prince ogling me and wanting favors, I wouldn't fuss about it, I'll tell you that." Deborah held out the corset cover, and Rosaleen positioned it so Molly could slip into it.

A quick tap on door preceded the entrance of one of the scullery maids. In her black uniform and apron, the diminutive girl looked to be younger than Kate. Her braids hung over her shoulders. She stared at the three women and settled her gaze on Molly. "It's true? They're letting you go to the ball?"

Molly opened her mouth, but before she could speak, Deborah jumped in.

"Yes, it's true, Dora. Shouldn't you be down in the scullery, washing up?"

Dora hiked up her chin. "They be serving dinner now. I'll get plenty of dishes to wash later. Though I'm not allowed to wash the prince's china. Lizzie does that."

"Oh, what do you get? The stuck-on pans?" Deborah sneered at the girl, and Molly felt sorry for her.

"I *am* going to the ball tonight, Dora, and I wish all the maids could go."

Deborah sniffed. "They wouldn't let *her* go. She's only twelve."

"Well, I'm sure there will be another ball in Charlottetown someday. Perhaps you'll get to go then," Molly said.

"All right, Deborah, time for the first petticoat." Rosaleen pointed to the garment she wanted. "The light cotton one first. Molly, lift your arms. Help me, Deborah. Up and over!"

Dora stood with her mouth gaping as they dressed Molly.

"Time for the crinoline," Rosaleen said. She and Deborah lifted the awkward hoop frame. Molly stepped into the middle, and the other women adjusted it and fastened the waist. "Now a petticoat to keep the gown from snagging on your hoops."

"Now the dress?" Molly asked a moment later.

"No, one more petticoat. We want a smooth look to your skirt."

"You should be a lady's maid, Rose."

Rosaleen laughed. "I used to aspire to be one. That was before I married my husband. Ah well, it was a dream. Marriage is better, if I do say so."

Molly swirled about, making the white underskirts and hoops of the crinoline sway. "These are heavy. I won't be able to walk, much less dance."

"Would you stop complaining?" Deborah tugged at the closure on the last petticoat once Molly stood still. "It's bad enough you're going, but then you let on you don't want to and that you hate wearing all these beautiful clothes of Thompson's."

Rosaleen darted a frown at Deborah. "Come, now, there's only the gown, shoes, and gloves left."

"I've got a question," Dora said.

"Oh, hush and get back to the kitchen," Deborah told her.

Molly smiled at the girl. "What is it, Dora?"

The scullery maid eyed Molly's wide skirt cage and then the narrow doorway to the bedchamber. "I just wondered…how are you going to get out of this room in that thing?"

*****

Peter stood behind the earl's chair at dinner that evening. The state dining room at the governor's mansion was full of dignitaries and their wives. Mr. Reynold had invited Peter to eat in the servants' hall, but the house servants would be eating late—after the Dundases and their guests left for the ball. He declined the invitation, determined to wait until supper was served during the ball.

He told himself he didn't want to cause the cook more work, but he had other reasons for not eating at Government House. Molly wasn't in the dining room tonight. If he ventured into the kitchen to eat, would he see her there? She would probably dine with the other servants tonight. He didn't want to embarrass her or betray his feelings for her with other members of the staff looking on. Though Washburn said he needn't stay, Peter was perfectly content to stand at the ready. If his master had the slightest need unmet, Peter would gladly fulfill it for him.

After dinner, the aristocrats briefly viewed the fireworks from the lawn at Fanning Bank, rather than venture down to the harbor in the rain. At last they were ready to depart for the ball. Mrs. Dundas left first, accompanied by her husband, so they would be on hand to greet the prince when he arrived. The others would follow in carriages. Peter held his master's coat and hat for him in the grand hall and saw Washburn out to the carriage he would share with Newcastle, St. Germains, and several others.

Although he held an invitation to the ball, Peter waited in the entry to the Colonial Building until all the titled guests and local dignitaries had entered. Then he ventured in. The improvised ballroom was the legislative chamber to the right, while the council chamber at the opposite end of the building had been designated a reception room. Peter stood in the shadows, a couple of yards down the passage, where he could observe the arriving guests.

The prince stood with Mrs. Dundas just inside the ballroom, ready to open the ball with his hostess. After that first dance, the prince would pick his partners from the ladies in attendance, according to a prepared list. He would dance with as many ladies as possible, showing no partiality. But Peter wanted only one partner.

Two women entered together—a short, petite brunette in bright plumage of striking magenta silk with green ribbons and ruffles. Peter recognized her as Mrs. Dundas's lady's maid. She accompanied her mistress to most social events. With her was a taller, more beautiful young woman. The blonde hesitated and said something to her companion, then relinquished her shawl to a footman, keeping only her fan in her gloved hands.

Peter inhaled slowly, savoring the moment. Molly. Her gown was of purest white, relieved only by rosettes of blue and a panel of what appeared to be intricate embroidery and lace at the hem. Nothing could have suited her better. The contrast to her daily uniform of dreary black was complete—she looked young, feminine, and eager, though a bit timid, as she gazed about her with eyes shining. The pristine gown set off her neatly coiffed hair and glowing complexion.

Where did she get such a dress? He didn't care. He only rejoiced that she was wearing it and that she had arrived. This night would be memorable for him if it ended right now. For her, it must be the culmination of a dream. Her weeks of service at Government House now ending in this splendid event—what island girl did not envy her?

Molly and the lady's maid paused a moment in the doorway, and the steward in clear tones announced their names. "Miss Thompson and Miss Orland."

The ladies crossed the threshold. Peter had the briefest glimpse of them curtsying before Mrs. Dundas. A man in a dress uniform and a woman wearing a magnificent dress with an emerald skirt yards wide filled the doorway and blocked his view.

When the ballroom was full nearly to bursting, the steward looked about the hallway and nodded to him. "Going in, Mr. Stark? His Royal Highness and Mrs. Dundas will open the ball momentarily."

"Yes, thank you." Peter stepped forward. "You needn't announce me. I'll slip in and find Lord Washburn."

"As you wish."

St. Germains stepped aside and let him pass unheralded into the chamber. Peter stepped up before Mrs. Dundas.

"Dear lady, thank you for inviting me."

"It's my pleasure, Mr. Stark. I hope you enjoy the evening."

Peter bowed before the prince and gravitated to the wall beneath the gallery, where the musicians were stationed, overlooking the dancers. He gazed about the ballroom. Local matrons had taken great pains to transform the chamber into a festive bower. Bunting, spruce boughs, and British flags hung all about the room. Swags of floral garlands hung between the green-draped windows and wound up the graceful white columns. Even the staid portraits of the island's statesmen were draped with gay streamers. Across the room, Lord Washburn conversed genially with another gentleman and looked to be perfectly at ease, so Peter didn't see a need to approach him yet.

Lord St. Germains took a few steps into the center of the room and announced, "Ladies and gentlemen, your hostess, Mrs. Dundas."

Mary Dundas smiled and looked about the throng of eager islanders and visitors. "My dear friends, it gives me the greatest pleasure, with the help of His Royal Highness, Prince Albert Edward of Wales, to open this ball in the name of our sovereign, Queen Victoria."

Cheering and clapping erupted, nearly drowning the first strains of the quadrille played by the orchestra in the gallery. The prince, resplendent in his evening clothes, led out the lieutenant governor's wife. Other couples of high social standing took the floor as well, to follow them in the intricate dance. Peter saw that Molly's hand was claimed early by a man twice her age. His master found a partner with one of the ladies who had attended dinner at Government House.

Although they'd had no practice together, the Prince of Wales danced well with Mrs. Dundas and set a spirited pace for the dance. The couples walked together, separated, reunited, and wove across the floor.

When the music stopped and a new tune began, gentlemen quickly sought new partners. Dundas claimed his wife's hand, and the prince turned to the wife of a prominent legislator. For many long hours, Mary Dundas had pondered the list of partners with whom the prince would dance, and after the royal party's arrival at her home, she had sat down with the Duke of Newcastle and Lord St. Germains to review her choices. Some were obligatory—but later in the evening, the young prince would get to waltz or polka with several single women, much to those ladies' delight.

Peter kept his post beneath the gallery. He kept track of Lord Washburn's movements—the earl was now leading the wife of a local judge onto the floor. His master seemed to be doing fine, and so Peter turned his attention elsewhere. Molly stood a bit apart from a cluster of ladies, but only for a few seconds. Before Peter could move toward her, Captain Grey, equerry of the prince, approached her and bowed gallantly. Molly's face flushed a delicate pink, and after a moment she placed her hand in the captain's.

Peter leaned back against the wall and smiled. Did Grey know she was one of the housemaids who'd cleaned their rooms and served their luncheons? He doubted it. Grey and his friend, Major Teesdale, had spotted a pretty girl and probably flipped a shilling to see who requested a dance with her first.

The colors of the ladies' dresses made a constantly changing mosaic as the guests whirled about. Molly's white gown, one with hoops of medium width, was easily spotted between the men's dark suits and the vibrant colors worn by the women. Peter watched closely as Grey led her about in time to the music. Molly's dancing was adequate but not polished. Grey didn't seem to mind. He chattered constantly down at her, and Molly smiled up at him—but with polite interest, not affection.

Noting that the couple moved gradually away from the entrance, Peter judged where he thought they would land when the tune ended and worked his way around the edge of the crowded room.

He wasn't far wrong, and Captain Grey and Molly came to a halt only a couple of steps away from his new position, laughing and panting a bit as they applauded.

Next to him, Governor Dundas said to the duke, "Let's see, I believe His Royal Highness is to dance with Mrs. Mayfield next."

The prince manfully worked his way down the prearranged list of local dignitaries' wives. After that, he would be free to dance with the single girls. His next partner was the mayor's wife. To Peter's surprise, Captain Grey dared to cut in on the prince halfway through the number. Prince "Bertie" laughed and whirled away to snatch a pretty young woman from her partner. Peter realized that securing a dance with Molly might be more difficult than he'd anticipated. He was determined to have his turn with her before the prince was able to approach her.

When the music ended, he drew a deep breath and took one stride toward her. Out of nowhere, Major Teesdale stepped up before Molly.

"Miss, I'd be honored if you would grant me this dance."

Peter watched in chagrin as the major whirled her onto the floor.

"Annoying, isn't it?" Grey said in his ear.

"Uh, yes, sir."

Grey chuckled. "She tells me her father is a farmer. She's a handsome little thing but a bit shy. Well, there are other ladies waiting to be run about the floor, though none other so pretty." Grey clapped Peter's shoulder and moved off toward a cluster of females who were chatting and flapping their fans.

Peter frowned in concentration as he followed Molly and Teesdale's progress. He hoped he didn't have to chase her about the room all evening to get a dance. As he gazed at them, Teesdale swung Molly around, and for an instant she faced Peter. Her eyes widened as her gaze met his, and her mouth opened slightly. A bolt thudded in Peter's chest. He managed a smile, and then the major waltzed her away again.

After a quick glance about to be sure that Washburn was pleasantly occupied, Peter sauntered along the wall, again aiming for the best place to intercept the couple at the exact moment the last bars of the tune sounded.

The music ended sooner than he'd expected, and by the time he reached the spot where she'd been, Molly had been whisked away by a junior legislator. Peter watched sorrowfully and began plotting a new strategy.

He mustn't neglect his duties. After the next dance, he promised himself, he would seek out the earl and ask if he needed anything, should that seem appropriate. But first…

He watched Molly and her new partner glide about among the other couples. There wasn't room to sweep across the floor, but no one seemed to mind the cramped quarters. Nobody would volunteer to leave the gathering to give the other dancers more space.

When the melody came to a stop, a half dozen men surrounded Molly. Peter could never get through that crush and claim her hand. He watched in despair as she blushed, smiled, and chose one of the supplicants.

*****

Molly staggered to a chair between numbers, hoping for a moment to catch her breath. She longed to slip off the borrowed shoes, but that would be most vulgar. She wasn't used to dancing, and her feet throbbed.

She opened her fan and waved it before her face. The temperature in the room had risen due to all the people and the activity. She found it just short of unbearable.

"Molly! You surprise me."

She looked up at the speaker. "Hello, Emmet. I didn't see you before. Is your mother here as well?"

"Yes." He looked around for a moment. "Under the gallery with the Earl of St. Germains."

"Ah." Molly fanned herself more vigorously.

Emmet leaned closer. "I hardly expected to see you here tonight."

She looked up at him and arched her eyebrows. "Perhaps you should raise your expectations."

Emmet's face colored. Before he could speak, another man stepped up.

"Good evening, miss. My name is John Harrold."

She looked into his face and dredged up a smile. "Good evening, sir."

"I wondered—"

"Miss Orland!" Another gentleman—this one wearing an amazing silver-embroidered satin waistcoat—crowded in beside Harrold. "Dear lady, I must have a dance with you."

Harrold fixed him with a cold stare. "I beg your pardon, Humphries. I just asked the lady to dance myself."

"No, you didn't. You hadn't got it out yet."

Someone tapped Molly's shoulder. "Pardon me, miss. Are you free for the minuet?"

Molly rose and looked helplessly around at them. Two more men appeared behind them, grinning at her. Emmet had faded to the fringe of the group, which suited her fine.

"I…" She gulped and extended her hand. Where on earth was Peter? If he were among the eager gentlemen, this would all be worth it. "I believe Mr. Harrold was the first to ask."

He gave the other men a superior smile and bore her a few steps onto the floor in triumph.

The dancers seemed to be getting more boisterous, and Molly wondered if some of the men had been imbibing. The couples jostled one another in the warm room, vying for the limited space. The air took on a hint of perspiration and whiskey fumes. Harrold held her delicately, as though afraid to touch her spotless gown.

"I've been in Charlottetown for eighteen months, at Mr. Evans's shipping firm," he said. "I can't believe I haven't met you before."

"Most remarkable," Molly murmured, peering over his shoulder in search of Peter.

"I had to ask three people before someone told me your name. I believe your father's a dairyman?"

"That is correct, sir."

"I should be delighted if you would allow me to call on you, Miss Orland. Next week, perhaps?"

Molly jerked her chin up and eyed his waxed mustache. "I—well—I shall have to think about that, sir." She kicked herself mentally for tacking "sir" onto every sentence, but she'd grown so used to saying "ma'am" and "sir" all day that the habit was hard to stifle.

"Ah, that will give me an excuse to consult you later." Harrold grinned disgustingly close to her face, and Molly drew her head back.

She didn't like to disappoint anyone, but this had gone far enough. "I—I am not sure I'm disposed to that situation, sir."

"You mean...that you do not wish me to call on you?"

She swallowed hard. "That is correct, sir. But thank you for the offer."

His mustache drooped with his lips. "I see." When the music ended, Harrold bowed to her and made a swift retreat.

Molly drew as deep a breath as she could in the restrictive corset.

"Finally!"

She whirled around and found Peter at her side. Her relief was so strong it made her feel shaky.

"Mr. Stark! How wonderful to see you."

He smiled, his brown eyes glittering. "Really? They're going in to supper. I wondered if you would like to—"

A half dozen men descended on Molly and attempted to elbow Peter aside.

"Miss Orland, may I escort you to the table?"

"Would you take supper with me, Miss Orland?"

"Miss, I'd be honored—"

"Gentlemen!" Peter's roar startled them all, and for an instant the suitors fell back and the entire room went silent. Peter flashed her a look of contrition but firmly stepped forward and crooked his elbow. "Miss Orland was about to join me in the council room for supper."

Molly tried to remain calm as she took his arm. "Yes, Mr. Stark. Thank you. And thank you all." She smiled at the circle of dejected gentlemen. "I hope you all have a lovely time."

The aristocrats had ceremoniously led the way out of the ballroom and down the hall. Beaming, Peter marched toward the door with Molly at his side, his head high.

Chapter Eighteen

"Quite a mob, isn't it?" Peter had to raise his voice so Molly could hear him over the swell of a hundred voices. The windows of the council chamber had been flung open to admit every wisp of a breeze, and several side rooms had been opened to give the revelers places to sit down. The long council table was covered in damask and laid with delicacies of all kinds—fruits, breads, pastries, and meat pies. At one end of the room, Mr. Reynold and two underbutlers poured a steady flow of punch and ale.

"Indeed," Molly smiled around the rim of her punch cup. She had removed her gloves while they ate, and her slender hands seemed too delicate to hold a scrub brush. "And to think the prince is supposed to dance with me yet. I fear I'll have melted and disappeared before he gets around to it."

Peter hesitated but decided to ask what was on his mind. "Do you know which number he'll dance with you? I saw the list of his official partners yesterday afternoon, but that was—er—before you received your invitation. I'm wondering if they've added an extra dance to the program."

"Oh no, I'm not certain." Molly looked about in confusion. Was there someone she could ask, or was it better to say nothing and wait?

"Well, I know I would like to have the next dance with you, immediately after supper, if I may."

Her cheeks went redder than the evening's warmth accounted for. "I should like that." She took out the pasteboard dance card she'd received at the door and handed it to Peter. He rummaged in his coat pocket until he found a short pencil. She hadn't filled in the card with names.

As though reading his thoughts, she leaned closer. "To be frank, Mr. Stark, several gentlemen asked me to put their names down, but I was afraid to do so. I didn't know when the prince might wish to dance with me, you see, and—" She faltered and looked away.

Peter's heart warmed. "Dare I think you also wished to save me a spot?"

"You did ask me earlier."

"Yes, I did."

"To be truthful, I didn't want to miss it."

For ten seconds he couldn't do anything but sit and gaze at her, grinning like a silly fool. He shook himself. "I believe I can solve your problem."

"Oh? How is that?"

Quickly he wrote his name on the lines for all the dances after the supper hour. "There. When His Royal Highness requests the pleasure of your company, you may erase my name. For one dance only."

She chuckled.

Peter's heart drummed a tattoo as he watched her. Molly, laughing, was the most stirring thing he'd seen in British North America. He never wanted to leave her side. He could gaze at her forever without becoming bored.

"I suspect that people would gossip about us if I were to give you eight dances," she said.

"Would it matter?"

"Perhaps not." She gazed at him, her china-blue eyes nearly the same color as the ribbons on her dress, eyes brimming with possibilities—in short, full of hope.

"Molly!" He leaned toward her and reached for her hand.

Her lower lip trembled. "Yes, Mr. Stark?"

"Peter. Can't you call me Peter?"

"Perhaps. For tonight."

His aspirations crashed to earth. It *was* only for tonight. In the morning, he would sail away from her.

At the other end of the room, George Dundas rose and raised his glass. The murmuring died.

"Friends, let us drink to the health of our illustrious sovereign, Queen Victoria."

"To the Queen!"

Everyone sipped his beverage, and a hearty cheer broke out.

The Duke of Newcastle rose, bowed to the governor and the prince, then raised his glass. "To the health of the prince consort, Albert of Saxe-Coburg and Gotha."

The toasts went on for several minutes as the crowd drank to the good health and long life of the Prince of Wales and several other dignitaries, as well as the prosperity and peace of the island. At last the aristocrats went back to their supper and Peter could once more give Molly his full attention.

"And how are your parents doing?" he asked. "Is your father's leg mending?"

"Pardon me, miss. Mr. Stark."

They both looked up. General Bruce stood beside them holding a memorandum book and a silver pencil. In his full uniform, he cut an imposing figure.

Peter stood. "How may we help you, General?"

"When the dancing resumes, His Royal Highness desires to take the floor with the young lady who is sharing supper with you."

"Oh." Peter looked at Molly. She kept her expression neutral. "Miss Orland? Is your next dance free?"

Molly made no pretense of consulting her dance card. "Of course, General. Please tell the prince it will be an honor."

Bruce bowed. "Thank you. I'm sure it will be an experience you will tell your grandchildren about."

Peter watched him go, fighting the knot that had settled in his chest. He had this moment with Molly and perhaps a dance or two later. He didn't really believe they could dance together for the rest of the evening. It would scandalize the dowagers of Charlottetown and do Molly no good—especially as he would depart just a few hours afterward. Unwillingly he looked at the tall clock in one corner. A few hours from now and he would be off to sea again, and then would come the rest of the prince's tour. How desolate each city would seem without her.

Molly's gentle touch on his wrist brought him back to the present, and he sat down abruptly. He would not waste another second of what he'd received.

She leaned toward him. "I meant to ask you if we danced together, but since we have a moment, I'll ask you now. Did all go well between my father, my grandpa, and the earl?"

He nodded. "They parted on good terms."

"I don't know how much you are privy to concerning our story," she said.

"All of it, or so I believe."

"And you don't think less of us?"

"Why would I?" He stared into her questioning eyes, hoping she could read his empathy and his longing. "Dear Molly, your father and grandpa seem like fine men. I cannot but admire the way your grandfather defended his sister so many years ago."

Her color heightened, but she did not draw back. "Thank you, Peter."

He reached for her hand again and squeezed it gently. "I shall let them tell you what was said, but I hope it comes out well for you all."

"Mrs. Dundas is rising." Lines of tension creased her forehead. "Peter, what is the prince like? What shall I talk to him about?"

"I expect you'll find him easy to talk to. He's a charming young man."

She nodded, though her face was still taut. "He seems a proper gentleman."

Peter hesitated but saw no point in disputing her assessment. "You have no cause to be nervous, I'm sure. Just remember he's younger than you are and pretend he's one of your brother's friends."

That brought a smile. "I may find that helpful, though I can't imagine Nathan running about with him."

Peter stood and tugged slightly on her hand to help her rise. "We must go back to the ballroom. Look for me when your dance with the prince has finished."

"I shall, sir." Though she addressed him as she would a man of high station, the gaze they shared was one of equals.

"I shall look forward to it immensely." He pulled her hand into the crook of his arm and they shuffled with the others into the hallway and down to the ballroom.

"Oh!" Molly stopped walking and drew in a sharp breath.

"What is it?"

"My gloves! I left them in the supper room."

"I'll get them." Peter dashed back to where they had sat and found the wilted white gloves lying on a chair. Servants were already clearing away the remains of the meal. He hurried back to Molly.

"Thank you so much." She swiftly slid her hands into the gloves and poked the fabric between her fingers. "How awful if I'd forgotten!" When her hands were once again hidden, she positioned her fan on its chain at her waist with her little mesh reticule, squared her shoulders, and looked up at him.

"Ready?" Peter asked.

"Ready."

He escorted her to the door of the ballroom, where Lord St. Germains stood, and gave a little bow. "My lord, Miss Orland is to be the prince's next partner."

St. Germains smiled at Molly. "Ah, Miss Orland. Delightful. Please stand here by me for a moment."

Molly gave Peter's arm a light squeeze and released it. "Thank you," she mouthed as he stepped back. He nodded and walked quickly between the milling guests to his original spot beneath the musicians' gallery.

The Earl of St. Germains spoke with Molly for a moment then led her toward Mrs. Dundas. The Prince of Wales stood between the hostess and General Bruce, watching Molly appreciatively as she approached. Peter told himself everything was fine. Molly would fulfill her obligation, and then he could reclaim her.

The look in the prince's eyes changed subtly. Peter's stomach knotted. *He's only a boy*, he reminded himself. *Of course he's eager to dance at last with someone near his own age—not to mention one of the prettiest women in the room.*

With sudden clarity, Peter knew he was jealous, which made no sense. The prince would be in contact with Molly for five minutes at most. And both Peter and Albert Edward would sail tomorrow. But the knowledge didn't stop his lungs from aching as he gazed across the room. Perhaps the best thing he could do would be to take a brief walk outside.

He made his way to the door, easing between clusters of chatting people and avoiding bumping into hoopskirts. The strains of a Strauss waltz followed him as he left the building.

A few gentlemen stood in the portico, catching the breeze off the harbor. A couple more wandered about the garden before the building, smoking their pipes. Peter sauntered into the shadow of one of the columns, leaned his head back against the cool sandstone, and closed his eyes.

"Mr. Stark, isn't it?"

Peter jerked upright and opened his eyes. In the shadow of the portico, a young man peered at him.

"Yes. Have we met?"

"Nathan Orland. You came to our farm with the prince."

"Oh, of course." Peter held out his hand and Nathan grasped it.

"Is the dance about over?" Nathan asked.

"Oh, no. It will go on for a while yet. Probably until two or three o'clock."

Nathan grunted.

"You're here to escort your sister home?"

"Yes, sir."

"That's good of you."

Nathan cocked his head and listened to the strains of the violins.

"Is our Molly dancing?"

"Yes. In fact, she's stepping with the prince right now."

Nathan grinned. "I'd like to see that."

Peter was about to suggest he go in and look but realized Nathan probably had no ticket, nor the sovereign to pay for one. "She...looks lovely tonight. You can tell your mum."

"I will."

Peter stepped away from the pillar. "Will you be out here?"

"Yes, sir. Might fall asleep if it goes on that long, though."

"I'll walk out with her and find you when it's over."

Nathan nodded. "I'd appreciate that, sir."

The number would end soon. Though Peter wished he could spend more time talking to Molly's brother, he knew he'd have to scramble if he intended to give her an excuse to turn down all those vying for her hand for the next dance.

*****

Molly tried to remember all the advice various people had given her that day. "Keep your back straight while you dance," her mother had said. "Look into his eyes"—this from Allison. Deborah had told her to compliment the prince's looks and deportment, while Rosaleen's prosaic counsel was, "Be yourself, dearie, and enjoy the moment."

The Prince of Wales bowed at the waist and extended his hand to her.

Molly gulped and placed her hand in his, glad for her short white gloves. Without them, her sweaty palm would touch the Royal Person. She shuddered.

"Nervous?" he asked.

She shrugged and lowered her gaze. "A bit, Your Highness."

"Don't be." He smiled at her as they moved onto the dance floor. Other couples left a swath of space around them, and they had more room to execute the waltz than Molly had had all evening with her other partners. Of course, more eyes were upon her now than ever before. Her cheeks flamed, and she had to remind herself to blink. She followed the prince's lead as he guided her into the first gliding steps. She was glad she'd had eight or ten dances earlier so that she'd become accustomed to the movement and knew what was expected of her feet, even if not what to say.

"At last," Prince Albert Edward said.

She stared up at him, not knowing how to respond.

He chuckled. "I'm tired of dancing with old women. At last I can have fun with the pretty young ladies of the island's society."

"Oh, I'm not part of high society here," Molly said.

He laughed. "I know. You are the maid who made such a charming entrance into the breakfast room this morning."

Molly gulped. Was it only this morning? It seemed years ago. She concentrated on her steps as they swept about their clearing in the middle of the floor. Other couples drew back, careful to stay out of their path.

"Your ensemble tonight suits you better than the black dress you wore this morning."

Molly stumbled and gasped as he tightened his hold on her.

"Uh-uh, watch your steps," he said. "People are looking."

She told herself that his playful smile was a compliment, but his eyes smoldered as he gazed down at her, and he didn't relax his hold. They were dancing too close. It felt all wrong.

"So, do you live at the governor's house?" he asked.

"Oh no, sir. Your Highness. My father's farm is not far from town."

She leaned back, resisting the pressure of his hand on her back. He only kept smiling and murmured, "You are lovely, you know. Much too lovely to be working as hard as you do."

"Thank you, but it was necessary."

"Oh? I'm sorry to hear that."

"My father was injured…."

The music's rhythm called for a turn. The prince swung her around and pulled her even closer. "Maybe between the dances we can slip outside. It's becoming quite warm in here."

"Oh, I—" Molly stared at his second button, not daring to look up into his face. Though she'd never attended a ball before, she knew instinctively that disappearing with a man would be frowned upon if not outright scandalous. "Surely you have partners lined up for every dance, Your Highness. I'm certain every lady in the room wishes to dance with you."

He shrugged. "The night doesn't hold enough hours for that. But you are right—I must spread my favors as broadly as possible. Pity." He gazed down at her again with a longing Molly found disturbing.

"Are you enjoying your stay on the island?" She hoped her tone conveyed her desire to keep the conversation light.

"Oh, yes, it's wonderful. But I've lacked for female companionship. There are ladies all around, but none who are approachable. Are you approachable, Miss…hmm…Orwell, was it?"

"Orland," she said.

"Orland. Of course." His eyebrows shot up. "Don't tell me you belong to the dairy I visited today…?"

"My family was delighted to meet you, Your Highness."

"Well, well." He swept her around with a flourish as the music rose in crescendo. As they met once more, he said, "So you belong to the farm where I stopped to imbibe in the excellent local ale."

"Yes, Your Highness."

"What a charming coincidence."

Molly suspected it was no coincidence but a machination of the Earl of Washburn's—however, she would hardly voice that to the Prince of Wales.

"You said your father was injured."

"He broke his leg in a farming accident."

"Oh, yes, I recall that he had crutches. I hope he recovers quickly."

"Thank you."

The music came to an end. They stopped dancing and bowed to each other.

"Thank you, dear lady." The prince bowed over her hand.

"My pleasure," she managed to say.

He leaned close to her. "Perhaps we shall manage to spend a few minutes together later."

He walked away, and Molly stared after him. Should she be flattered or outraged? Her face flamed, but most people watched the prince's departure, waiting to see what lady he would dance with next. This might be the ideal time to slip into the hall and retire to the ladies' powder room. She might be able to hide there until her face returned to its normal color. At least the other young gentlemen had held back after the prince left her. Molly whirled toward the door and nearly collided with Peter.

"May I—would you—"

She smiled at his discomfiture. Peter always seemed so calm, but tonight he looked anxious. "Of course. I was hoping you were close by." Her desperate urge to leave the ballroom evaporated.

He took her into his arms and swept her around as the music started again. She was relieved that she wouldn't have to wonder any longer when he would claim his dance…or deal with a bevy of other young men.

"I stayed too long outside, and I was afraid I'd missed my chance," Peter said. "Either that or I'd have to beat off a dozen fellows."

"No, I think they lost their ardor."

"More likely they were making sure the prince was well out of the way before they approached you."

Molly looked over his shoulder. The Prince of Wales was dancing with the daughter of a shipbuilder. Molly had waited on her the previous evening at Government House and knew her by name. The young woman wore a gorgeous blue gown, but unfortunately, her long, plain face and her intimidating father had kept suitors from her door.

She turned her attention back to Peter. He moved gracefully, steering her around the other dancers, but his gaze barely left her face.

"I met your brother outdoors."

"Nathan?"

"Yes, he's waiting for you. I told him it would be awhile."

"Thank you. He's very good to me."

"Molly." Peter bent his head slightly until his lips grazed her hair. The gentle pressure sent a tremor through her. "I've anticipated this moment all day," he whispered. "Ever since I heard you would be here tonight."

"So have I."

The song ended all too soon. As they came to a halt amid swirling skirts, bowing gentlemen, and fanning ladies, three young men wound their way to Molly.

"Miss Orland, are you free for this number?" asked the first.

"Oh, I—"

Peter took a step back from her and bowed. "Thank you very much. Perhaps I shall see you later?"

"Why, yes, Mr. Stark. I've promised you the last dance."

Peter smiled and nodded. As he disappeared into the throng, Molly's heart sang. She couldn't give him every dance and maintain propriety, but the promise of one more was not too bold. It would give her something to anticipate and an excuse to hold off the more aggressive of the young men clamoring for her attention.

"Let's see. I believe you asked first, sir." She took one man's hand, knowing she'd seen him before at Government House, but she was unable to put a name to him.

"I don't believe we've met," he said as they settled into the rhythm of the music. "I'm Philip Draper."

"And you live here in Charlottetown, don't you, Mr. Draper?" she asked.

"Yes. I'm a physician. My father and I have a surgery office on Allen Street."

Molly nodded and tried to portray a serene lady. Where were all these young men before the prince noticed her? None of them had ever come around to the Orland farm asking to court her. She supposed she'd lived a rather isolated life on the farm. She'd attended the small rural school and a church outside the city. If her mother were here tonight, she'd no doubt urge Molly to encourage her dance partners to call on her. This might turn out to be a rare chance for a country girl to draw the attention of potential husbands in the city.

But there was only one man Molly would care to have calling on her, and he would be gone at daybreak. She glanced about the room and spotted Peter, back in the place he seemed to like—in the shadows, where most people overlooked him. He could stand there and watch the dancers—watch her. She smiled, and he smiled back, trusting, waiting. Now that the dreaded ordeal of dancing with the prince had passed, Molly realized she was more worried about Peter's departure in the morning. How could he be so calm, if he really cared for her? Of course, he wasn't really as calm as he managed to look—she'd seen his agitation earlier.

The music wound to its final strains. Philip Draper still talked, and she tried to focus on what he was saying.

"—and if you would agree, I could come by next Friday evening."

"Oh, I–I'm not certain. Did you mean… I'm sorry—would you please repeat that?"

Already, aspiring dance partners pressed through the hoopskirts toward them.

"I should like to call on you at your home. Next Friday evening?"

"I… " She glanced about at the others. "I'm sorry. I can't answer that just now. Perhaps we could talk later."

Draper's fretful expression changed to a brilliant smile. "Of course, Miss Orland. I'd be happy to." He bowed.

Molly wondered what she had just agreed to. Would Peter come around now, hoping for the next dance? No, she decided. He'd wait for the last one. She cast her gaze over the waiting gentlemen. The eager young men fell back, giving way to a uniform. Molly sucked in a breath.

General Bruce smiled down upon her once more. "Miss Orland, the prince would like to reserve the quadrille with you."

"I—uh—" She fumbled in the small reticule at her waist and brought out her dance card. The quadrille was two down the program, and three from the end. "Certainly, sir."

"I will tell His Royal Highness." Bruce bowed and marched away.

After a moment's silence, one of the perspiring gentlemen made a bold move. "Miss Orland, I beg you to dance with me. I've been waiting all evening."

"Surely."

He took her hand and tugged her away, leaving the others gaping.

Molly followed his lead about the floor. The prince had requested another dance with her? What did it mean? He hadn't danced more than once with anyone else. She'd thought he was spreading his royal presence around as much as possible. Could it be that he actually liked her as a person and wanted to spend more time with her? The thought was flattering, but it made her uneasy. Peter was the man who filled her heart. The prince was two years younger than her, and she didn't want to embark on a flirtation with him—or any other man—that would end in regret.

She put the prince out of her mind and conversed with her partner. Her heart felt a hundredweight lighter since her time with Peter. And she would have the last turn about the floor with him. That prospect put her in such good spirits that she was able to respond merrily to Draper's jokes and questions. When he asked if he could come a-calling, Molly put him off with a vague answer. If she flatly turned them all down, her mother would probably take her to task. And after Peter had sailed out of her life, wouldn't she eventually wish to settle down with a nice young islander?

No! Again she sought Peter. He'd left his post beneath the gallery. For a moment her heart fluttered. Until it was his official time to leave, she didn't want to lose track of him.

"And do you like opera?" Philip Draper asked.

"Opera? I've never seen one."

"We must remedy that. Might I escort you to the next one staged in Charlottetown?"

Molly gulped. "Perhaps. Why don't you ask me when the time comes?"

"All right, I shall."

They turned and whirled, and suddenly another young man tapped her partner on the shoulder and swept her away from him.

"Oh. Er…hello." Molly gazed up at him, uncertain what to say.

He laughed. "Hello to you, Miss Orland. I'm Timothy Rollins. I've hoped to meet you, but you're always the center of a crowd, it seems."

"Well, we've met now." The remark sounded inane in her own ears.

"Yes. I decided that if the prince can cut in, so can I."

"Indeed, sir." She looked around and saw the Prince of Wales grinning as he hopped about with one of the merchants' daughters.

She bumped against someone and jumped closer to Rollins, at the same time turning her head to say, "Excuse me!"

Emmet returned her gaze. His surprised expression slid into speculation. "No harm."

The music pulled them apart. A young man in an officer's uniform from the Volunteers regiment cut in on Rollins, and Molly tried to catch her breath as he led her about the floor at a near gallop. All the dancers seemed to have become less inhibited, and during the next five minutes, Molly changed partners seven times.

She almost felt relieved when the Prince of Wales once again claimed her hand.

"Your Highness." She swept a curtsy, and he bowed before her.

"Lovely Molly, I've longed to speak to you again."

"Truly?" She was still short of breath from the last polka, and she found his charming smile alarming.

"Certainly. No other woman here draws me as you do."

"Th–thank you." She swallowed hard.

"It's getting stuffy in here," he said. "Perhaps we can catch a breeze out in the garden."

"Oh, I… Surely that's not allowed, Your Highness."

He laughed. "Not allowed? How do you mean? Are the chaperones of Prince Edward Island so strict?"

"No, Your Highness, I meant…" What did she mean? She looked about the room. Peter was speaking with Lord Washburn, not looking her way. Near them, however, the general stood straight as a pillar, watching them with a critical eye. "General Bruce—"

"Fie on the general. Come on. For my sake?" He guided her between the other couples, away from the general, toward the door. Everyone leaped to get out of their way.

As they reached the doorway, Molly looked back. The path had closed behind them, like water after a stone has sunk. If Peter hadn't seen them leave, he would have no idea where she was.

The prince tugged her hand. "This way."

Lord St. Germains stepped out of a recess. "Your Highness, may I help you with anything?"

"I should say not. It's hot in there, and we're going out to get some air."

St. Germains faded into the shadows. Molly gulped. Would she be considered, by association, someone who'd been rude to an earl?

The prince guided her around the corner, into the entry. A footman hastily shoved open the door and held it. They burst out into the cool night air, and Molly stopped to inhale deeply.

"Oh, that sea air *is* refreshing."

"Isn't it? Come, let's stroll down below, through the shrubbery."

A garden of rosebushes and evergreen shrubs, with several plantings of late summer flowers chosen especially because they would bloom while the prince visited, lay before the imposing building. Molly descended the steps cautiously, with the prince holding her elbow. She glanced around, wondering where her brother was. A couple walked slowly along one of the paths, and several gentlemen lingered in the lamplight, smoking. She didn't see any sign of Nathan. Had he given up and gone home? Molly felt vaguely uneasy and wished he was nearby.

The prince seemed to want to walk in the darkest corner of the garden. The farther they strayed from the portico, the louder rang the alarm bells in Molly's brain. The only light was from the windows behind them and the gleam of the lanterns along the distant walkway that led from the street to the steps of the Colonial Building.

She shivered. The prince slid his arm about her waist.

"Please, Your Highness, I'd like to go back now."

"Oh, Molly, Molly, surely you wouldn't deny me a kiss."

She caught her breath and stopped in her tracks, staring at him. "I beg your pardon, sir. I can't think why I shouldn't. It isn't seemly."

"Not seemly?" He laughed.

Molly hoped his retainers would hear and come to them. Where were they all, anyway? The equerries and General Bruce either had not noticed their exit or didn't care. And where were Lord Washburn and Nathan and—and Peter?

"Come, now," the prince said smoothly, pulling her toward him. One arm went about her waist, and with the other he reached toward her face. "I've been kept caged up for weeks and I've had no chance to enjoy the company of a pretty girl like yourself. Won't you make me happy tonight, Miss Orland, and send me off to Quebec with a favor?"

Molly threw back her shoulders. "Really, Your Highness! Is this way you behave everywhere you go?"

"Not everywhere." He pulled her closer.

"Please! Let me go." She struggled, but his grip on her tightened.

"Don't be coy. You ought to be flattered to have a little fun with me."

"Let the lady go."

210

Peter's tall form materialized behind the prince. Molly took advantage of His Royal Highness's surprise and jerked backward, pulling her wrist from his grasp.

"I beg your pardon?" the prince's acid tones would have wilted an oak tree.

"What on earth do you think you're doing?" Peter glared into his sovereign's eyes.

Molly clapped one gloved hand to her mouth as the two young men took each other's measure.

Chapter Nineteen

Through narrowed eyes, Peter gauged Albert Edward, heir apparent to the throne of the British Empire. He couldn't think of Albert's position now. He had to think only of Molly. No man—not even a prince—should insult a woman so.

"Stark." The prince's lips drew back in a strained smile. "What's the meaning of this?"

"Miss Orland asked you to release her. Any gentleman would do so at once."

The prince kept his arm around Molly's waist and yanked her toward him. "Ah, I see. And does knowing that make *you* a gentleman, Stark?"

Peter's blood rushed to his face. No doubt the prince knew of his background. No doubt at all. And he wouldn't hesitate to use it against him in this embarrassing situation. Molly pushed against the prince's chest with both hands now, in an effort to keep some air between them.

"Call me whatever you like, Your Highness, but let the lady go. Now." Peter put steel into the last few words.

"How dare you?" The prince squared his shoulders. "Leave us at once."

Molly shrank away from him. "No, don't, Peter. Please."

Peter glanced at her and back at the Prince of Wales. He couldn't ignore the panic in Molly's voice or the pleading in her eyes, whatever the cost. "The lady obviously does not want to be alone with you, Your Highness. I suggest you let me escort her back to the ballroom."

"And what will you do if I refuse? Are you forgetting to whom you are speaking?"

"Not for an instant." Involuntarily, Peter clenched his fists. How had it come to this? No doubt the prince had received years of training in self-defense and pugilism, along with diplomacy, etiquette, horsemanship, and a score of other disciplines. But could he fight like an orphan who'd been taunted since infancy?

He watched the prince carefully. Any change in his posture, even a slight shift in weight, could signal a coming blow.

"Back off now, Stark."

"Not without the lady," Peter said.

"Here, here, what's going on?"

Peter whirled at his master's voice. Washburn and General Bruce strode toward them across the garden.

"A simple misunderstanding, my lord." Peter ducked his head. "Miss Orland wished to return to the festivities."

"This man attacked me," the prince cried. "I want him arrested."

"Attacked you?" General Bruce stepped forward and grasped Peter's arm. "What's the meaning of this?"

"Stark?" Washburn turned to him, his face etched in lines of disbelief and pain.

"I assure you, my lord, I haven't laid a finger on the prince," Peter said quickly. "But it seemed the lady did not wish to continue their walk and His Royal Highness wouldn't listen to her. She asked him to release her, and I—I merely stepped forward as any gentleman would to—"

As Peter spoke, the earl's eyes widened and his color heightened. Several other men appeared behind Bruce and Washburn.

"What's the trouble?" one asked.

"No trouble, gentlemen," Washburn said. "Just a little discussion. General Bruce will handle it." As the men moved away, he leaned close to Peter and whispered, "Have you lost your mind?"

"N–no, my lord, I don't think so."

"What are you even doing out here?" Washburn's voice rose and cracked.

"I came out to have a word with—with a friend, and I saw the prince and—and his dancing partner." Whatever happened, Peter knew he must keep Molly's name out of this if at all possible. "I heard her ask to return to the ball, and she sounded upset. I couldn't turn my back on a lady in distress."

Washburn's gaze bored into him. After a moment, the earl turned and looked at the prince. "Well, now, Your Highness, what say you?"

"I say this man is jealous of the attentions paid to me by a local farmer's daughter. Perhaps he's been casting his eye on her himself this week. So when he saw her—shall we say, viewing the stars with me, he got angry and—"

Molly stepped forward and faced the earl, her eyes snapping. "That's not what happened!"

"Silence, woman!" The prince glared at her.

Molly cringed.

"Here now, Your Highness!" General Bruce stepped to Peter's side. "Let's not be rash."

"My lord, it didn't happen like that." Peter reached toward Washburn, but General Bruce's grip on his arm was like iron.

"I think we'd best have this man confined until we sort things out," the general said.

Washburn frowned at him. "Do you really think that's necessary?"

"Yes, take him away," the prince said. His eyes darted from Bruce to Washburn and back. "I shan't feel safe if you let him go."

Peter's heart leaped into his throat. What would happen to him? Would he be hung for supposedly attacking the prince? Imprisoned? Sent back to England in disgrace? He turned to his master.

"Lord Washburn, please believe me. I only stepped up when the lady begged him to let her go. I wouldn't have presumed to interrupt if I didn't think she needed assistance."

While Peter spoke, Bruce had somehow conjured two soldiers out of the darkness.

"Take this man to the governor's residence and guard his door," the general said. "Restrain him if you must."

"You won't need to do that," Peter said. "I'll go with you willingly, so long as someone takes care of—of the lady."

"I shall see to her," Lord Washburn said.

As the soldiers shoved him toward the street, Peter heard the prince say, "Really, Washburn, the man was insufferable. He should be hung—or flogged at the least."

*****

Molly's stomach tightened. Her throat hurt and tears burned her eyes. How could this happen? Should she have let the prince kiss her and kept quiet? Peter could be killed for dashing to her aid.

"Wait, Bruce." Lord Washburn said. "Let me speak with the lad for a moment. He is in my employ, you know."

The general hesitated and looked toward the prince. "Your Highness?"

Albert Edward shrugged and spread his hands. "I'll allow it. But I realize, Washburn, that Stark is a favorite of yours. Don't think I'll let this insult go unpunished."

Washburn bowed from his waist. "Thank you, Your Highness. I understand."

Bruce yelled to the two soldiers to stop, and they waited on the walkway with Peter between them.

The prince strode past the general without another glance at Molly. Major Teesdale and several other gentlemen who'd waited a few yards away fell in behind him and mounted the steps of the Colonial Building.

Molly exhaled and kept her place in the shadows as they went back to the ballroom, not sure what she should do. General Bruce stood by with his hands on his hips, and the two soldiers continued to hold Peter by his arms.

Washburn walked over to where they stood. "Peter, my boy." The earl's voice was thick with emotion. "I'm so sorry. I have no doubt things happened as you say."

"Thank you." Peter raised his chin and looked his master in the eye. "I regret that I've caused you embarrassment."

"It cannot be helped. If it's possible, I'll convince His Highness and the duke that we must kept this quiet. We can't let it get back to the queen and prince consort. That would spell disaster for the prince and shame for the Crown." Washburn shook his head. "He should know better. He can't afford a scandal on this tour, especially so early into it. He has the Canadas and the United States to visit yet."

"He's behaved well up until now," General Bruce said tersely.

"Yes, you're right. Perhaps between you and Newcastle, you can talk him into reverting to that good behavior." Washburn's tone was so sad that tears of empathy sprang into Molly's eyes. The earl rested a hand on Peter's shoulder. "I'm afraid I cannot help you now, but I shall try. I'll do everything in my power."

"Thank you," Peter choked out.

"I suppose I might be able to persuade the prince that discharging you from my service would be punishment enough."

"But I was to leave in the morning, my lord, to make arrangements for the royal party at the next stop."

Washburn sighed. "I'll have to send someone else to take care of those duties."

"Come, now," Bruce said. "Let's not drag this out all night."

"All right. Peter, I shall come to you later at Government House. Do not lose heart. I shall find you, even if they take you to some other place of confinement. I won't leave the island without making sure you're all right."

"Thank you, sir." Molly could barely hear Peter's words.

The earl pushed in, ignoring the two soldiers, and drew Peter into a hug. "No matter what the crown prince says, I will not abandon my nephew."

In the darkness, hot tears streamed down Molly's cheeks. At first she thought she'd misunderstood Washburn's words, but Peter returned his embrace for a moment and murmured, "Thank you, dear uncle."

*****

"Molly! Molly, where are you?"

She snapped from her reverie and flung herself into Nathan's arms.

"Where were you, Nathan? Oh, where were you? I needed you!"

"I'm sorry. I thought it would be a couple of hours yet, and I walked around to the back. They were giving out punch and sweets to the servants who were waiting for their employers to be done dancing."

Molly sobbed, and he pulled away from her.

"What is it? Tell me what happened. I saw Mr. Stark being hauled away!"

The Earl of Washburn stepped closer. "Allow me to introduce myself."

Nathan swung around to see him and caught his breath. "You were in the carriage today. At the farm."

"Yes. My name is Washburn."

"I know who you are." Nathan straightened his spine and eyed the earl belligerently. "What have you done to our Molly?"

"Nothing, lad. Come sit down over here, and I'll tell you how things are."

The earl led them to a stone bench, and Molly sat down with a thud. General Bruce and the other onlookers had melted into the darkness. Nathan settled beside her, uneasily watching Washburn.

"First, Miss Orland, are you all right?"

"Yes, sir." She dashed at her tears with the back of her hand. "I'm sorry."

"Why is my sister crying?" Nathan demanded.

Molly reached over and patted his arm. "It's not his lordship's fault, Nathan. I had some trouble out here with—with a gentleman I'd been dancing with, and Peter came to help me. There was a misunderstanding. The—the gentleman claimed

Peter hit him, but he didn't. I was right there, and I know what happened."

"We'll straighten this out insofar as possible in the morning, I'm sure," Washburn said gently.

"You won't let them hurt him, will you?" Molly asked.

"I shall do all in my power…which seems very small at the moment."

"I shan't be able to bear it if they mistreat him." Molly sobbed.

"Peter means a great deal to me," Washburn said softly.

"You said…" Molly glanced at her brother, wondering if she ought to raise the subject in front of him. But why shouldn't Nathan hear everything? He was as old as the prince. "My lord, you said Peter is your nephew."

Washburn nodded gravely. "So he is."

"I thought—that is, we all thought—he was your servant."

"He is that too." The earl hesitated then cleared his throat. "Peter Stark has been in my employ for six years. He began as a footman, and he is now my understeward. But his mother, Catherine Stark, was my sister—a sister I never knew."

"Catherine?" Molly asked.

Nathan eyed her uneasily. "That's the name Papa and Grandpa said the baby was given—Aunt Mary Orland's baby."

Molly looked from him to Washburn and back. "When did they learn this?"

"They told Mum and me about it when they came home from Government House—before I left this evening. They said Lord Washburn told them Mary's little girl was named Catherine, and that she's still alive and has a son."

"Yes," said the earl. "Catherine was the child conceived by Mary Orland, your grandfather's sister. My own father…was Catherine's father as well." He looked away.

Molly's face flamed with heat, but the darkness would conceal that. Her mind raced as she followed the implications. "Then you—you are the connection. I never thought it out before, but…oh, dear." She clapped her hands to her cheeks.

"Yes," Washburn said. "David Orland and Catherine Stark are cousins. Peter is your second cousin."

Nathan leaped to his feet. "Peter Stark? He's our…"

"Yes."

"Does he know this?" Molly asked.

"He knows."

She wilted against the stone bench. "He knew all along?"

"He knew as soon as I did, I daresay—when your grandfather showed up at the levee yesterday."

"Not before?"

"I don't believe so. Why? Is it important?"

"No. It's just…"

Washburn and Nathan both stared at her.

"I wondered if he knew when he first met me."

"I think not, my dear." Washburn smiled down at her. "He was quite taken with you before he suspected you were an Orland. And when he found out, it didn't change his regard for you."

She swallowed with difficulty. "I just don't understand. If your father had this other child…"

"He never acknowledged Catherine." Washburn bowed his head. "Publicly, he denied she was his offspring. But he did make some provision for her and her mother. When I grew up I learned the full story, and I made contact with them. After my father died, I got to know Peter. He's become very dear to me—in fact, I don't shrink from saying that I love him as I would a son."

Molly stood and reached for the gray-haired man's hand. "Peter loves you too. He's always spoken well of you to me, and I heard what passed between you a few minutes ago."

"Thank you for saying so. He is a delightful young man, and I'm proud to claim him. I only wish my father had acknowledged Catherine as his daughter."

"He had no idea what he was missing," Molly said.

"That is true." Washburn cleared his throat. "My father's act of renouncing his own child made me lose all respect for him when I was old enough to understand what had happened. The rift between us never healed."

"I'm sorry. And you will help Peter?"

"If I can. I shall go to Government House now and see what they've decided to do with him. But what of you?" Washburn glanced toward her brother.

Nathan stood and walked closer to him. "I shall see Molly home, sir. That's why I came here to begin with. I'm angry with myself for leaving my post in the portico. I never should have gone around back."

"Lad, these things happen. See to your sister now, and you'll have fulfilled your duty. That is all we can do in this life." He smiled down at Molly. "My dear, no matter what happens, think of this: Peter Stark is not such a bad fellow to be related to."

Though she tried to hold them back, Molly burst out in fresh tears. She fumbled in her reticule for a handkerchief. Washburn and Nathan both had theirs out before she could find her own. She gave a shaky laugh and took one in each hand.

"Thank you, my lord," she said to Washburn as she wiped her eyes with his pure linen one. "And thank you, sir." She nodded to Nathan, holding his plain cotton square.

Nathan drew in a deep breath and gazed at the earl. "I can't stand to see history repeated this way. Here's Peter, who seems to be a fine man, being punished for the same offense for which our grandfather was deported."

The earl patted Nathan's shoulder. "Ah, lad, you're right. In my opinion, Anson was no guiltier than Peter is."

"It isn't right." Nathan clenched his teeth.

"There, now, Nathan, let his lordship handle this," Molly said. "We Orlands have shown that we don't do well when we get mixed up in the affairs of the aristocracy."

"You're probably right." Nathan sighed. "Do you have to go back inside?"

"I left my shawl at the booth in the entry."

"Then I'll escort you in to retrieve it." Nathan offered her his arm.

"Thank you. I suppose I should also say good-bye to the hostess, but—"

"Under the circumstances, it might be better if you let me express your regrets to her," Washburn said. "I'll be sure to tell her that you did not misbehave and that she should think none the less of you or your family because of this incident."

"Thank you, my lord. We may never meet again, and so I bid you farewell."

"I hope we shall indeed meet again and I shall get to know you better." Washburn took her hand and bowed over it.

Chapter Twenty

"All right, you, get down, and don't give us any trouble," one of the police officers guarding him said.

Peter swung his shackled legs over the end of the wagon and slid to the ground. He staggered and flailed his arms, also bound at the wrists, to keep from falling on his face in the street.

"There now, up them steps."

Slowly he mounted the stone steps before the police station, laboriously raising one foot at a time. His stomach roiled. The earl had not appeared during his brief stay at Government House. General Bruce had placed a guard of two Volunteers at his door and two more outside the house. He had apparently hashed over the entire incident again with Newcastle and decided to get Peter out of the governor's mansion before Dundas and his wife returned from the ball. The prince, meanwhile, was kicking up his heels at the ball as though he had not a care in the world—or so one of the guards told the other in a voice so loud Peter could easily hear it through the pine door panels.

After a half hour, two police officers had come to haul him away. On his protest, the Irish officer now herding him into the building had told him he was acting on orders from the prince via General Bruce, so it would do the prisoner no good to make a fuss.

"Whatcha got there?" asked a sergeant who was sitting behind a desk in the front room. "Drunk from the festivities?"

"Seems to be sober," the officer replied. "He's the gent we picked up at Fanning Bank."

"Ah, the one what hit the prince."

"I did not hit the prince," Peter said. "Please, could I have the services of an attorney?"

"Maybe tomorrow." The sergeant wrote something in a large book lying open before him. "Every lawyer in town's up to the Colonial Building, no doubt dancing."

"But surely—"

"Surely nothing, mister," the officer holding him growled. "You can do your business tomorrow."

He shoved Peter toward an imposing plank door and rapped loudly on the wood. Another man looked through a small, barred window in it and the sound of a turning key was followed by the door swinging inward. The guard pushed Peter inside.

"Come on, now, over yonder."

Kerosene lanterns hung at intervals lit their way. At a long deal table, another man took the paper handed to him by the guard.

"Ah, so you need some more appropriate clothing." He eyed Peter's evening clothes. "It would never do to put you inside in those."

The guard laughed. "They'd tear him to shreds."

Peter clenched his teeth and said nothing.

"Quite the dandy, ain't he?" asked the man behind the table. He rose and took a pile of folded clothing off a shelf behind him. "Here you go. It'll be too large, but you're too tall for the others."

"Come on." The guard shoved him toward the far side of the room. He took out his keys and unlocked the shackles. "Strip and put your things on that table. You'll get 'em back when you're released."

Peter hesitated. His wallet was in his pocket and contained his letters of recommendation and the money Washburn had advanced him for his trip to Quebec, Montreal, and Toronto. "Will I get a receipt?"

The guard laughed and called to the other man, "You hear that, Jack? He wants a receipt."

"You should be so blessed," Jack replied.

Peter felt ill, but he could see no alternative to obeying the guard's orders. Reluctantly, he took off his jacket, folded it, and laid it on the small table provided. He began to undo his onyx cuff links. They were his last Christmas gift from the earl. What would become of them?

Ten minutes later he was thrown unceremoniously into a cell. He caught himself against the end of a double-tiered bunk and slowly lifted his head. Three other men stared at him.

One of them grinned through a beard resembling a rat's pelt. "Well, now, we got us a gent."

"Doesn't look drunk," said the one lying on the bunk above him. He was leaning up on his elbow to look over the newcomer. Peter couldn't judge his size very well, but the prisoner's broad shoulders and large, shaggy head gave him no reassurance that he'd spend a peaceful night.

*****

Papa lumbered, yawning, into the kitchen when Molly and Nathan entered through the back door. He wore an undervest and a pair of workaday trousers, and his light hair was tousled.

"Well, well, there's our Molly back from the ball. Look at you!"

Molly glanced down at the skirt she'd had to crush to get through the door. She hoped she hadn't damaged Thompson's crinoline.

"Oh. Well, you see, I left my things at—oh, Papa!" She hadn't meant to cry. In fact, she'd hoped she and Nathan could sneak in without awakening their parents. But the storm of tears burst so suddenly she couldn't hold it back. She dashed across the floor and threw herself into her father's baffled embrace.

"There now, what's the fuss about?" His words were gentle, but she felt the tension as he swung his head toward Nathan.

Molly tried to curb her sobs.

"She had a bit of trouble," Nathan said.

"What kind of trouble?"

Nathan didn't answer right away. He stepped to the table and turned up the lamp that was burning low.

Molly raised her head and wiped her face with the back of her hand. "It's Peter, Papa. He's been arrested."

"What?"

"It's true—the prince's orders. And he's our cousin, Papa!"

Her father stared at her. "The prince is your cousin? What on earth are you saying?"

Nathan let out a guffaw, and Molly threw daggers at him with her eyes. "No, no. Peter Stark is our cousin, and the prince claims that Peter hit him, which he didn't, and now who knows what will happen to poor Peter, and we haven't even gotten to know him."

Her father held her at arm's length during this torrent, watching her lips and nodding mechanically. When she'd finished, he swiveled his gaze toward Nathan again. "Is she talking nonsense?"

"No, Papa." Nathan walked over to the stove and lifted the coffeepot that simmered there. "Maybe you'd better sit down. There seems to be some coffee." He patted the side of the pot experimentally. "Though it's not very hot."

"I don't want coffee. I want to know what happened tonight and what all this is about Stark."

"David," Mum chided from the doorway to their bedroom, "what's the trouble? You'll wake Da and the children with all this noise." Her gaze settled on Molly, and her expression softened. "Look at you in that dress! Sweet Molly, how beautiful you are." She stepped forward, clutching her dressing gown together over her nightgown, and circled around Molly's voluminous skirt. "It's the prettiest dress I've ever seen in my life."

"Thank you, Mum." Molly felt fresh tears prickle her eyes, but the wild, incoherent feeling was gone. She was glad that in this turmoil her mother had found a moment's delight before the force of the storm hit.

Mum smiled at her and touched her cheek. "I'll have to help you out of that gown, unless I'm mistaken." She sobered abruptly and shot a glance at her husband. "Now, what's all the commotion about?"

Nathan lifted the lid of the firebox on the cookstove and set it aside. He pulled a few sticks of kindling from the wood box. "Why don't you all sit down? I'll build up the fire and heat the coffee and teakettle."

"Just tell me you're not hurt, Molly," her father said.

"I'm not, but my heart is breaking for Peter."

She sat on the edge of a chair, fighting with the crinoline. Her parents sat down in the places they always sat for meals. As Nathan worked at the stove, Molly took a deep breath and blinked back her tears.

"Everything was going well at the ball—so beautiful, and the music was lovely. We danced and danced."

"Who's 'we'?" her father demanded.

"Oh, everyone," Molly said.

"Hush, David." Mum reached over and took his hand. "Let her tell it."

*****

Peter woke in the fetid cell. The high, barred window showed a gray sky. He rolled over on the upper bunk, setting the frame to swaying.

The man below him kicked the bottom of Peter's bunk. "Quit."

Peter tried to lie still. His three cellmates had cuffed him about last night, not so badly that he needed a doctor, but they'd threatened to do worse if he didn't behave as they told him. So far that entailed promising to help them if he was released before they were and keeping quiet while they played cards. Peter was content to stay out of their business—one boasted that he was confined because he'd slashed a man's face with a knife, and another had been caught stealing from the ship's cargo he'd been hired to help unload. The third man didn't volunteer to tell his offense, leaving Peter to imagine the worst.

When did they feed the prisoners here? His hunger surprised him. He wanted to get up and wash, but that would probably draw the other men's displeasure.

He lay on his bed, close to the ceiling, alternately praying and fretting about Molly. Where had she gone? Had she escaped the grounds of the Colonial Building and fled for home? Had she met up with Nathan outside? He hoped she had made it back to the farmhouse and was there with her loving family. In the haze of his memories of the night before, he clung to the earl's promise to take care of her.

He thought back over everything that had happened—how he'd spotted Molly and the prince from the portico moving into the shadows near the edge of the garden, and how he'd sensed that Molly held back, unwilling to go farther from the building with the prince. Peter had told himself he would only go close enough to determine that she was not uncomfortable with the situation and then retreat silently. But he couldn't do that when he heard her protests and then her demand that the prince let her go.

He gritted his teeth. He could not have acted otherwise. Even though he'd been unjustly accused and thrown in this awful place, he could not regret confronting the prince for his vulgar actions.

Steps in the passageway between the cells drew his attention. A guard appeared, accompanying another man who wheeled a cart with trays on it.

"Breakfast," the guard said.

Peter sat up and swung down from his bunk while his three cellmates groaned. Two of them began to rise, while the last only pulled his gray wool blanket higher over his ears.

"Are you Stark?" the guard asked.

"Yes."

"Clean up after you eat."

The guard walked away. Peter hurried to the door and peered out, but the man had gone on down the row.

He claimed his bowl of grayish porridge and tin cup of milk. No use in thinking of the lavish breakfasts at Fanning Bank. The city jail wasn't serving kippers or hot biscuits and jam. He forced himself to eat the bland porridge. The two men who had risen scraped their bowls and eyed the fourth dish still sitting on the tray.

"Hey, Blackie, you going to eat your swill?" one of them called.

The man still in bed didn't move.

"Well, then, let's have it."

"Give me half," said the other man.

Blackie sat up with a roar.

"All right, all right," said the first prisoner. "Take it, then." He retreated to his bunk.

Peter limped to the corner where the tin washbasin sat on an upended crate. His muscles ached more than he'd realized, both from the light beating he'd received and the hard bunk he'd slept on. His ankles itched—his bedding no doubt harbored assorted insects. His face throbbed, and he suspected it was bruised and his left eye blackened, but he had no way to relieve the pain or cover the marks.

He poured water in the basin, being careful not to take more than the others might construe as his share. There didn't seem to be any soap, so he made a meager ablution, carefully cleansing the swollen skin around his left eye. He dumped the wash water into the slop pail and put on his shoes.

"Where you going, gov?" The sleepy man, Blackie, had risen at last and sat on the edge of his bunk wolfing his porridge.

"I'm not sure," Peter said. "The guard told me to clean myself up."

"Expect the worst," muttered one of the men.

"No, that ain't right. Expect the best," said another.

"Do that and you're sure to be disappointed." Blackie tipped up his bowl and licked it out.

"Tha's right," said the one who'd predicted the "worst." "They're like to hang you this morning."

"That's all you know about it," Blackie sneered. "They don't hang folks with money. More like, they'll try to squeeze a bribe out of 'im."

Peter climbed to his upper berth and sat, out of their immediate reach, waiting to be summoned. At last the guard returned and put the key in the cell door's lock.

"Come on, Stark. Time to meet your fate."

Peter gulped. Maybe they *would* string him up…but he hardly dared think it. Deport him, more likely. Put him on the next ship to Australia. What would become of his mother? His mother! The thought of her grief when she'd hear the news pierced his heart. For her sake, he should have restrained his impulse last night. But no. He couldn't sacrifice Molly for the sake of his mother's comfort.

"The rest of you, stand back." The guard swung the door open.

Peter stepped out and walked before the guard. Men in the other cells called out insults as he passed. Another uniformed man opened the door at the end of the passageway. They went up some stairs, and the guard ushered him into a small, bare room.

"Peter!" The Earl of Washburn rose from one of the two stools in the room and stepped toward him. His face was drawn, and dark smudges showed beneath his eyes.

"My lord!" Peter's relief was so strong his knees wobbled. "Thank you for coming."

Washburn rested his hand on Peter's shoulder for a moment as he studied his face. "My boy." His voice cracked. "Did the police beat you?"

"No, my new friends in the cell. But it's nothing, really. I'm fine."

Washburn nodded, though his face was still drawn. "Sit down. We have but a few minutes."

"What has happened?" Peter took one stool, and the earl settled on the other.

"The prince has reached a decision."

"Oh?" Peter dared not let his hopes rise too high.

"His Royal Highness does not wish to embarrass the governor or to cast a pall over his tour—and even more than that, he has no desire for his parents to hear of this incident."

"I should think not."

Washburn nodded. "After Bertie had danced his fill at the ball, Bruce and Newcastle tried to persuade him to drop the charges he'd insisted on. He refused, but after lengthy discussion, he finally agreed to hush it up. I think it helped that Miss Orland stated you hadn't touched the prince's person, and that I believed her and adamantly took her side."

"Molly wasn't dragged any further into this sordidness, was she?" Peter eyed his face anxiously.

"Nothing beyond the regrettable scene you were witness to. Her brother appeared shortly after you were taken away, and he escorted her home."

Peter exhaled and closed his eyes for a moment. "That brings me comfort."

"I think we managed to keep the business from Mrs. Dundas's ears as well. Her husband was most anxious that she not hear of it. So unless some of the soldiers talk, no one should be the wiser. The governor agreed to let the prince pronounce sentence and avoid having you prosecuted through the colonial judicial system."

Peter frowned, trying to follow him. "So...what is to become of me, my lord?"

"We debated that until dawn."

"I'm sorry you were up all night on my behalf."

"Think nothing of it. The others are sleeping now, and I hope they have no regrets over the decision that Bertie reached an hour ago."

Peter waited, nearly mad with dread.

"You can't go home, lad."

"I..." Peter's chest tightened. "You mean, they'll keep me here in prison? Or will they ship me to a penal colony?"

"Neither. You shall be released this afternoon, provided you never set foot in England again. And I..." Washburn's face crumpled, and tears formed in his eyes. "I must discharge you from my employ at once. I'm sorry, Peter. He wanted me to declare your disgrace publicly, but Bruce pointed out that all the islanders, including Mrs. Dundas, would hear of it then and the papers would make hay with it. So the prince agreed to keep silent to save his own dignity."

Peter drew a careful breath. "He doesn't want it known in England."

"Not on your life. His father would go mad, and his mother—well, the queen would be vastly disappointed."

"Yes, I can see that."

"And so we're all going to forget that last night's unpleasantness ever happened. The prince never insulted Miss Orland, you never came to her aid, and no charges were ever brought. You simply…left our entourage and disappeared. If anyone asks me, I shall let it be known that you took a fancy to Prince Edward Island and decided to try your hand as a colonist, with my blessing."

"Thank you." Peter looked deep into his uncle's eyes and saw pain, regret, and love there. This parting would be as difficult for the earl as it was for him. "And so I shall live the same fate as my grandmother's brother."

"Yes."

"But what shall I do?"

Washburn shrugged. "You can do whatever you wish, once we are gone. You can remain here or travel on into Canada or down into the States. But you can never set foot on Great Britain again."

Peter nodded slowly. "All right. I can bear that. It's better than hanging. But what about my mother?"

Washburn pursed his lips for a moment. "If you wish to write a letter, I will carry it to her myself and visit her as soon as I return home. I'll explain everything to her. And I suppose that, if you wish, once you've settled somewhere, you could send for her."

Overwhelmed, Peter dropped to his knees and grasped the earl's hand. "Thank you so much. I don't care what becomes of me, so long as I know that Mother will be all right and that Molly's name hasn't been besmirched by my actions."

"I shall see to your mother's comfort—have no fear. After all, she is my sister. I think it's time I invited her to live in my home if she wishes."

"My lord, if you do that, I can cheerfully accept any punishment."

Washburn hauled him to his feet and hugged him. "Peter, my boy, it grieves me that you're receiving any punishment at all, though some would call this a light sentence. I know you did no wrong."

"Thank you."

"And you must call me "Uncle" from now on. Can you do that?"

"I—I shall try. I know I would like to, very much."

"Good, because you have made me proud. I am not ashamed of you, nor of Catherine. If I could, I would leave my estate and even my title to you. You know that, don't you?"

Peter's throat constricted. "I don't know what to say."

Tears gleamed in the earl's eyes. "The Lord saw fit to take my wife and little boy away, but later He gave me you. I'll always be grateful that we had each other's company for a while."

"I feel the same. Thank you for everything you've done for me and for Mother."

Washburn reached into his pocket and took out a pouch. "Take this."

Peter caught his breath. "My lord—I mean, Uncle—the money you gave me for the voyage, and my letters of reference. They took them from me with my clothing and all I had on me last night. Will you be able to get those back? Whoever goes in my place will need them."

"We've already sent Captain Grey on ahead, so put your mind at ease. And I spoke to the police sergeant when I came in. I told him you'd best have every penny and every stitch of clothing returned to you. He blustered a bit about how his men were trustworthy, but I assured him I'd make him regret it if any of your things had been pilfered."

"But I won't need the money now—"

"Won't you?" The earl looked somberly into his eyes. "Peter, the amount I'm giving you now isn't half what you had on you for the trip. You'll need to live until you either establish yourself here or get to some other place to do that."

"You mean…I should keep it and use it, as well as this—if they give it back to me?"

"It will be little enough for all you've done on this journey and the pain you're suffering now. The prince may say what he likes, but I shall make sure that every man among our party knows you are innocent."

"Thank you."

The earl rose. "Very well, then. I have enough cash left so that I can get by until we land in the next sizable town, and there I can draw on a bank draft for more money. I only wish I had a larger amount on hand so that I could do more for you. They won't release you until we sail after luncheon. I don't suppose you want to take that money to your cell with you?"

"I should lose it very quickly if I did, sir."

"As I thought. Peter, I'm very sorry."

"I know. But I can survive until this afternoon."

"Good. Unfortunately, the prince insisted you be kept in bonds until he's left the harbor. He has some misguided notion you might try to harm him—or wants other people to believe that. But I shall speak to the chief of police, I think, before I set foot in the street again. I'll entrust that money to him and tell him to the penny what you should have when you are released, and I'll ask Dundas to check on it later to be sure you were not robbed or ill-used."

"And then, sir? Should I take the ferry and leave here? I don't wish to embarrass Mr. Dundas any further than I already have. He's been very good to me, and if my presence would shame him, I shall leave as soon as possible. Have you any counsel for me on what I should do?"

"If I were you, boy, I'd stay on this beautiful island. I've told Dundas how the wind blows, and I think he'll be tolerant, though you mustn't expect him to receive you socially."

"I would never presume that much, sir."

"No, you wouldn't, would you, my lad? I do think you'll find your niche here after awhile. It's a good place to live. And after all, you have family here."

Peter drew in a deep breath. "Yes."

Washburn smiled. "Don't underestimate your cousin David or your great-uncle Anson. They are good people, and they, more than anyone else, will understand your plight."

"They have a thriving farm," Peter noted.

"Yes. You've always shown an affinity for my tenant farmers and a love of the soil. Think about it. Perhaps they could help you find a place here in the colony." Washburn put on his hat. "It's a good thing to have family near when you're in a strange place. I'd be very surprised if the Orlands didn't welcome you into their circle. And don't forget that lovely second cousin of yours."

Peter's face warmed at the mention of Molly. "I shan't, sir."

"I thought not. She shed tears for you last night. That's not a bad thing, either."

Chapter Twenty-One

Molly rose after only four hours of sleep and put on her black dress. She groomed herself carefully. In the kitchen, she found her mother at her worktable, scrubbing the wide hem of the white gown in a large pan of water.

"I don't know if I can get all the mud out." Mum sighed. "Probably the folks at Government House can do better, but I didn't want to send it back all spattered like that."

"I never intended to wear it home," Molly said.

"I know, dear." Mum gave her a weary smile. "Eat some oatmeal. The tea's steeping."

"What if they turn me away when I get to Government House?" The fear had come to Molly before she fell asleep. What if Mr. and Mrs. Dundas refused to let her come back to work because of her part in the prince's embarrassment?

"Then you come home." Mum raised the stretch of fabric she'd been washing and scrutinized it. "I'm going to press this dry and send you in the wagon with Nathan driving. You can't carry the crinoline all the way in to Charlottetown."

"What about Allison?" Molly asked. "Shall we give her a ride? She'll know something's happened."

"She'll know if you don't stop too, now, won't she?"

"I suppose so."

Mum walked to the stove and lifted the teakettle of hot water. "Do you really think it won't be the talk of the island today?"

"I don't know." Molly bit her lower lip, trying to remember everything the earl had said in the garden at the ball last night. "Lord Washburn was going to try to hush it up, and since his nephew is involved, he'll do his best to make sure Peter isn't slandered and…" Tears filled her eyes for the umpteenth time since she'd seen Peter arrested. "Oh, Mum, what if the prince insists they punish him to the fullest? He's innocent."

"I know, child. Mr. Stark shouldn't be punished at all, or even put to shame. He should be honored for what he did. But because the man he confronted is royalty, his life could be ruined."

"Worse than that. You don't think they'll hang him, do you? Oh, Mum!" Molly threw her arms around her mother's neck and clung to her, sobbing once more. "He did it for my sake, and it was all so unnecessary. It would have been better if I'd simply refused to walk outside. There might have been a little fuss and I might have been snubbed, but what does that matter? Peter's life is in danger now."

"There, there." Mum patted her back. "You didn't feel you could say no to the prince, did you?"

"I suppose not. But I should have—Papa warned me about this very thing. I didn't think it could happen to me."

"We've got to trust the earl and the Good Lord, Molly dear. Come on, now. You can't go to work with a red nose. Sit down and eat your breakfast. I'll wake Nathan and have him harness the horse. And then I've got to finish with this dress."

An hour later, Nathan and Molly carefully carried the gown and crinoline, with the rest of the borrowed clothing, out to the wagon and mounted the box. After further discussion, they'd decided to say nothing to Allison or anyone else on the chance that somehow word of the incident hadn't become public knowledge. Nathan would pick up a newspaper in town so they would know whether the journalists had gotten hold of the story. If Allison already knew, it would be hopeless, but if she'd heard nothing, there was still a chance the earl had managed to quash the scandal.

Nathan stopped the wagon near the Johnsons' gate. Allison ran out of her parents' house, grinning, and climbed to the seat beside Molly.

"We get to ride today? How jolly!"

"Yes." Molly waved a hand toward the sheet covering the borrowed finery in the wagon bed. "It was late when I got done last night and Nathan brought me straight home, so I have to return the gown and all the other things this morning."

Allison's eyes shone. "Hello, Nathan! Molly, what was the ball like? Tell me everything! Did you dance with him?"

"With whom?" Molly asked uneasily.

"The prince, silly. Did he speak to you?"

"Of course. He…asked me about my family and…basic things about the island. The kind of things he probably asked every woman he danced with."

Allison laughed. "Did you do the same? 'And what's it like, living in a palace, Your Highness? Do you like having eight brothers and sisters? Do they all share their toys nicely?' Ha!"

Molly smiled at that. "I don't believe I said anything of the kind. I did ask how he enjoyed his stay on the island."

"Brief as it was." Allison sighed. "They're still planning to leave today, I suppose."

"Oh, yes, it's all settled. His Royal Highness will meet the representatives of the Indian tribes this morning and tend to a few other details, and after luncheon the prince will board the *Hero*."

"Ah, but I heard a slight revision of that plan from Mrs. Randolph last evening just before I went home." Allison leaned toward Molly, eager to impart her news. "The prince's chef will prepare luncheon aboard the ship, and the governor and Mrs. Dundas will eat with him on the *Hero*, in the harbor, while the *Flying Fish*, the *Ariadne*, and the *Cossack* stand by. After the meal, the Dundases will come ashore and then the salutes will be fired and the prince will set sail."

"It sounds like a fitting send-off," Nathan said, without meeting his sister's gaze.

Molly couldn't help being a little bit glad that "Bertie" wouldn't be dining at Government House that day and there would be no chance of her being called upon to serve the royal guests at luncheon. But what about Peter? she longed to ask. Where will he be while all the pageantry takes place?

They rode along listening to Allison chatter about the distinguished visitors and what the other kitchen maids thought of them all, and the bracelet the prince had bestowed upon Mrs. Dundas.

"Did you see it at the ball, Molly?" she asked eagerly. "They say it's fabulous."

"Only from a distance. It has a blue enamel medallion."

"I heard it bears the Prince of Wales's crest and plume in diamonds," Allison said.

The nearer the wagon came to Government House, the more Molly's nerves stirred. Her stomach clenched as they passed through the gate and into the back garden.

"Do you want to go in first and see if the way's clear?" Nathan asked. "I can help carry that contraption up the stairs if they don't mind."

"Perhaps Allison and I should take it." Molly glanced warily toward the door of the laundry.

Nathan eyed her soberly. She'd told him before they picked up Allison how much she dreaded meeting Mrs. Bolton or Thompson. "Just pop in and see what's what, then. I'll wait."

Molly hopped down and hurried to the door. She heard and felt Allison behind her but didn't speak to her friend for fear that her voice or her expression would give away her anxiety.

No one had begun work in the laundry yet. They hurried into the kitchen. The cook was measuring out ingredients at the table across the room, but the American chef was nowhere to be seen, and only two kitchen maids had started their morning work.

" 'Morning," one of the kitchen maids called.

Allison stopped to chat with her while Molly ventured to the passageway leading to the back stairs. As far as she could tell, all was clear. She dashed back outside. Nathan arched his eyebrows.

"Let's do it quickly. Cook is puttering about for breakfast, and Allison will be expected to pitch in soon."

Nathan tied the horse and went to the back of the wagon. By the time they had the draped gown and crinoline out, Allison had returned.

"Can you grab the shoes and that small bag?" Molly asked.

"Got it."

Molly went in first, holding up her side of the awkward frame for the hoopskirt. Nathan followed, keeping his gaze downward. The cook glanced their way but said nothing, while the maids stared openly at Nathan.

"We got a new useful man?" one of them asked.

Molly laughed. "He's my brother."

"Ah." The way she said it spoke volumes, and Nathan flushed to his hairline.

"He's useful on occasion," Allison said with a chuckle.

At the stairway, Molly halted. "You go first, Allison. Make sure no one's about the upper halls and that we can get into Deborah's room."

"You don't want to take it directly to Thompson's wardrobe?"

"We might meet someone." The thought of coming face-to-face with Mrs. Dundas or even the prince made Molly cringe. It was early yet for the aristocrats to be about, but the governor often rose at sunup for a ride. Even that thought distressed her, as the last time she'd known Dundas to do it, Peter had gone with him.

After much maneuvering of the hoops and histrionics by Allison as she peered around corners, they arrived at Deborah's chamber. Allison quickly placed her burdens inside and came back into the narrow passageway.

"I'll help from here on, Nathan. 'Twouldn't be proper for you to go in, seeing as you're not employed here."

Nathan released his end of the crinoline. "All right. Shall I find my own way out?"

"No, wait for us," Molly said. "We wouldn't want anyone to find you wandering the halls alone. If one of us is with you, we can explain things."

They soon had the clothing placed where Molly could get it easily after she'd had a chance to speak to Thompson about returning it.

"I must dash," Allison said. "I'll see you this afternoon if not before."

Maybe, Molly thought. *If I don't get sacked.*

She sighed and turned to Nathan in the hallway of the servants' quarters. "Well, I guess there's no way around it. I've got to report for work. If Mrs. Bolton tells me I'm fired for promoting a scandal last night, I'll…I'll just… " Tears splashed down her cheeks onto the frill of her apron.

"There, now." Nathan touched her shoulder. "They won't dismiss you."

"Won't they? The prince was very upset, and not just with Peter. He was angry with me for resisting his advances. I think that's why he was so harsh with Peter."

"Maybe so, but you can't change that."

Molly nodded. "You're right. I just hope I don't have to see His Royal Highness ever again."

Together they scuttled down the back stairs. Molly slipped into the laundry with Nathan. The two laundresses were pouring the day's first wash water into their big galvanized tubs.

"Do you want me to wait a while?" Nathan asked.

"No, go on home. Papa needs you. If they toss me out, I'll walk home."

She went back to the kitchen.

"Ah, there you are, Molly." The head parlor maid, Roberts, stood in the doorway to the passage. "We need to set up the breakfast things quickly. The master has gone out riding this morning, and he and the gentlemen with him could be back soon."

Molly hurried into the breakfast room and mechanically set out dishes. Plates, flatware, bowls, cups, saucers, finger bowls. Eustace, the footman she'd met at her initial interview, came in with a steaming silver coffeepot.

"Good morning, Molly."

"Good morning to you."

Eustace set the coffeepot down. "They say that Mr. Stark has already left, and so has Captain Grey. The prince and his suite will want breakfast before His Royal Highness inspects the Volunteers and meets the tribal leaders, though."

"And when will that be?"

"I believe they're to be at the Colonial Building by eleven, which means they'll probably start ringing for breakfast trays any time now."

Mrs. Randolph peeked in from the kitchen. "The Duke of Newcastle just rang, Eustace. Take his coffee and toast straightaway, and don't forget the cream pitcher this time."

"Yes, ma'am."

Molly reached into the sideboard, took out a small tray, and handed it to Eustace. Milton came in with a larger serving tray that held several covered dishes.

"The governor and his riding party just returned to the stable," Milton reported.

The men who had been out on horseback would most likely take their breakfast downstairs before going up to change their attire. Molly closed the cupboard and strode toward the door.

"Ah! The hot dishes are ready. Charming."

Molly looked over her shoulder. General Bruce had come in to look over the prospects of breakfast and now headed back toward the hall door.

"Teesdale! Snag Bertie and tell him they're just putting breakfast out. Quicker to eat in here than to have them carry it up."

So the prince had joined the riding party this morning. Molly gulped and picked up a dish. Any excuse to leave the room before he came in.

Major Teesdale looked in over Bruce's shoulder. "Right you are, General." He spotted Molly and grinned. "Miss Orland, isn't it? I enjoyed our romp across the boards last night."

Molly opened her mouth and closed it again.

Teesdale laughed, and she flushed uncomfortably warm.

By now Bruce had turned around to stare at her. "By George, it *is* Miss Orland. Good morning to you, miss."

"Th–thank you, sir." Molly edged toward the kitchen door. "If you will excuse me."

Teesdale stepped out into the hall and cried, "There you are! Look who's serving our breakfast."

The Prince of Wales appeared in the doorway with a faint smile on his lips. "Who? Oh." He stared at Molly.

She gulped and dropped a curtsy, managing to hold onto the dish she held.

The prince nodded. "Well, then, coffee ready or what?"

Chapter Twenty-Two

Peter held his arms out so the turnkey could unlock his shackles. When the chains were off, he rubbed his tender wrists. "Thank you."

The policeman grunted. "Come this way, sir. You can pick up your things out front."

"Bye, now," called one of Peter's erstwhile cellmates.

"Don't forget us, will you, Petie-boy?"

Peter waited until the door was safely secured between them and then replied, "Never."

The three inmates' raucous laughter followed him down the passageway between the cells.

Once in the front lobby of the police station, he was handed his clothing, his wallet, the pouch entrusted to him by Washburn, his penknife, cufflinks, and the handkerchief, a few coins, and a small tinderbox he'd had on him at the time of his arrest. The last item the sergeant placed on the pile was a dance card with the name *Molly Orland* written on the line for the one dance they'd shared.

"I believe you'll find everything in order, sir. I regret that we had to keep you, but the *Hero*'s just passed out of the harbor. The prince's orders—you understand."

Peter nodded.

"If you find all your plunder intact, sign here, and you can change your duds in yonder." The sergeant pointed to a doorway.

Peter opened his wallet. The letters were there, just as he had left them. He counted the money he'd been given for the journey.

"I'm short a fiver, but everything else seems in order."

The sergeant eyed him cautiously. "Are you certain, sir? I made sure my men hadn't disturbed anything. They all swore they hadn't."

"I'm willing to overlook it."

The sergeant nodded. "Good of you, sir."

Peter picked up the pen, dipped it into the inkwell, and signed *P. Stark*. He bundled his belongings into his arms. As he walked into the small, bare room where he was to put on his civilian clothing—his formal evening clothes from the ball—he once more considered leaving the island. He had enough cash to do so. But the red soil and his newfound family had won him over. He knew he couldn't leave, now that he'd gotten to know Molly. Could he fit in here and find a way to earn a living? Or would he be looked upon as an outsider and a felon?

A bath and a shave—the routine he'd begun to take for granted in the earl's service—were only to be dreamed of. He shucked off the prison garb and quickly pulled on his own trousers, stockings, and shirt.

He tied his necktie and put on his cutaway coat. He'd get some stares walking down Great George Street wearing evening clothes in the afternoon, but what of it? He placed his wallet, the money pouch, and other sundries in his pockets. No mirror graced the room, so he ran a hand through his hair and pulled in a deep breath. Time to face his new life.

He gathered the coarse uniform he'd worn overnight and opened the door. A familiar figure stood by the sergeant's desk. Peter walked out slowly and placed the prison clothing on the desk.

"Mr. Stark." Milton, the footman, quickly covered a look of astonishment and bowed slightly. "The master asked me to bring your luggage over here to save you the trouble of going to Government House for it."

Trouble, indeed, Peter thought. More like to save Dundas the embarrassment of having him show up at the mansion, seeking his belongings.

"Thank you, Milton." Peter reached into his pocket and took out a coin. He passed it to the footman.

Milton frowned as he pocketed it. "I...trust all is well with you, sir?" He was staring at Peter's face.

Peter touched his cheek with his fingertips. The bruising must be colorful by now. At least he could still see out of the injured eye. "Yes, thank you."

"You're free to go, Mr. Stark," the sergeant said.

Peter nodded, picked up the valise at Milton's feet, and headed for the door and fresh air.

"Sir?" Milton was on his heels as Peter hit the sidewalk outside.

"Yes, Milton?"

"Mr. Dundas asked me not to speak of your situation among the other servants."

"That was good of him."

"But I wondered—"

Peter stopped and turned to face the footman. "Yes?"

"We all thought you'd gone ahead of the prince this morning, but your clothes were still in your room. And now—well, sir, it's just—I know you're not a drinking man, sir."

Peter smiled. "No, I'm not. Milton, you may as well stop calling me 'sir.' I'm as much a commoner as you are, perhaps more so. And I've decided to stay on your fair island."

Milton nodded, his eyes thoughtful. "If there's anything you need, Mr. Stark, I'd be honored to help you. My family lives on the north edge of town, and we'd welcome you any time."

A surge of achiness swept over Peter. He wasn't sure if it was from gratitude or mere fatigue. "You would trust me, Milton, after seeing me walk out of the local prison?"

"Yes, sir, as you've trusted me this week. I daresay if you wasn't trustworthy, Mr. Dundas would have said so. But he didn't. He only said to bring your things down here and not to revile you among the others, because you didn't deserve what you'd got. Didn't say what that was, but I took it he thought you'd got the short end of the stick somehow. So here I am, and

I'll let on to the other staff that you've gone away, if that's what you want, sir. Or if you want to stay, I'll trounce anyone who tries to blacken your name."

The young man's open friendship nearly overcame Peter. He extended his hand. "Thank you very much, Milton."

They shook hands solemnly.

Milton looked up at him hesitantly. "If you need someplace to board, sir…well, I don't want to insult you, but my mother rents rooms now and again. Mrs. Bracey, on Kent Street. I could take you there. She has a good, clean room to let just now."

Peter smiled. "That is one of many things I'm in need of. How can I thank you, Milton?"

The young man rubbed his chin. "Well, sir, I'd be pleased if you'd speak to me when we meet in the street."

"I'd be proud to."

*****

Molly worked all day, cleaning the bedchambers the royal guests had vacated. She expected to be questioned about the previous night's events, but no one mentioned it to her. No lunch was served upstairs, as the Dundases had gone to the harbor to eat with Prince Albert Edward and his retinue on board the *Hero*. Cook had control of her kitchen back, and she outdid herself in preparation of the servants' hall lunch.

After her brief encounter with the prince in the breakfast room, Molly didn't see him again, and she was glad. She'd slipped away with an empty serving dish and left Milton to see to the royal diners' needs.

In midafternoon, Molly and Rosaleen were stripping the linens off the guests' beds when they heard the firing of the cannons at the forts.

"He's gone, then," Rosaleen said.

"Aye." Molly glanced toward the window.

"What was it like, dancing with him?"

"The prince?" Molly sighed. Three other maids had asked her the same question.

"No, not him. Mr. Stark. You did dance with Mr. Stark, didn't you?"

"Oh. Yes. He's...a very good dancer. Far better than I am."

Rosaleen laughed. "That's the first smile I've seen from you all day, dearie. You'll miss him, won't you?"

Tears threatened, and Molly blinked hard to keep them back. "Yes, I expect I will."

"Did he give you any indication that he'd write to you?"

"No."

Rosaleen picked up a pillow and shook off the case. "Ah, men. I'm sorry that. He seemed such a nice young man. Perhaps he knew there was no future for the two of you, so he didn't dare presume. Probably best that way."

"Yes." The tears were thick in Molly's throat now, and she gave a little cough.

"I heard the prince was quite rambunctious during the latter part of the ball." Rosaleen unfolded a clean pillowcase. "Miss Thompson said he danced his heart out. Impressed everyone, I guess. Cutting in on couples too. She said Major Teesdale even cut in on His Royal Highness once. Did you see it?"

"No. I—I left early."

"Oh?" Rosaleen peered keenly at her.

"After I'd danced with him and—and with Peter, there seemed to be no point in staying longer."

"Oh, and did Mr. Stark see you home?"

Molly's face flamed. "No indeed. My brother Nathan was waiting for me outside, and he walked me home."

"I see."

They continued to work in silence for a while. When that room was finished, Molly scooped up the dirty linens and Rosaleen picked up the broom, dustpan, bucket, and cleaning rags.

"You're taking this quite hard," Rosaleen noted. "I'm sorry, Molly. Is Peter Stark the first young man you've lost your heart to?"

Molly thought it best to dodge the question. "It's not so much that. I'm worried about him."

"While he's traveling with the prince? Surely he'll be all right."

"I…hope so." Almost Molly poured out her heart to Rose, but she thought better of it. The fewer people who knew, the better. She wished she'd seen Lord Washburn again so she'd know whether or not his intercession for Peter had succeeded.

She managed to get through the rest of the day without engaging in another conversation about the ball and the gentlemen involved in last night's fracas. When Roberts finally released her from her duties, she told her to go to Mrs. Bolton's room. By now Molly had heard from several others of the domestic staff what this was about, so she didn't fret and stew as she climbed the stairs.

"Good afternoon, Molly." Mrs. Bolton seemed almost cheerful now that the gentlemen had left the house. "As you probably know, the temporary staff's service is now at an end."

"Yes, ma'am. I'm thankful I was able to work here this summer."

The housekeeper nodded. "You acquitted yourself well. You may come in Monday morning to pick up your wages. And you can keep the clothing issued for your uniform."

"Thank you, ma'am."

"I heard that the gown you wore to the ball suited you admirably."

Molly found it difficult to respond. She could hardly believe that Thompson had spoken well of her to the housekeeper. The lady's maid had ignored her once they'd entered the ballroom. The last time Molly had seen her, Thompson was dancing a waltz with Emmet Price. But perhaps Mrs. Dundas had mentioned the festivities to Mrs. Bolton.

"Th–thank you."

"You're dismissed."

A vague sadness enveloped Molly as she climbed to the servants' quarters, retrieved the white gown from Deborah's room, and carried it to Thompson's chamber. She knocked on the door, and Thompson bid her to enter. The lady's maid sat near her window mending a chemise.

"I'm returning the gown you loaned me. I'll go back for the crinoline and other things." Molly laid the gown on the bed. "I do need to show you the hem. I soiled it last night, I'm afraid. My mother worked on it this morning, and I believe she got most of it out."

Thompson came over to the bed and lifted the edge of the skirt.

"I'm sorry," Molly said. Would Thompson want her to pay for the gown? It really didn't look bad, now that Mum's laundry job had dried and been pressed.

"Why don't you just keep this dress?" Thompson said.

"I—I beg your pardon?"

"It never fit me right anyway. If you think you can wear it again, take it."

"Why…" Molly inhaled sharply. "Thank you. That's most generous of you."

"Think nothing of it. But I want to know…" She squinted a bit as she appraised Molly. "What happened last evening? You stepped outside with His Royal Highness, and a quarter of an hour later, he came back alone. Mrs. Dundas said Washburn made your excuses to her. What happened out there?"

Molly sucked in a breath. Was the gift of the gown contingent on revealing the prince's indiscretion?

"I'm sure I don't know what you mean. My brother was waiting for me outside, and when I met up with him, I decided to go home early."

"You left the Prince of Wales in favor of your brother?"

Molly started to protest but decided she was better off to let Thompson think what she may. Anything discussed now would surely be passed on to Mrs. Dundas later, and so far as Molly knew, the mistress had no idea that her most illustrious guest had insulted one of her employees. Yes, best all around to keep silent.

"I believe His Royal Highness returned to the ball and enjoyed the rest of the evening very…energetically."

Thompson smiled. "You might say that. I danced a polka with him myself." She laughed. "Yes, he's quite the charmer, isn't he?" She picked up the billowing gown. "Here. Keep it. Perhaps someday you'll have another ball to wear it to. Or you can sell it, if you prefer."

Molly knew she would never sell the beautiful white dress. Though it held a mixture of memories for her, when she looked at it she would always remember Peter and how he'd smiled down at her as he held her in his arms.

"Thank you so much. It's a wonderful gift." She scooped it up and hurried away with it before Thompson could have second thoughts. How she would get it home was a quandary she could deal with.

*****

Peter reached the farm lane just before five o'clock. He'd settled with Milton Bracey's mother for the rent of a cozy back bedroom and declined tea with her and the family. A walk into the countryside had beckoned him.

In the distance he could see Nathan and his younger brother guiding the cows toward the byre. Their grandfather waited by the gate.

For a moment, Peter stood gazing at the scene. This was the best of the island life. It epitomized his dreams. Did the Orlands realize how fortunate they'd been? He picked his way down the lane, dodging the few remaining puddles. The rain had ended, and the sun would soon dry them up. Milton's mother had assured him that as they headed into autumn, they'd have some balmy days for harvest.

When he reached the byre, the Orland men were beginning to milk the cows. Nathan and his grandfather had already set to work, and David had leaned his crutches against the wall and was settling onto a stool near another cow. Joe was inside a pen with several calves, picking out forkfuls of manure.

David looked up as Peter stood in the doorway. "Good evening, sir."

"Good evening, Mr. Orland."

Anson turned to stare at Peter in the dimness of the barn, but Nathan appeared not to have heard the exchange and went on with his milking. Anson rose and ambled toward Peter with a bemused expression on his face.

"We thought we'd seen the back of you, lad." Anson stuck out his gnarled hand and Peter clasped it.

"Only if you wish it, sir. I've a mind to stay on the island."

"You're most welcome here." Anson squinted at his face. "You took some hard blows last night."

"I'm all right."

"Good. Our Molly was concerned about you."

David swiveled around on the stool and held out his hand. "Pardon me for not getting up. It's not worth the trouble in my present state."

"Think nothing of it, sir." Peter took his hand. "May I help with the chores? I'm a better hand at milking than I am at dancing the quadrille."

Nathan turned his head and spotted him. "Peter!" He smiled and shoved his milking stool back and strode to where they stood. "You're free."

"Yes, thanks to my uncle and your sister." He shook Nathan's hand heartily.

Nathan winced as he eyed Peter's swollen face. "You didn't have that black eye when they hauled you off."

Peter shrugged. "A delayed consequence."

"We're all most appreciative of what you did," Anson said.

Joe scrambled over the low wall enclosing the calves and came to stare at him, wide-eyed.

"You've met Joseph?" David asked.

"Only in passing, sir. I saw him when the prince came a-calling yesterday."

"Ah. You shall get to know him better if you're staying in these parts." David looked at Nathan. "Find a barn frock for the lad. Can't have him spoiling that elegant shirt."

Peter smiled as Nathan grabbed a worn homespun jacket from a hook near the door and held it out to him. He pulled it on over his own clothing and turned back to Anson. "Put me to work, sir. I'm your man."

*****

"They kept you late." Mum was taking a beef roast out of the oven when Molly got home, and Katie was laying the table.

"Yes. Today was our last day, and I'm to go in Monday for my final pay." Molly summoned up a smile she didn't feel. All day she'd had to hold back tears, and soon she would probably lose that battle.

"Ah, well." Mum straightened and set the pan on top of the stove. "How did things go today?"

"Fine. No one seemed to know anything about it, which I found odd."

"Perhaps the earl greased a few palms."

"Yes, you may be right."

"Nathan brought home the newspapers, and there was nary a word in them about what took place."

"That's good." Molly went to help her sister. "Katie, you've put one too many plates out."

"Go and call the men in, Kate," Mum said.

As her little sister scooted out the back door, Molly picked up the extra ironstone plate.

"No, leave that," her mother said. "We've a guest tonight."

"Oh?" Molly eyed her suspiciously. "Not the minister, I hope. I'm exhausted, and he always stays late."

"No. Could you fetch the butter, please?"

Molly frowned as she went to do as she was bid. Mum was certainly avoiding telling whom she expected to dine with them. She stopped for a moment as she considered the awful prospect that one of her eager dance partners from the ball had come calling already and secured an invitation to supper.

When she returned with the butter dish, she noticed that her mother had prepared enough food for a regiment. Besides the beef, she'd set out potatoes, gravy, biscuits, beans, carrots, and creamed onions, as well as jam and pickles.

"This looks like a feast."

"Just a hearty supper for our men."

Molly placed her hands on her hips. "All right, Mum, what's going on? You may as well tell me."

The back door burst open. Katie and Joe ran in.

"Slow down, you two," Mum said.

"I want to sit beside Peter," Joe said.

"No, me." Katie elbowed him aside.

"Peter?" Molly's heart lurched. She stared toward the door. Nathan came in next. He held the door while his grandfather shuffled in first, then his father with the peculiar swing-step gait his crutches gave him, and last of all Peter, dressed in clothing far too fine for a man with straw in his hair and traces of cow manure on his shoes.

She was staring. But then, so was he. A slow smile lit Peter's face. She stepped toward him, her hands outstretched.

"You're here."

"Yes. They released me as soon as the *Hero* sailed past the fort."

They stood for a moment gazing into each other's eyes. Molly hitched in a breath and nodded slowly. She would get his story, one precious word at a time.

"Well then, are we going to have supper?" her grandfather asked.

"We are," her father said. "And our new hired man will join us. We've much to be thankful for this day."

Chapter Twenty-Three

April 1861

The rattling of wheels on the frozen lane and the *clop* of shod hooves alerted Molly that Peter had arrived. She whipped off her apron.

"Mum, they're here!" She grabbed her shawl from its hook and hurried outside as the farm wagon came to a halt before the Orlands' house.

As Peter wrapped the reins around the brake handle and climbed down, Molly surveyed his two passengers. The Earl of Washburn, bundled in a woolen overcoat and a beaver hat, well swathed with a muffler and gloves, climbed down precariously on the near side of the wagon. Meanwhile, Peter was helping a middle-aged woman emerge from the voluminous driving robe and ease her way to the ground on the other side.

"Lord Washburn." Molly stepped forward, her hands extended. "We're so glad you could come back. It's a joy to see you. I know it's eased Peter's mind, having you with his mother on her journey."

Washburn grasped her hands and chuckled. "My friends think I'm mad to make an ocean voyage so soon after the last one, but I've enjoyed nearly every minute of it. We had a couple of rough days when poor Catherine kept to her cabin, but for the most part, considering the time of year, it was not an uncomfortable voyage." As he spoke, Washburn looked at Molly from head to toe. "My dear, you look marvelous. You've made me so happy, because you've made Peter happy."

Molly's face flushed, but she was able to return his delighted smile. "Thank you."

Peter led the woman around in front of the team while solicitously holding her arm. When they reached Molly and the earl, he stopped. "Mother, this is Molly."

Molly hesitated for only an instant. In Mrs. Stark's eyes she saw the same uncertainty she felt. She smiled. "I'm so glad you're here."

Peter's mother held out her arms, and Molly hugged her close.

"Dear girl," Mrs. Stark said in her ear. "This is a happy day indeed."

"Come in!" Molly stepped back, laughing. "Mum and Papa and the rest are eager to meet you, but they've let me have this first moment with you all to myself. Now I get to share you."

She led the guests inside. After the introductions to her parents and siblings, Nathan slipped out to help Peter with the horses. Mum welcomed the guests into her small but spotless parlor. Grandpa Anson was waiting there, and he rose.

"Mrs. Stark, this is my grandfather, Anson Orland."

Grandpa stepped forward eagerly with tears in his eyes. "You look like Mary."

Mrs. Stark's eyes misted as she grasped his hand. "So you are my uncle Anson who took my mother's part so gallantly. At last I get to meet you." She stepped closer and kissed him soundly on the cheek. "Thank you so much, dear uncle."

Anson flushed to his hairline but smiled on her, with satisfaction smoothing his face. "I'm so very, very pleased to meet you." He looked past her then and settled his gaze on the earl. "We meet again, sir."

Molly was always a bit chagrined that her grandfather refused to call Washburn "my lord," but the earl seemed to understand his stubbornness and take it in good grace.

Washburn laughed and shook Grandpa's hand. "It does me good to see you looking so well."

"What, you thought I was so doddery that I wouldn't make it through another island winter?" Anson offered the earl his comfortable chair, but Washburn declined, taking one of the straight chairs Joe brought in from the kitchen.

"Our little home is crowded but happy," Mum said. "Please sit here, Mrs. Stark." She gestured toward her own rocker.

"Thank you. But you must call me Catherine."

"And I am Eliza."

The two mothers sat down and began to chat about their children as though they had known each other for many years.

Molly's father's injury had taken its time in healing, and he had used his canes all winter, hobbling about the farm, careful not to take another fall. He sat down near the earl and Grandpa and inquired after the Washburn family.

"Those that matter most to me now are here," the earl said with a smile. "I haven't much family, really."

"I'm sorry to hear that," Grandpa said.

The earl shrugged. "My wife died after we'd been married but two years, and my only child died with her. It was a long time ago, but I've never remarried. So my estate and title will pass to my cousin when I'm gone. I don't mind—he'll be good at it."

"Surely it's not too late for you to marry and produce an heir," Grandpa said.

Washburn waved his hand in dismissal. "I fear it is. I loved and lost, you see, in my youth, and I've never felt inclined to pursue marriage again. A pity in a way...but since I can't leave my worldly goods to Peter, I've decided to make the best of it and help him all I can while the estate is still mine."

Peter, across the room, was listening to something Molly's mother said and didn't hear the earl's statement, but Molly took note of it and his wistful look as the earl's gaze rested on the young man.

"So how is His Royal Highness doing?" Papa asked with a grimace.

"What, Bertie?" Washburn asked. "He's getting on all right, I guess. He'd like to have a military career, but they won't let him because he's heir to the throne. He goes and takes part in training and exercises, but they won't let him near a battlefield, you can be sure of that."

Grandpa nodded. "According to the papers here, he earned a lot of diplomatic cachet during his tour over here."

"That's true. And I must say, he was on his best behavior after we left here. The model representative of the Crown, if I do say so." Washburn chuckled. "I think General Bruce had a little man-to-man chat with him. Anyway, I never saw him misbehave again. He had a grand time down in the States. President Buchanan showed him a good time."

"I'm glad to hear it," Molly said. "Everyone here thought he was so charming—I could hardly believe the way he treated me that night."

"Most unfortunate, my dear." Washburn shook his head. "I'm so sorry it happened."

"But if it hadn't, Peter wouldn't have stayed around," Grandpa said. "Then where would our Molly be? Most likely moping around and pining for a certain English gentleman."

They all laughed.

"The prince is back at Oxford now," Washburn said. "Not the best scholar, or so I've heard tell…and there was a little incident with an actress, so perhaps he's cutting up again. They say he'll go to Germany in the fall with his regiment, to observe military maneuvers. And Prince Albert wants him to go to Cambridge after that, I think. Seems the lad has a penchant for history, and the best professor is at Trinity College. Or maybe Albert just wants to change his venue and get his son away from his Oxford friends, I don't know."

"Well, the boy's sowing his oats while his mother rules the empire," Papa said. "That can be boring, waiting around for the older generation to vacate the place for you." He caught himself and grimaced. "Begging your pardon, my lord."

"Think nothing of it. That sort of thing does happen. I only wish my father had stayed on this earth longer. But you can be sure no whiff of scandal during the Canadian tour reached Queen Victoria's ears."

Peter came over and sat down beside his uncle.

"Are you staying at the farm with Peter?" Grandpa asked the earl.

"No, I shall be comfortable at the Wellington in town. I'm afraid I've grown used to the amenities. Catherine is moving right out to the farm immediately, though. I shall stay a couple of weeks and make sure she's well settled before I leave her."

"Well, cousin," Papa called to Catherine, "we all hope you'll like it here and stay on the island."

Catherine smiled and darted a glance at Molly. "I still can hardly believe Peter and Molly have invited me to live with them. Peter and I struggled to make a go of it for years in England, but he is confident he'll be able to establish the farm this year and make a good crop of potatoes."

Papa nodded. "You'll see. In a month, all this snow will be gone and he'll be out harrowing his fields. That's a good farm Peter has leased."

"Yes," Grandpa said. "It's quite a choice spot—and less than two miles from here."

"We were discussing the wedding," Mum said. "I assume you young people are still planning on Saturday."

Molly looked at Peter.

"Of course," he said. "We've no reason to delay any longer now that Mother and Uncle Edwin are here, have we, Molly?"

She smiled up at him. "No reason at all."

A few minutes later, Molly rose to help her mother fix tea for the guests, and Peter followed them to the kitchen.

"I'd be happy to help you serve, Mrs. Orland, but then I thought perhaps I'd snatch Molly away for a minute."

"Step right on out into the dairy if you want," Mum said. "Just don't linger too long or David will send one of the boys after you."

Peter laughed. "Just for a moment, Molly?"

Molly gladly put on her shawl and led him out into the milk room. "Your mother is a dear, but I knew she would be."

Peter closed the door firmly and held out his arms to her. Molly melted into his embrace. Peter kissed her and then held her against his chest, stroking her hair.

"Darling, I couldn't wait to tell you. Uncle Edwin is giving us the price of the farm."

"What?" Molly pulled away and studied his deep brown eyes. "Giving us…" She clamped her lips together.

"You know he questioned me closely in his letters about the soil and the buildings. When I picked him and Mother up at the pier, one of the first things he asked me was whether I still felt the farm I'm leasing was the one I'd like to own. I told him yes and that in ten years we should own it. He said, 'Sooner than that, I hope, lad.' The money will be our wedding gift. If you've no objection, that is."

Molly let out her pent-up breath. "Why would I object? Oh, Peter! It seems…too easy."

He laughed. "I know. Eight months ago, I thought I was facing the gallows. And now I have you, and Mother's safely here too, and we'll have our own farm. It's more than I ever thought to see in my lifetime." He ran his finger down her cheek. "And you're certain you don't mind Mother living with us?"

"You've asked me that a hundred times. I don't mind."

He kissed her lightly. "You don't know how happy you've made me." He pulled her close and kissed her again.

A moment later, Molly reluctantly eased away from him. "We'd best go in, or Joe will be out here pestering us."

"Brothers," he said. "That's another thing God has given me. And a sister too. I love your family."

She chuckled. "I love your family too. It's a bit odd, since I spent so many years hating the Washburn clan."

"Well, I'm as much an Orland as I am a Washburn, with a generous helping of Stark thrown in too. Don't forget that."

"No, I shan't. I wish I could have met your father. But I'll take his lordship as a stand-in."

The kitchen door opened, and Joe peeked out into the dim milk room. "Mum says enough sparking, and the tea is ready."

"Does she now?" Peter grinned at Molly and crooked his elbow. "May I escort you in, Almost-Mrs.-Stark?"

*****

The church bells rang out as the Orland family's wagon drew up before the church in Charlottetown on Saturday afternoon. Peter strode forward to meet them. A ten-year-old boy trotted at his side.

"Good morning, Mr. and Mrs. Orland." Peter nodded to Anson as well. "Sir. This is Milton's brother. He'll watch the horses while we're inside."

Nathan was already helping Molly from her perch on the wagon seat beside her mother while Joe and Katie scrambled out of the back. Peter gazed at Molly. His heart swelled, and he found it difficult to breathe. She'd arrived in the wagon with her dress swathed beneath a travel robe, but now she'd thrown that off and the frothy layers of her gown dazzled him. A veil of flimsy netting draped over her golden hair.

The dress looked the same…but different somehow. Gazing at it, Peter realized she had edged the bodice and sleeves with the fine lace his uncle had ordered be sent over from Honiton, in Devon. The aristocratic brides of England would have no other, and though Molly wouldn't have cared, the earl would take delight in seeing her wear it today.

"That's the gown you wore at the ball last summer, isn't it?" he asked.

Molly smiled gently. "Yes, it is. I hope you don't mind."

"Mind? When I saw you in it that night, I knew you were the most beautiful woman in the room—on the whole island." He stepped forward and took her hands in his. "My mother and uncle are waiting in the church. Milton's here, too, to stand up with me." The footman had become his close friend during the weeks Peter had boarded with Milton's family last fall.

Molly's blue eyes shone up at him. "I'm so glad your mother and Lord Washburn came."

"Yes." Peter's contentment knew several levels—they'd gone all winter with only a vague wedding date in mind. With the money given him by the earl at the jail, he'd leased the small farm with a snug house and a small barn. He hoped to make a good crop this summer. With Molly's encouragement, he'd written to invite his mother to share the home he'd found on Prince Edward Island.

Things had taken a turn when, after New Year's, his mother's letter had arrived saying that she would come and her half-brother would escort her and see her safely settled. Molly and Peter had agreed: when the two special guests arrived from England, they would be married. If the journey had been delayed, so would this splendid day. But now the ship had arrived and Peter's mother was ensconced in her room at the farm, while the earl took temporary rooms at the Wellington Hotel in Charlottetown.

"Look, Peter!" Katie crowded close and tugged at his sleeve. "I've a new dress for your wedding."

He surveyed her pink sprigged muslin dress and grinned at her. "You look wonderful, and so grown up." He'd have reached for the nearest pigtail, but they'd been replaced by a coronet of braids wound close around Katie's head…no doubt modeled after Molly's coiffure.

Molly's friend Allison hurried out of the church, holding the skirt of her blue gown just above her shoes.

She embraced Molly. "You're a beautiful bride! I think everyone is here now."

Peter glanced toward Molly's parents and grandfather. "Shall we go inside?"

"You go on and take Liza in," David said. "I believe I'm supposed to wait out here with the bride."

Peter nodded and stepped toward Mrs. Orland. He offered his arm, and she slipped her hand inside his elbow. Grandpa Anson and the two boys went inside. Peter sneaked a final glance at Molly in that magnificent white gown with blue trim. Her smile was breathtaking.

Inside, he took Molly's mother to the front pew. She paused to speak to his own mother. With tears in their eyes, the two women embraced.

"Such a blessed day," Mrs. Orland murmured. Peter seated her in the box pew across the aisle from his mother and Washburn. He took his place at the front of the church with Milton and the minister. Milton looked good in his new suit, a somber contrast to his usual bright livery.

Molly's grandfather and her two brothers sat next to Mrs. Orland and beamed at him. Peter had claimed Molly's brothers as his own and been enthusiastically welcomed by them into the family. He intended to enjoy Nathan and Joe to the hilt.

As the organist played Mendelssohn's "Wedding March," Katie entered the church and walked slowly down the aisle, grinning at the family and small group of friends gathered. Her pink dress swished as she walked, and she let out a giggle as her gaze met Peter's. He winked at her and noticed his mother's smile. Allison came next, in her wide-skirted blue gown. Though not as pretty as Molly, she still cut an elegant figure in her unaccustomed finery, and Peter sensed Milton's appreciation as they watched her. Milton had confided recently that he'd begun calling at the Johnsons' farm on his half day off each week. Allison took up a spot opposite the footman, and all eyes turned to the door of the church.

Molly and her father walked slowly down the aisle. David still limped, but today he had abandoned his canes and stood upright, his chin high, his face glowing with pride as he brought Molly down to the altar. He stood beside her until the minister gave him his cue, when he placed Molly's hand in Peter's and sat down with his wife and the boys.

"Dearly beloved," the minister intoned.

Peter's eyes misted so that he could barely see Molly's radiant smile.

Author's Note

Dear Reader,

    Though the prince for whom Prince Edward Island was named never set foot on it, his grandson was the first member of the British royal family to visit there. In 1860, Queen Victoria sent her oldest son, Prince Albert Edward, then Prince of Wales, on a "goodwill" tour of British North America (now Canada) and the United States. Prince "Bertie," who later became King Edward VII, traveled during the summer and fall of the year, making a two-day stop on Prince Edward Island in August.

    His journey was tightly scheduled, and the eighteen-year-old prince performed many official duties along the way, such as opening Victoria Bridge in Montreal and setting the cornerstone for the parliament building in Ottawa. All accounts report that Bertie was on his best behavior throughout the tour and drew much praise and admiration from the public. His misbehavior in my story is completely fictional. However, accounts of his life laid enough factual background to make it believable. He was later known as a womanizer and, during his long wait to take the throne, came to symbolize the fashionable, leisured aristocracy.

    Even as a young man, his father (Victoria's husband, Prince Albert) had to take Bertie to task several times for his escapades. Both at school and while away at military training, he engaged in incidents that brought his parents' displeasure and might foreshadow just such an event as I've presented in this book. So I hope any historical purists will forgive me for making the prince misbehave when there was no indication that he did so on the tour. I'm sure his other antics made up for it.

    In reading newspaper accounts from the time and books and articles about the royal tour of 1860, I was caught up in the pageantry and the enthusiasm of the people in seeing their prince for the first time. Bertie was perceived as a handsome and energetic young man who cared about his subjects. It pained me to cast a dark shadow over that image, but not so much as to make me change my story.

I've tried to stick to the facts concerning his tour. The levee and ball took place as described. His ride into the countryside, stopping at a local farm and taking a glass of ale, entertainments, official appearances, shooting party, and other activities were squeezed into his forty-eight hours on Prince Edward Island.

Most of the people included in his "suite" or "retinue" in this story were real, with the exceptions of Peter Stark and the Earl of Washburn. Lieutenant Governor George Dundas and his wife were, of course, real, as were the Duke of Newcastle, the Earl of St. Germains, Dr. Acland, General Bruce, and the "equerries," Grey and Teesdale. All of the servants named in this book are fictional, as is the entire Orland family and their neighbors and friends.

I extend my thanks to the very helpful people at Province House and the Public Archives and Records Office in Charlottetown and to Heather Peters and her family at Swept Away Cottages in Cavendish. I hope you enjoyed this story and our journey to Prince Edward Island!

Susan Page Davis

About the Author

Award-winning author Susan Page Davis has published more than eighty novels in the historical romance, suspense, mystery, and romance genres. She's a past winner of the Carol Award (formerly American Christian Fiction Writers' Book of the Year Award) and is a two-time winner of the Inspirational Readers' Choice Contest, a two-time winner of the Will Rogers Medallion, and a runner-up in the WILLA Literary Awards.

A Maine native, she now resides in Kentucky with her husband, Jim, a retired news editor. The Davises have six children, ten adorable grandchildren, and two feuding cats. Susan loves to read and does logic puzzles and genealogy research. She's a longtime homeschooler and former schoolteacher. She's also a certified farrier but no longer practices the art. Visit Susan at her website: https://susanpagedavis.com, where you can read a short story, sign up for her newsletter, and enter a monthly drawing for books.

More of Susan's historical novels you might enjoy:

Echo Canyon (set in 1860)
River Rest (set in 1918)
My Heart Belongs in the Superstition Mountains (set in 1866)
The Crimson Cipher (set in 1915)
The Outlaw Takes a Bride (western)
Mrs. Mayberry Meets Her Match
The Seafaring Women of the Vera B. (Co-authored with Susan's son James S. Davis)
The Ladies' Shooting Club Series (westerns)
    The Sheriff's Surrender
    The Gunsmith's Gallantry
    The Blacksmith's Bravery
Captive Trail (western)
Cowgirl Trail (western)
Heart of a Cowboy (western collection)
The Prairie Dreams series (set in the 1850s)
    The Lady's Maid
    Lady Anne's Quest
    A Lady in the Making
Maine Brides (set in 1720, 1820, and 1895)
    The Prisoner's Wife
    The Castaway's Bride
    The Lumberjack's Lady
Mountain Christmas Brides
Seven Brides for Seven Texans
Seven Brides for Seven Mail-Order Husbands
Seven Brides for Seven Texas Rangers

See all of her books at https://susanpagedavis.com.

Printed in Great Britain
by Amazon